the
one
for me

The One for Me
Copyright © 2020 Corinne Michaels
All rights reserved.
ISBN—paperback: 978-1942834502

Cover Design:
Sommer Stein, Perfect Pear Creative

Editing:
Ashley Williams, AW Editing

Proofreading:
Michele Ficht & Julia Griffis

Formatting:
Alyssa Garcia, Uplifting Author Services

Cover photo © Brian Kaminski

The Arrowood Brothers Series

the
one
for me

CORINNE MICHAELS

To Melissa Erickson, thank you for being an incredible friend and always making me laugh. However, Sean isn't yours. Me dedicating this is actually proof that he's not. So, in case you were confused, this is me clearing it up.

one

"I am so done!" Devney gives a small little giggle before covering her mouth.

We've spent the last four hours in her barn, laughing, drinking, talking about life . . . I had forgotten just how much I love being with her.

"One more drink," I urge.

"No. I have to meet Oliver tomorrow."

I roll my eyes. I don't know what the hell she sees in him. He's the complete opposite of the kind of guy she needs. Devney is strong and defiant, and yet, she has many weaknesses she doesn't let people see. Like how she wants to make everyone around her happy, even at the cost of her own wants. He doesn't see that or know her heart. Oliver is just . . . nice.

That's the best I can come up with.

He's. Nice.

She doesn't need nice. She needs someone to rival her and

bring out her spark and fire. A long time ago, it raged inside her. I hadn't thought there would be a chance it would be extinguished, but then, about nine years ago, it went out.

I don't know why or what happened, but she changed.

No one stays the same, I know this. Hell, I'm not even close to the same man I was before the night of the accident that changed my life, but Devney doesn't have some dark secret. She tells me everything, and I withhold that one story.

Oliver, though, he doesn't know her secrets.

"How is our perfectly nice friend Oliver?" I ask. I'm just on the fringe of being drunk enough not to care that I'm being a dick.

Usually, I mask it. The feelings that simmer are able to stay down, but tonight, I just don't care.

"He's going to propose."

My eyes lift, and I find myself staring into her coffee-colored irises, hating the words that came from the lips I've dreamed of kissing.

She can't marry him.

Not when . . . not when the lies we've been telling each other for all this time are between us.

I have to stop this. "Dev—"

"It's good, though. He's . . . he's really good to me, Sean. Oliver will take care of me, be here, and he won't push me. You should be happy and not looking at me like that."

"Like what?"

She tucks a lock of brunette hair behind her ear and shrugs. "Like I just kicked you in the face. You know, you looked like this the day that Debbie Sue tried to kiss you."

"Well, Debbie Sue also kissed two of my brothers."

"She was on a mission to be struck by the Arrowood brothers."

We both laugh. "Yeah, she was."

Devney shifts, leaning her head on the back of the couch and angling her body toward me. "It's not any different than the girls you hook up with now. What do they call them? Homeplate Hussies?"

I roll my eyes. "You have no idea what I look for."

"Right. Ohhh"—Devney lifts her head with a smile—"that's right, they call them Bat Rats! Or maybe Cleat Callers?" She taps her chin. "Strikeout Sluts? Homerun Hoes?"

"Cleat chasers." I give her one of the many names they have for the girls who want to fuck a ballplayer.

"Not nearly as much fun as mine. And what do you mean I have no idea what you look for?"

She has no clue that I am not the guy who is out there, trying to rack up my batting average with women who aren't . . . well, her.

Devney is the girl I keep searching for, even though she's right in front of me.

My brothers give me shit, and they're right, but we can never be. Not because of the promises I've made to stay single and never marry. It's that I can never marry Devney. She wouldn't be able to handle the fact that I'd never be here. I travel too much, train too much, work harder because, if I don't . . . I will get cut.

The only dream I've ever had was to play ball. I dealt with the abuse of my father, the pain of losing my mother, and the constant worry for my brothers because I always had baseball.

I couldn't give it up. Not for anyone.

And Devney would need me to. She can't love half in, half out, which is exactly what my life is. I'm married to the game, and she would be my mistress.

"Nothing, ignore that," I say and then grab my beer. I can't go down this road with her. I've had enough wrecks in my life and this friendship is worth taking a different road.

"No, I want to know."

"I don't think you do."

She pokes my chest. "Yes, tell me."

My lips part and the words stall. If I release them, there is no taking it back.

I take her glass, fill it again, and hand it back to her. "Just drink more and we can go back to making fun of my brothers or we can talk about why you're still living in Sugarloaf when you had dreams to leave."

That usually takes care of it.

What bound us was the want for more. Devney was going to be an architect, and I used to rarely find her without a pencil and sketchbook as she doodled buildings, houses, and any other kind of structure.

Then, when she came back from college, that all stopped.

"Sean," she whines, "I am so drunk already. Oliver hates when I drink because I get too unpredictable. He likes that I always behave, that I'm always proper, and he never has to worry about me."

I laugh. "Then Oliver doesn't know you."

"Oliver knows who I am now."

"Well, it's a good thing that I know who you are in your soul."

We both raise our glasses, clink them, and then drink.

"I'm so going to regret this in the morning," Devney complains as her head falls back.

Not as much as I will.

"Well, tell me about Oliver and his proposal plans." I bring the conversation back to where I want it.

Her eyes lock on mine, and she shrugs. "I don't know what

to say other than he mentioned that it was time that we move things along. He loves me, and he's good for me. He's that steady kind of guy, you know?"

"Sounds like the makings of the perfect marriage."

"Don't even. I don't judge your relationships—well, not that you have any."

I smirk. "Damn right."

Devney rolls her eyes and sighs. "Don't play that crap with me, Sean Arrowood. I know you better. You want the wife and kids. You always have. The issue that you have is that you're stupid."

"Stupid?"

She nods. "Yup. S-T-U-P-I-D. And dumb."

"They mean the same thing."

"It required the extra punctuation at the end."

God, I love the side of her that is smart-mouthed, fearless, and relaxed. She's only this way with me. Or at least, that's what I'd like to think.

The last ten years have been hard on our friendship. We both went off to college, I had baseball and she was studying. We'd see each other on breaks, but after the accident that changed the trajectory of my life, I stayed in Maine, and we rarely saw each other.

However, when I had a series in New York, Devney came. If I was in Philly, she would find a way to meet me, and I flew her down to Tampa a few times.

Now, though, I'll be around her so much more, and I know these feelings aren't going to go away, they'll get stronger.

Yeah, I guess I really am stupid.

"Well, I may be stupid, but at least I'm not settling."

She sits up, slapping her hand on the couch cushion. "Settling?"

"Yeah. You may love Oliver, but he doesn't make you crazy."

Devney shifts back. "You're making me crazy right now."

"Good."

"You're infuriating!"

I shrug. "You love me."

"It helps that you're hot." Devney quickly covers her hand over her mouth. "I did not mean it like that."

I grin and lean toward her. "You think I'm hot?"

"I think you're mediocre. God knows your harem of . . . whatever you call them . . . think you are."

For so long I've fought against telling her anything about how I feel. How those women are faceless and mean nothing to me. It's always her. Always a brunette who I seek out, hoping to find just a piece of something like her that I can cling to, but I never say it.

Then I wonder, maybe this is the perfect time. Oliver is going to propose. Oliver will marry her, and I won't have a goddamn thing to say about it because I will have never told her.

Plus, she's drunk.

Maybe she won't remember it.

"Maybe so, but I'm not asking them. Plus, all the girls I'm attracted to look like you."

Devney laughs while shaking her head. "Well, it has to be tough kissing your best friend, right?"

And in that moment, I know what I'm going to do. It doesn't matter that it's stupid or wrong. I no longer care about her boyfriend or how this moment will undoubtedly change everything between us because she will marry him when he asks. Devney won't falter. She'll cling to the safe, and I am not that, but I love her.

I lean closer and her eyes study my movement. With a

trembling hand, I cup her face and brush my thumb against her soft skin. Everything freezes around us as I feel the warmth emanating from her. Our breaths mingle as the distance closes. "I don't know, but I'd like to see if it's tough to kiss you."

I wait, giving her one last chance to push me away, but instead, her tongue moves against her pink lips, which is all the invitation I need.

I lean in, my lips touch hers, and I know my life hasn't just changed, it's been completely upended.

two

"A re you okay?" Oliver asks as I push the food around on my plate.

"I'm fine."

I'm not fine. In fact, I'm a mess. It's been four days of avoiding his calls. Four days of replaying that kiss over and over again in my mind. There's no making sense of it.

Sean Arrowood kissed me. He kissed me, and I liked it. A lot.

"You seem a bit out of it."

I plaster a smile on my face and shove all my confusion aside. It's our monthly date night, and I should be happy. Oliver came to the office with flowers and a smile so warm it could have melted ice. He's safe and good for me. I know this, and yet . . . I feel horrible.

He deserves to know.

"Oliver," I say carefully. "I . . ." *I kissed Sean.* "I . . . I'm not sure what to say." *I kissed Sean, and I'm a horrible person.*

"Just talk to me, Dev. There's nothing you can't tell me."

I put the fork down and release a few heavy breaths. I already live with secrets, and they fester, eating away a bit of my soul each day. I can't handle living with another one. While he may think there's nothing we can't discuss, there are some things that no one wants to hear.

Still, I won't do this to him. I won't agree to something more when everything is a lie.

I made a mistake.

I screwed up, and I have to own it.

"The other night, when I was with Sean." I take a long pause, hating that I'm going to hurt him. He doesn't deserve it, but more than anything, he deserves the truth. "We were drinking a lot."

Oliver smiles and shakes his head. "If I remember correctly, you paid for it the next day."

I've been paying for it since it happened.

"Yes, but there's more . . ." God, I want to throw up. "We were really drunk. Both of us were, well, we should've stopped drinking much earlier. I need to tell you this because I love you. I do. I love you, and I love what we have."

"Devney, did you . . . did you sleep together?"

I jerk back, eyes wide with shock. Why the hell did he make a leap like that so fast? "No," I say quickly. "No, we didn't. But we . . . well, we kissed."

Oliver sits back, adjusting the napkin on his lap. "I see. Not like you normally do with hello or goodbye?"

I shake my head. "No."

He swallows and then takes a drink of wine. "I'm not surprised."

Well, I am. "Why do you say that?"

"Did anything else happen?" he asks with a shake of his head. "I'm assuming you're telling me because there's more."

"No, I swear. It was stupid, and I haven't talked to him since then, but I wanted to tell you. I'm so sorry. I love you. I hate that I hurt you and destroyed what we have. I wish I could go back and stop it. I'm so *so* sorry, Oliver."

Oliver, the sweetest man in the world, who has never once questioned or pushed me to do something I didn't want to, the guy who put me back together when I was falling apart and no one else knew, is going to hate me. And the sad part is, he has every right to.

I wipe away the tear that hangs on the fringe of my lashes. There is no excuse for the choice I made.

"Do you love him?"

My stomach drops. Yes. No. I don't know. The way I feel about him is muddy. "I have loved him for a long time, but I don't love him the way I love you."

"I'm asking if you're in love with him. Not if you love Sean the way you always have." There's tension in his voice that I've never heard before. I hate that I'm breaking his trust—and his heart.

"I know what you're asking, and I have never thought of him in any other way than . . . Sean."

"And how is that?"

My heart is pounding loudly. Everything feels as though it's falling apart around me, and I don't know how to stop it. I rest my hand on my neck, playing with the necklace Sean gave me when I was sixteen. And for some reason, that single unconscious movement tells me the truth.

"He's my best friend."

Oliver nods. "And that's all I've ever wanted to be for you." And that's no less than he deserves. I watch him, swallowing hard, but his face is a mask I can't read. "You know what this means for us, right?"

A tear falls down my cheek, and I nod. "I've broken us."

"It's not the kiss. I could get over the kiss," he says with a laugh. "How sad is that? I'm here, telling the woman I planned to ask to marry me next week that I could forgive her kissing another man."

I open my mouth quickly to try to say something—anything to make this better. "Ollie."

"I can't do this to myself, though. I can't love you when you love another man. If I asked you to choose between us, you'd pick him."

Denying it is all I want to do, but it would be a lie. I may not love Sean the way he thinks I do, but I love him enough to know that if Oliver made me choose, I would never let Sean go.

Which leaves us at this impasse.

Ollie rests his hand on the table, palm up. "Take my hand, Devney." I place it in his. "I won't lie and say that I'm not hurt. Your friendship with Sean has always been hard on me, mostly because I don't understand it. However, I accepted it. I love you and want to marry you, but I can't marry him too, do you understand?"

I nod. "I would never ask you to."

"But you have. You love him even though you have never allowed yourself to feel it. Maybe not until now. The friendship you have with him is unbreakable, and I am always competing for the top spot in your heart . . . the one that belongs to him."

Sean is always the man I measure people against. He's the guy I look to when I'm hurting or alone. I don't know why I try to pretend otherwise. "I wanted it to be you," I confess, letting the tears spill. "I wanted for it to be us."

"I did too." Oliver's voice shatters at the end. "I just knew that I was fighting a losing battle."

God, how horrible I am. "Do you believe me that I didn't know?"

His lips turn to a sad smile as his thumb rubs the top of my hand. "I've known you were in love with him since the first time I met him. I knew that you both were in love, and I prayed that I could make you love me."

My lip trembles. "I do love you."

"I know."

"Do you?"

Oliver nods but pulls his hand away, leaving me feeling bereft. "But now, you've seen something else, and I don't have a chance. So, I'm going to do what's right for both of us and walk away while we can still be friends."

"Ollie . . ."

He stands, placing his napkin on the table, and comes around to my side. His lips press against the top of my head. "I want you to be happy. I want you to heal and find a way through whatever it is that troubles you."

My heart is pounding hard in my chest as Oliver walks away.

I've just lost the best man I've ever dated.

The mistakes just keep piling up.

"So, you told Oliver?" Sydney asks as I sit by her bed. She had a few false contractions, and Declan refuses to let her out of bed other than to pee.

Which she apparently does often.

"And he broke up with me."

I open the folder, ready to move on from my disaster of a personal life, but Sydney isn't.

"He broke up with you?"

I sigh and close the file. "Yes, and I don't blame him for it, either. Oliver should be with someone who loves him madly. Not someone who is unwilling to give her heart to him."

"Why are you unwilling?"

"I just am."

Syd's head jerks back. "That sums it all up. Is it because of something in your past? Something that you're trying to keep hidden, but sucking at it? Or maybe because you're afraid of something?"

"I'm unwilling right now because my boss is asking too many questions," I say defensively.

Sydney pulls the papers from my hand and tosses them onto the other side of the bed. "You know I'm not a patient person. I like to *know* things and help people. You have something you're upset about that doesn't involve sticking your tongue in Sean's mouth. Tell me."

There are some truths that can't be spoken, this is one.

So, I go with something else that is part of it. "It's about why I stayed away so long."

"You mean from Sugarloaf after college?"

"Yes, I . . . loved someone when I was in Colorado. I loved him a lot, but I didn't ever tell anyone." She smiles and waits for me to continue. "We never should've been together, which is why I don't talk about it. Christopher was older and in a position of authority. Anyway, the last few weeks have been hard because he's been on my mind a lot, and now with Sean, it's like I don't know who I am anymore."

Sydney's lips pull into a tight line. "I can't tell you who you are, only you can do that. What I can tell you is that you're brave, beautiful, smart, and a wonderful friend. You didn't have to tell Oliver about the kiss, it was a drunk night that no one would fault you for, but you did. You face your mistakes head-on. You deal with the consequences, and that is something you should be proud of."

Oh, how wrong she is. There is no facing my mistakes, I run. The minute I could, I escaped the college I was at and all that surrounded him. I run from it all, and I'm doing it now with Sean.

"I wish that were true. I still haven't answered Sean's calls or texts."

"You need to talk to him. Trust me. This won't go away, and it's better to know where he stands before he's back in town and in your face."

My phone pings with a text.

"Speak of the devil," I say, shoving my phone away without reading it.

"Why don't you head home? Declan keeps pacing by the door, and I'm getting a little tired. Thank you for bringing this over." Her hand taps the folder.

"Are you sure?"

"Positive. I'm here if you need me."

I squeeze my friend's hand and then head out to the hall where, sure enough, Declan is wearing a hole in the floor.

"You okay?" I ask.

"No. This is insane. I'm nervous, frantic, and afraid to leave the house to get food. She makes a noise, and I'm leaping to my feet." He runs his hands through his hair.

I smile at my lifelong friend, somewhat enjoying his misery. "This is payback for being such a tool the last few months."

"I have a feeling I'll be getting payback for a long time."

"Yeah, I think you will. I'll see you later."

I start to make my way downstairs, but Declan calls my name. When I look back, he seems to waver with saying something. "I promised him I wouldn't get involved," Dec starts, and I tense.

"He told you."

Declan nods. "I know Sean, and he doesn't do something without thinking it through. I know you two have history and don't want to complicate things, but for what it's worth, sometimes complications become miracles." He looks back toward the room where Sydney is. "And believe me, you want the miracles."

"Sean and I will figure it out," I tell him, not wanting to get into it.

"I'm sure you will."

"Call me if you guys need anything," I say and then rush out of the house.

Once I get in my car, I pull my phone out and look at the text.

Sean: Dev, we need to talk. I'll be in Sugarloaf next week, and avoiding each other isn't going to work. Call me.

My fingers hover over the keys because, while I claim the kiss was a drunken mistake, it wasn't. What if that was all it was for him, though? I don't know that I'm strong enough to hear that. Then again, it might be exactly the right answer.

Instead of texting him, I press the call button. Now is not the time to be a chickenshit. Declan is right, this is complicated, but I need Sean in my life. I always have, and I can't keep pushing him away.

"Hey." Sean's deep voice fills my ears, sending a rumble down to my stomach.

"Hey. Sorry I didn't respond or call, but . . ."

"But we sort of crossed the line the other night."

I guess we're going to get right to it.

I sigh as I stare out the window. "Yeah, we did."

"I'm sorry, Dev. I don't know what got into me. I never should've kissed you. It was a mistake. A horrible one that I regret so much."

Those four words just broke my heart. I close my eyes to stop the emotions that are robbing me of breath and then let them go. It was one night, we drank too much, and things got carried away.

"It was," I confirm.

Sean is silent for a second before saying, "It won't happen again."

There's a strain in his voice, and I know I have to say something to salvage this. "We were drunk and . . . there's been a lot going on for both of us. You're my best friend, and I don't want to lose that."

"You'll never lose me," he says with promise.

"Good. Then, it's fine, we'll pretend it never happened and go back to the way things always have been."

Sean laughs, but it sounds forced. "Sounds good to me."

Sounds like hell to me, but what other choice do I have? Tell him that I want something more when he clearly thinks it was a "horrible mistake"? No. That would be stupid and reckless. Not to mention, I can't leave Sugarloaf. There are things here that matter to me, more than my own heart. I have to be smart and think of what is important.

I look over at the clock and sigh. "I have to go. I'm heading to my brother's for dinner and I have to be up at like four in the morning to see Austin's baseball game tomorrow and . . ."

And I'm lying because I can't talk to you right now.

"That early?"

"Yes. His game is early. You remember how those tournaments go."

Even if there isn't one, Austin will have something baseball related.

"Yeah, I remember. I talked to your brother the other day about working with the kids one-on-one. It'll be good to help out and not be stuck on the farm, twiddling my thumbs or trying to learn about the damn cows."

I smile, knowing Austin will absolutely love it. There's nothing like getting to hang out with your idol. He adores Sean, mostly because he's a famous baseball player, which is what he hopes to be some day.

"I'm sure the kids of Sugarloaf will be happy."

"At least someone will be about me being back there."

I stay silent because I was so excited when I found out he would be back for six months. I couldn't wait to spend time with him and have my best friend around. I have Sydney and Ellie, but it isn't the same.

They aren't Sean.

They don't know the crap I deal with from my mother or how much I wish I could be doing something different with my life.

Since Sydney gave me a raise, I'm a bit closer to that freedom. It helps because the sooner I can get out of my parents' house, the better. I can't stand being under their thumb, but with the student loans I racked up after my scholarships were cancelled, I haven't been able to do it.

All that time and money wasted. I have a degree in architecture, and thanks to my piss-poor decisions regarding men, I have no chance of ever using it.

"All right. We're okay?" Sean asks after I don't say anything.

"We're good."

Other than I want to know if kissing you again will be like that night. Oh, and Oliver and I broke up.

"I'll see you in a week," he says.

The flutter in my stomach makes it hard to keep my tone even, but I manage it. "Can't wait."

Yeah, the next six months are going to be a test I pray I don't fail.

three

I have a new countdown in my head.

Three days until S-day.

Sean Day.

Three days before I have to pretend I haven't relived that stupid kiss and haven't realized that I'm in love with my best friend.

Super fun.

I get up, check myself in the mirror, and then head downstairs. My parents are in the living room, looking at some article in the newspaper. Mom looks up. "Where are you going this early?"

"To the stables."

She huffs. "Aren't you being the dutiful daughter. Now you suddenly care about the animals here. Because it suits you?"

I swallow the acid response I want to toss at her.

My mother was once a very loving and sweet woman. We would spend hours in the garden, planting and harvesting vegetables. She would take me into the stables and allow me time with the horses. That was always my desired place to be.

She has a strong belief in values and did her best to instill them in me.

For years, it seemed as though I surpassed her hopes.

Until I didn't.

"Lily," Dad says softly. "She's not doing anything wrong. She's helping out on the weekends."

I smile at my father, who has a full head of gray hair and is a bit rounder than he likes to believe. He doesn't look at me as though I'm a failure, and I love him even more for it.

"A lot of good it does us during the week when she's working a job that is beneath her."

"I enjoy working for Sydney."

She places her hand on the cover of the book she was reading. "Your family's farm needs help. Your brother at least comes and works on the machines. We would've closed things down, but you encouraged us to keep going when you decided to move back home after college."

Yes, it's all my fault. I am the one who destroyed everything for her. "I didn't encourage it, Mom. I said that I was here and if you and Dad didn't want to get rid of the animals, I would help."

"But you don't," she counters.

No, I do anything I can to stay the hell away from her censure.

Dad places his hand on hers. "Let's not blame anyone, please." He nods toward the door, and I take my cue.

"I'll be back later."

My mother waves her free hand as though she can't be

bothered, and I head out to the barn.

My family is sort of eclectic on what we provide as a farm. We have a bit of everything and cater to whatever people might need. We have cattle because Sugarloaf is primarily a dairy town, but we also have horses, goats, chickens, and sheep.

We not only sell animals but also help local farmers by purchasing and rehoming animals they can no longer keep for whatever reason.

However, the horse I'm standing in front of is all mine. "Hey there, Simba," I call to my beautiful oatmeal-colored gelding that I've loved for the last ten years.

He lifts his snout and makes his way toward the apple I have in my hand.

"That's a good boy. Want to go out for a ride?"

He takes the food and bobs his head as though he is actually agreeing.

I tack him up, and we head out to the open fields. I love when I can let him run free. He's getting older and doesn't go nearly as fast as he once did, but I give him the reins and let him go.

I smile as the wind whips through my hair, the sun beats down on my face, and the fresh air fills my lungs. The freedom I feel as Simba and I ride through the countryside is indescribable. For this brief moment, I can be who I am. There is no forcing a smile or pressure to make my life better. I just . . . am.

I'm the girl who has given up so much that I can never get back.

I'm the woman who is trying to find her way in a sea of uncertainty.

I'm also the person who is working to forgive herself.

And I will. I must.

When I get to the back end of the field, I head across the creek and over to where my brother's property is.

After I cross his fence line, I make my way toward where my brother, Jasper, is usually working. I tie up Simba, patting his neck and kissing his nose, grateful that we were able to spend some time together, and then I go in search of the one person in this world who has never made me feel bad about myself.

Sure enough, I find him tinkering with something on an older-looking tractor.

I clear my throat. "Hello there, brother."

Jasper slides out from under the engine. "This is a surprise."

I say the one word that binds us. "Mom."

"Say no more."

My mother treats my brother much better than she treats me, but it's still . . . not great.

"What are you working on?" I ask.

"I'm trying to fix this for Connor. He says he fixed it twice, but . . ."

"Connor is not really mechanically inclined."

He laughs. "No, I'm not really sure what the hell he fixed, but I'll get it working enough for him to sell it."

I lean my hip against the workbench that is littered with tools. "Of course you will."

"So, what was Mom after you about this time?"

"Who knows, but one day, I won't be such a disappointment."

Jasper has always understood me. It doesn't matter that there is seven years between us because, when we were kids, we were inseparable. As we got older, we drifted a bit, unsure of how to navigate him being an adult, working full-time and marrying Hazel, while I was a kid. But he's been kind when my mother has been anything but that and never pushed me away. Instead, he's been grateful for the relationship we've established.

"Don't listen to her. She's just . . . her. Any luck finding somewhere to live?"

"No, I just have to be patient." I have just about enough money to rent somewhere, but the crux of the issue is where to move. I don't want to leave Sugarloaf. I want to be close to my brother and there isn't exactly a plethora of housing options.

"Have you talked to Sean?" Jasper asks.

My throat goes dry at the mention of his name. "About?"

"Living with him for the six months. I mean, Connor and Ellie moved into their new house, Declan is living with Sydney, and Sean will be in town. You could easily crash in that box thing that Dec lived in."

There was not a chance that I was going to stay in the big house, not after that kiss. However, I hadn't considered living in the tiny house. I could totally do that. Of course, I'd need land to put it on, and I know mother would have a conniption if I asked. Heaven forbid she have to accommodate any changes for me.

I could always ask Jasper, but . . .that might cause her to flip on him and I'd rather not do that.

"I'll think about talking to him. Thanks for the idea."

He smirks. "I'm full of them."

"You're full of something, all right."

"Hazel would agree with you there."

"Hey, did you decide to take on another mechanic?"

Jasper straightens up and shrugs. "I'm not sure what to do. Bringing another employee into the business means I need more work."

"Jasper, you have plenty of work. In fact, you have too much work."

I've been encouraging him to expand for a year. He could do so much more if he was able to bring in some help. With all the money he spends on Austin's baseball, I know he needs the help financially.

"Your business plan was interesting."

"It was also detailed and the projections were very conservative."

He wipes the grease off his hands and stares at me. "You think I would make more than what you put in that graph?"

I nod. "I do."

"You know I love you?"

"Yes. How could you not?"

His smile is wide and causes the skin around his eyes to crinkle. "My point is that you're way too smart for your own good. If I did this, I'd need your help."

"You don't even have to ask. If you do it, I'll be here each step of the way."

Jasper pulls me to his chest, the smell of gasoline, oil, and wood fill me as I hug my brother. "Good. Now, go get me some customers and hire a few people."

I laugh and shove him back. "I didn't say I'd run your business."

"Really? I swear I heard that."

"You need your hearing checked."

"And you need a life outside of this family."

This is a conversation I am not ready to have. I look toward the house, knowing there's only one thing that will get him off this topic. "Are Hazel and Austin home?"

Jasper nods. "They are. I'm sure they'll be happy to see you. Hand me that wrench, will you?"

There are six wrenches on the table, so I just pick one. I crouch down, kiss my brother on the cheek, and head off in search of my sister-in-law and my nephew.

Before I can reach the back door, the nine-year-old bundle of energy comes flying out the door. "Aunt Devney!" he yells and launches himself at me.

I catch him—barely—and laugh as he wraps his arms around my middle.

I love this boy.

I love him more than anything in the world, and I am so grateful for the time I get to spend with him.

"Look at you, you've grown in the last few days." I squeeze him a bit tighter.

"It's because Mom is feeding me gross vegetables. She says they will help me play baseball better."

And Austin will do anything that might make that a reality. "At least it's working."

He releases me and smiles when he spots something behind me. "You brought Simba?"

"I did."

"Can we ride back and get my horse from Grandma and Papa?"

I'd rather eat nails than go back home, but for Austin, I just might do it. "Maybe. Do you have practice today?"

He groans. "Yes. I can skip it, though!"

There's not a chance in hell that's happening. Hazel and Jasper indulge him in a lot, but the amount of money they spend on his private lessons, special teams, and gear means that he is absolutely not allowed to skip.

"I doubt you really mean that. Would you want to explain to your coach or Sean when he gets here that you skipped out?"

Austin kicks a rock. "I guess not, but can we ride soon?"

"Of course, we'll ask your parents and find a day."

"Is Sean coming to Sugarloaf soon? Hadley was telling *everyone* at school how her famous uncle was coming to town and how cool he is. And then she was going on and on about her stupid tree house and how her uncle is buying her a horse. I have a horse! I don't know why she thinks we care. She's just a girl."

I bite my tongue and try to keep from smiling. He's such a typical boy in the girls-are-dumb phase. "She is a girl, but so is your mom and so am I."

"Yeah, but you're not *Hadley*." He sneers her name.

I crouch, taking his hands in mine. "Austin, you liked Hadley last week."

"Yeah, but now I'm going to have to listen to her talk all the time."

This time, the smile will not stay hidden. "She's your friend, isn't she?"

"Sometimes."

"Well, she's excited just like you are that Sean is coming to be your coach. Don't you think she's allowed to be the same way?"

He rolls his eyes and groans. "I guess."

"Right. Well, he'll be here soon, and then you can both talk about how cool he is. Just remember that I knew him when he was not so cool."

"He was always cool."

There's no way to burst his bubble. Telling him the stories of when we were younger will probably only cement his status instead of showing that he is a mere mortal like the rest of us. To who knows how many boys with dreams of the big leagues—he's a God.

"Anyway, you will have plenty of things to be excited about once Sean arrives and works with your team."

There's a glaze that falls over Austin's eyes as he smiles.

"It's going to be the best. I'm so glad you know him!"

"Me too."

There are a lot of reasons I'm glad I know Sean Arrowood, not just because he makes Austin smile like that. Years of friendship and trust and now, who knows what.

Three days until I have to figure it out.

Austin and I turn to go inside just as Hazel opens the door. "Hey, you."

"Hey, sorry to just drop in."

She rolls her eyes. "Like you'd ever not be welcome? However . . . I was coming out here because something showed up at the front door that I think you might want."

"For me?"

She nods. "Yup."

"Here?"

I never send anything to my brother's place.

"Yeah, I think it's a surprise."

Just then, a tall figure steps out of the house, and my three days become zero.

four

Not sure if this was my best idea, but it's too late to go back now.

When I got to Devney's house and her parents said she went riding and probably came here, I was unable to stay away from her another minute.

Looking at her has everything in my head all fucked up again. For days, I've wondered, thought about her, wished I could be here so I could try to figure out what to do. Kissing Devney was like nothing I could've prepared for.

Years of listening to people tell us we were more than friends, thinking they were all ridiculous only to realize that was utter bullshit.

However, she has Oliver.

The nice guy.

The one who is here for her, who takes care of her when I . . . well, I can't.

Still, I want to see her. I'll have her any way I can get her.

There she stands, dark brown hair in a braid and the prettiest brown eyes I've ever seen are staring back at me. Her lips part, and I can see the heavy rise and fall of her chest.

"You're early," Devney says as she watches me watch her.

"I am."

"Sean!" Austin breaks the moment as he heads to me.

"Hey, little dude." We do the customary fist bump, and he is practically bouncing.

"This is so cool. So cool. I can't believe you're here . . . Mom! Mom! Do you see who is here?"

Hazel laughs and touches my shoulder. "I see him. He's real. Who knew?"

The kids are the best part of my job. I've always made sure to sign balls and autographs, and I try to be a role model for them. While I may not have had a father figure in my life, I've had great coaches. The men who taught me how to grow up and find humility in the world that offers so little.

I'm a normal guy who just happens to play baseball.

To these kids, I'm a hero. Someone they aspire to be, and I never take that for granted.

Devney heads toward us, and suddenly, I'm not sure what to do. Do I hug her? Do I confess that I want her and ask that she get rid of the idiot she's with? No, that would be unfair and selfish. I need to do what I've always done. I pull her close and kiss the top of her head.

"It's good to see you," she says, head against my chest.

"You too."

"You're so short, Aunt Devney," Austin comments.

"She is, right?"

"I am not short." All too soon, she's out of my arms and standing there, glaring at Austin, attempting to appear angry.

Austin tilts his head, and I mimic him. "I think she is."

He nods. "I agree."

"Great, now I have the two of you ganging up on me?"

"We speak the truth, Shrimpy," I say, knowing she'll get pissed.

"I'm going to kill you!" she yells and then rushes toward me.

I dart to the left, and she goes right. Austin laughs and chases us as I go in circles, zigging and zagging to get away from them.

There's not a chance in hell she's going to catch me.

After a few more rounds, I stop and turn the tables, advancing on her.

"Sean," she warns.

"You should run, Dev."

"Don't do it."

If I catch her, then it's game on. She laughs and takes off, lifting Austin in her arms, carrying him against her hip as he squeals.

"I'm getting closer."

She stops running and falls to the ground. Without thinking, I cover her with my body, and we all roll in the grass. Austin moves to the side and jumps on my back as I start to tickle Devney.

"Surrender!" I say with a mocking tone.

"Never!"

There is nothing she hates more than being tickled. "Say uncle!"

Devney laughs so hard tears are coming from her eyes as I continue my assault. "Aunt!" she yells.

I love that no matter what, giving in isn't a part of her

makeup.

I take that as her version of a truce, and all three of us lie on the ground, facing the sky. I can't remember the last time I played like this. Each time I've seen Connor, I've spent time with Hadley, but she's usually forcing me to a tea party or play with dolls in the tree house that my brother built.

Not just . . . playing.

"I hate you," Devney says after a few moments of silence.

"You'll get over it. You always do."

I turn to look at her, and she does the same. There's an easy smile on her lips. I worried that, when we were together again, it would be awkward. It was the last thing I wanted to be true.

There's only been one time when we haven't been on speaking terms, and that was in fifth grade when she told Marley Jenkins that I liked her. I didn't, but she chased me for weeks.

"I got over it because she started to like Jacob and irritate him."

Devney smirks, knowing exactly what I'm talking about. "I put that in motion too."

"You're a whole world of trouble, Devney Maxwell. A whole world of it."

Austin sits up. "Are you going to come to my practice tonight?"

I forgot the kid was here. Jesus, how easy it is to get lost in her eyes.

I face Austin. "Would you like me to?"

"Of course!"

"Then consider it done."

Austin jumps up. "I have to go tell Dad!"

And now, it's just Devney and me.

She tucks the stray hair that fell from her braid behind her ear and leans on her arm. "You have no idea how much he likes you."

"I think it's a Maxwell thing. You are all drawn to my undeniable charm."

"Oh please." She scoffs. "The only thing undeniable about you is that you think you're charming. Spoiler alert, you're not."

"I've always been able to tell when you're lying. Which it seems you were before."

"What did I lie about?"

"You told me that you couldn't talk on the phone because Austin had a game."

Her eyes widen and she lets out a nervous laugh. "I meant practice."

"Did you?"

I think there's more to it, and I'm going to push her a little.

"Obviously."

I smile at her. "It wasn't about the kiss?"

Devney releases a long sigh. "No, Sean, it wasn't. We're both in agreement that it was a mistake and we weren't going to talk about it."

I guess that I'm the liar now. Still, I need to play it cool. "Right. We did."

"Why are you here early?"

"I needed to see you." The words slip from my mouth so easily. There's a new tension in her body that makes me wish I had thought before I spoke. "The last time we were together, things got messy. I don't want messy with you, Dev."

She gets to her feet, brushing the grass from her jeans. "Nothing is messy. We're fine. We were drunk. I'll just put that on the long list of things that we need to atone for."

There are a lot more things that I'd like to add to the list. Like taking her in my arms and kissing her until she can't think. I'd lay her in the grass, feeling every contour of her body, using my hands, lips, tongue—

"Sean?" Devney waves her hands in front of my eyes. "You there?"

"Yeah, sorry . . . I'm tired from the early flight."

Devney extends her hand, and I clasp it, fighting back the pulse of electricity that happens at her touch. I rise, towering over her and can't stop myself from pulling her close, needing to have the connection we've always shared.

Her arms wrap around my middle, head tucked under my chin. "There are only two things that will make these six months bearable."

"What are they?" she asks, peering up into my eyes. Her soft smile makes me believe we'll be okay.

"You and spending time with my two brothers. But you're number one, Dev. You're always my number one."

She looks away and then steps back. "You've got me, right?" It's the phrase we've used since we were kids.

"Always."

I just pray I don't let her down.

five

"**H**e's absolutely perfect," I say, holding Deacon James Arrowood—also known as DJ—in my arms.

"I love him so much already." Sydney smiles, lying in the bed after the easiest birth in history.

I swear, it was as if she commanded him to obey, and he did. Instead of laboring for hours, Sydney woke up, told Declan it was time, they went to the hospital and five hours later, he was here. After how rocky her pregnancy was, I think this was a welcome revelation.

"Of course you do. He's beautiful." I sway slightly, loving how innocent and sweet he looks. "Where's Declan?" I ask.

"He went with his brothers to the burial site."

Some might not understand the importance of that, but Sydney and I do. Their mother was a formidable woman who they loved, as we did as well. When she died, nothing could illuminate the darkness that seeped into that house.

"I'm glad they're together again. Well, almost."

Syd nods. "It's been hard on them, and even though I think their father was a bastard, him forcing this has been a good thing."

"Well," I say softly, bouncing Deacon, "I know of at least two good things that have come from them returning."

"Ellie is desperate to have the baby already."

"I can imagine. She was uncomfortable when I saw her last week."

Sydney yawns and then winces. "I'm so sore, and it's so . . . weird, not having the pressure anymore."

"The pressure is in my arms, huh?"

I love babies. They're so perfect and untouched. Nothing has hurt them or jaded them. They just are, and it's magnificent. One day, I might have this. I yearn for it, more than anyone can ever understand.

It was once in my grasp, but then it was gone just as quickly.

Still, I would love to raise a child someday.

Deacon squirms a bit, and I tighten my hold, remembering how much Austin loved to be swaddled tightly. He would fuss until someone would make him unmovable in his cocoon.

"Dev?"

"Yeah?"

"Are you going to tell me anything about what's going on with Sean? I've been patient, but you're killing me. It's been two weeks since you told me he kissed you."

I sigh, moving to the edge of her bed. "It's nothing. He said it was a mistake, and well, he's right. So, we're moving on."

Sydney stares at me for a moment. "It's not easy to just move on. Not when you realize you're in love with him."

"I'm not in love with him."

At least, I'm not willing to be. I can't be in love with my best friend. It doesn't work that way. Not when he's been the best part of my life since the second grade.

"Look, I'm not going to call you a liar, but you're not exactly being honest."

"You have a baby to mother now, Syd, you don't have to do it with me."

She laughs once and then sighs. "I'm not mothering you— or at least, I'm not trying to. I'm just saying that loving him, more than as a friend, is common knowledge to everyone but the two of you. He's here for another five and a half months and then, who knows what will happen?"

"Exactly!" I say in a whisper-yell. "He's going to leave, and if I remember, *someone*, didn't want to get involved with a certain Arrowood for the same reason. *And*," I stress, "I have zero chances of being pregnant with Sean's baby. So, taking five and a half months to . . . date . . . or whatever the hell it would be only ends with me having a broken heart in Sugarloaf and an Arrowood in Florida. No thanks."

"Maybe that will be the case, but what if it isn't? What if he's the one for you and you let him go?"

"What if? I can't play those games, Syd. I'm not a kid anymore. I have responsibilities and desires. I want to get married, have kids, have a life . . ." DJ starts to fuss, and I place him back in his mother's arms. "I love you, and I know that what you're saying is from the goodness of your heart. I really do. But Sean is my best friend. Blurring those lines would destroy not only my heart but also my soul. If we didn't work out, we could never be friends again. We were drunk and kissed, but in a few months, he'll go back to his life, and I'll go back to mine."

Sydney's eyes look to her son and then back to me. "Yeah, I thought that too. Good luck, my friend."

And she was wrong, and I'm sure I am as well.

I enter the house, battle gear on, ready for whatever war my mother is about to declare. I'm never sure how I will disappoint her, but it's always there.

"There you are," Dad's warm voice says from the couch. "Everything okay?"

"Yeah, everything is great. Sydney had the baby."

"That's great. I'm sure the family is happy. Is Sean back now?"

I sit on the couch beside him, laying my head on his shoulder. "He is."

"I'm sure that means we'll be seeing a lot of him?"

Between Jasper and Sean, not many boys would dare approach me. Jasper was bad, but Sean was a nightmare. Just a look from him would send any guy running in the other direction. It was inconvenient and irritating, but Sean would say that any guy who wasn't willing to push him back wasn't worth a moment of my time.

My father agreed, which earned Sean my father's love.

"I don't know. He's going to work with Austin and some other local kids on the team, do something on the farm with the cows, and I'm busy, so . . ."

"So, we'll see him when those things aren't happening." Dad chuckles. "That boy can't stay away, Shrimpy. You're just too damn irresistible."

"Yes," my mother says snidely as she enters the room. "Men, boys, all creatures just can't resist, can they?"

I let my guard down, and now I must pay. "I guess not, Mom."

"That was not what I was saying, and we all know it," Dad corrects her. "Not to mention, when Sean was around, Devney smiled more."

"Yes, we could all use a little of that, I guess."

In other words, she really doesn't care.

The doorbell rings, bringing this enlightening conversation to a close before it turns ugly. When I open the door, my heart nearly stops.

"Oliver?"

"Dev." He smiles warmly. "How are you?"

I glance toward my parents and then step outside with Oliver. I don't want them overhearing any of this. "I'm good, you?"

"I'm good."

"I didn't expect to see you," I say as we move over to the chairs on the far side of the wraparound porch.

Oliver looks different. Even though it's only been two weeks, something has changed with him. As though he's . . . lighter.

Guilt hits me as I wonder if the relationship was what weighed him down. I know I'm not an easy person to love. I'm stubborn, closed off, and untrusting by nature. It took Oliver asking me out for almost four months straight before I agreed to go on a date. He was persistent and wore me down.

I loved him in the only way I could, but it wasn't enough.

I let him into very select places of my heart, but it was never deep enough for him to have the ability to truly hurt me.

Someone before him taught me that.

We both sit, and he sighs. "I wanted to drop off a few of your things that you left at my place, but I also wanted to let you know about something."

"Oh?"

"A month ago, an opportunity within my father's company was brought to me. I was reluctant to accept."

"Because of me?"

He smiles and nods. "I knew that you wouldn't leave Sugarloaf, and I wasn't going to ask you since I knew the answer."

God, what a bitch I was. "That's . . . so wrong."

"Wrong?"

"Yes, Ollie, it was wrong that you wanted to spend your life with me and couldn't ask me to move with you. I should never have made you feel that way. It's not fair to you. I am so sorry that I ever made you reluctant to take a job offer that would further your career."

"Stop. Please. I really didn't want the job, and I think I used our relationship as the reason to turn it down. I knew my dad would never force me to choose, but now that we're not together, I sort of lost that bargaining chip. I'm not as honorable as you'd like to think I am."

That's where he's wrong. "No, I think you are."

He laughs. "Well, at least one of us does."

"Still, I owe you so much."

"I'm going to take the job in Wyoming."

"So far?" I say the words on a breath.

"He bought an ungodly amount of land and wants to expand our cattle business. It's a smart move, and if I go, I'll run that farm."

He was right that I wouldn't have gone. I would never go that far. My family is here, and I need to be close for selfish reasons. They may be difficult, but they helped me when I was lost.

"It's a good opportunity for you."

Oliver takes my hand. "I think it's good for both of us. If I leave, then we don't have to worry about running into each other or any awkwardness."

The sad part is that I don't feel awkward around him. I don't feel sad or hurt. It was a friendship that was always between us. The only regret is that I let him think a life together could be more. Now, I'm going to give him whatever comfort I can.

"Maybe you're right. I don't know how I'd feel if I saw you with someone else."

"I can't stay when I know Sean is here, Dev. I can let you go because I love you enough to want you to be happy, but I can't watch it."

I look into his deep blue eyes and see the pain there. "We're not . . ."

"Maybe not now. Maybe not in the next six months, but someday, the two of you will be, and I can't be here. So, I've come to say goodbye."

"Is it wrong to say I hate this?"

Oliver chuckles. "Is it wrong that I'm glad you do?"

I smile. "No."

"Then we're not wrong."

We get to our feet, and he pulls me into his arms for a sweet hug. I'm going to miss him. Oliver has been good to me and for me. There were no secrets or lies. No tawdry meetings in closets or whatever stolen kisses I was allowed.

He loved me in the open.

He loved me for who I was.

And now I have to let him go—for good.

I push onto my toes, and press my lips to his. "Thank you, Ollie."

My body is tugged forward into a tight embrace.

As we release each other, I turn and Sean is walking up the drive. His hands are in his pockets, light brown hair hanging slightly in his eyes. He wears an easy smile, but I can see the tightness around his eyes as he climbs the stairs.

"Oliver," Sean says, extending his hand.

Oliver, ever the gentleman, returns the gesture and then clears his throat. "Sean, take care of her."

Without another word, he walks away, leaving me with Sean, who has a million questions in his eyes.

six

"Devney?"

I need to know what that was. Did she tell him?

"Oliver is leaving for Wyoming."

I shouldn't be happy by this. No, I should be sad because Devney looks as though she's about to break down. Her coffee-colored eyes are soft and glossy. When she cries, I fucking lose it. There's nothing that breaks my heart more than that.

"You told him?"

She nods. "I told him before you got back, actually. We broke up then."

"Fuck." I groan. "I should've . . ."

"Should've what?"

There's no way I'm going to answer that because I don't know what I should've done, really. If it never happened, she'd still be with him, and I'd be lying if I said I'm not happy this is the outcome.

For weeks, I've tried to convince myself that we'd be stupid to attempt a relationship. I'm still not sure it's smart, but each time I talk myself out of it, I'm right back here—in front of her.

I came here now because I needed her. Standing with my brothers at the grave the other day, listening to them tell my mother about their lives, I felt hollow. There was nothing to tell her.

Declan, the one who was the most steadfast about avoiding marriage, kids, and roots in Sugarloaf bought a fucking farm and has started his family. Connor, who probably had it the worst and had the hardest time coming back here, is married and his wife is about to have another baby.

There I was. Kid-less, wife-less, and feeling as though I was floundering, which makes no sense. I'm the one who has it all.

I have the career that every kid dreams of.

A ridiculous penthouse apartment.

A car that other men drool over.

But all of that felt inconsequential as they told her of their treasures.

Now, I'm here, looking at her, wondering if I've had something for all these years that's infinitely more valuable and was just unable to see it.

"I don't know, apologized to him at least."

"He wasn't angry," she says, her voice low. "He wasn't even surprised."

Well, I sure as fuck am. "He wasn't?"

"No, Oliver took it graciously, far more than he should've been, and then he let me go."

I take a step closer. "And how are you taking it all?"

Her brown eyes meet mine, searching, probing deep inside me until my skin feels taut. "I'm fine. I'm sad because Oliver truly did love me, and I hurt him."

She hasn't once told me that she loved him beyond reason, though. I could—and want to—call her out on it, but that wouldn't help this conversation. I owe Oliver a lot more than an apology. He was my friend as well, even if it was only because he was dating Devney, but still. He trusted me, and I broke that.

"So, why is he leaving for Wyoming?"

"Why do you think?"

"Because I'm here, and he thinks . . ."

Devney shrugs and moves over to the rocking chair. "Yeah, I guess he doesn't want to watch what will never happen between us."

I don't miss the emphasis on the word *never*. "Right."

She sits and starts to move back and forth as I sit beside her. After a few seconds of amiable silence, she reaches over and takes my hand. We've always been affectionate, but this time, it feels different, more intimate, more like a couple. "Why did you come over? Was it the visit to your mother's grave?"

How she knows me so well. "Yes."

"You haven't gone since you buried your father, have you?"

Shame fills me. The loss of my mother was hard on all of us. I can't say that one of my brothers took it worse or better. We all grieved. We all felt the absence of her and it tore us apart. Elizabeth Arrowood was the most beautiful and perfect woman alive.

And I miss her more when I'm here.

"What's one truth about an arrow?" Devney's voice is soft and coaxing.

I look at her, feeling a myriad of emotions. I don't want to answer. I don't want to say the words my mother forced from me each time I was at the driveway.

Devney squeezes my hand. "It's okay, Sean. I've got you."

The words we've spoken to each other so many times over the years cause my throat to close. Being back here is fucking agony.

Not because of my father but because of all I have lost.

I close my eyes, letting her comfort give me the strength to say what I haven't in almost two decades. "Just because you don't hit the bull's-eye, it doesn't mean the other shots don't count."

"We don't always win, Sean. Sometimes we lose. Sometimes we don't hit the mark, but at least we tried, right?" Devney asks.

I think she might need the answer more than I do. Now, I have a little over five months to decide if the shot I took a few weeks ago was a miss or not. We have time to get to the bottom of the feelings we have and the ones we've been ignoring over the years.

"Are you asking for me or for you?" I ask. When she attempts to pull her hand back, I tighten my grip, unwilling to let her off the hook. "You've lost too, Dev. You've struggled to get back up. I don't know what you're keeping from me, but I wish you'd tell me."

"I'm not holding back." She gets to her feet, and I follow.

She's lying.

"Then what is going on? Why are you being so distant?"

"I'm not being distant, Sean. In the last few weeks, a lot of shit has changed. I broke up with my boyfriend, a new guy started working at the office, Sydney had her baby, Ellie is going to have hers . . ."

"And I kissed you."

She rubs her hands over her eyes and refuses to look at me.

"Yeah, then there's that."

"Why did you let Oliver go?"

Devney turns, eyes piercing mine. "Do you think I ever want to be 'that' girl? Do you think I would start my marriage to a man when I'd done something like cheat on him?"

"No."

"Then why are you asking?"

I move toward her, and she retreats. My heart pounds harder the closer I get to her. For the last two weeks, I've berated, promised, and done everything not to feel this way. Not to want her because she wasn't free. Now she is. I need to see if that kiss was nothing more than the lie I've been telling myself or if my heart knows more than my head. "Because I think, if it were just a drunken mistake, you would've fought for him."

"Sean, don't."

"Don't what?"

There are so many things she could be asking. Don't kiss me. Don't say anything I can't take back. Don't break her heart. I need to know what she's asking me.

"Don't do something we can't deny or take back."

"I won't," I promise her and then pull her into my arms. I give her another beat to make sure she understands this kiss won't be a drunken mistake. It won't be anything we can brush off or excuse away. This will be because I want to kiss her more than I want to draw breath.

Her hands rest on my chest, long eyelashes fan across her cheeks, and then slowly, she lifts her gaze to mine. I see the heat, wonder, and fear lingering there. I don't want to live with any more shame for not doing the right thing.

For not kissing her sooner.

And I'm not going to wait any longer.

seven

Oh God.

Oh God, oh God, oh God.

The litany is on repeat through my head. He's kissing me. For real, no drinking, no excuses, no lies-to-tell-ourselves-tomorrow kissing me.

And it is everything.

His lips are soft and coaxing. Each breath passing between us feels like a conversation.

Do you want me?

Yes.

Is this really happening?

Yes.

Should we stop?

Yes.

But I don't. I can't stop. I've wanted this every second

for a little over two weeks. Now that I feel his warmth and strength, I never want it to end.

It proves I'm a total idiot.

My hands move up his chest and across his jawline. The coarse hairs prick the sensitive skin as I move to his neck. I tangle my fingers into his soft hair, loving the way they slip through it without resistance, and then he moans.

He moves me back against the side of the house where no one can see anything through the windows. His arms hold me securely, and I press closer to his chest.

Everything in my mind is centered on him. I've wanted this so bad, thought about nothing else, and now we're kissing again. It's as though the world I've always known has flipped upside down. This is Sean.

Sean.

He is not supposed to kiss me. I'm definitely not supposed to want him to do so much more.

And then, like ice dumped on my head after a hot day, I remember that Sean isn't staying in Sugarloaf. Sean will go back to his fancy life, and I will stay here.

I turn my head and then he steps back. "We can't do this," I say once I'm able to catch my breath.

I can feel his gaze on me, and I meet it. "Devney, the last thing in the world I would ever do is hurt you."

Oh, how wrong he is. "You're the one man in the world who would destroy me."

He runs his fingers through his hair and starts to pace. I know him so well. Right now, he's figuring out all the ways to get what he wants. He's forming a plan, creating backup plans, going over outcomes, and trying to attack the best way.

Only, the end result will always be the same.

He might think there are a million reasons he can give me to leave, but there's one for me to stay that he can never compete with.

"Why?" Sean asks as he moves across the wooden floor.

"Because you know my entire heart and soul. I've given you more of myself than I ever gave anyone else. You know all my defenses, Sean, and if you wanted to use them, I wouldn't be able to stop it."

"That just means we could make things work."

"Oh, please. Stop it. I know you and your romantic heart, but I also know that you stood at that grave with your brothers and saw what you didn't have."

Sean's eyes lift to mine, awareness flashing between us. He may know me, but I know him just as well. "That's not why I kissed you."

"No, you're not cruel. You're worried, going through a lot of things, and I'm comfort, which is something I will always be."

He moves closer and then stops. "I feel something, Devney."

"And I do too, but we've been friends for damn near twenty years and have never felt anything until now, why? It doesn't make sense." I pull my jacket a little tighter as the cold air whips around us.

"Maybe not, but that doesn't mean it's not real."

"No, but it doesn't mean it's right."

His breath is forced out through his lips. "I see."

I'm glad he does because I have no idea what I'm saying. I feel something too—fear. I worry that I'll fall so head over heels in love with him and then end up broken on the ground when he leaves, which he will. It's not a matter of if but when he will go. His entire life is baseball and mine is not.

My insecurities are far beyond what he could try to guess. I can't live a life with someone who wants his cake and wants to eat it too.

"Our situations wouldn't change," I add.

"No, they wouldn't."

"I don't want to leave this town."

He runs his hand through his thick brown hair. "And I won't come back. Even if I wanted to, which I don't, I'm bound by contract to stay in Florida."

"Right. And . . . that leaves us here."

"At an impasse it seems."

At the beginning and the end of a relationship that was never meant to be. "I love you, Sean. I really do, so please, let's not do this and mess up the friendship we share, okay?"

He sighs and pulls me to his chest. "Okay, Shrimpy. We'll stay the way we are and I'll do my best not to kiss you."

I laugh. "I'm sure you'll find a way to manage."

Sean's arms fall away, and I step back. "Can we at least hang out? I'm in that . . . house . . . and I'm all alone."

"You live alone in Florida!"

"That's different."

"How so?"

He shrugs. "I don't like anyone there, and I happen to like you."

"Yeah, yeah. I'll bring a scary movie over tomorrow, and we can make fun of it."

The smile that paints his face is so beautiful. "Perfect. It's a date."

Friends. We are friends. Friends don't date. "Right."

"Say hello to your parents," Sean says as he heads down the stairs.

I watch him go and wonder how we're going to find our footing again. Each time he kisses me, a little bit of my resolve melts. It's been so long since I felt such an intensity with a man.

And I know where that got me.

Once I head back inside, my parents are in the kitchen at the small table.

"Everything okay with Oliver?" Dad asks.

"Yeah. He's . . . he's moving."

My mother's eyes meet mine. "He's what? Are you going? Did he propose?"

Oh, this is going to go over like a load of bricks. My mother thinks Oliver is the sun and the stars. He was her only hope of getting rid of me. "Oliver and I broke up, Mom."

"Excuse me?"

"A couple of weeks ago, we ended things. It was very amicable, and we're better off as friends."

Dad shifts a bit. "Did he hurt you?"

"Of course not," Mother speaks quickly. "We all know who is at fault here. This was your chance, Devney. The first time for you to find happiness since . . . since all of the mistakes you made."

"Oliver and I weren't happy."

She throws her hands up. "What do you think life is? Rainbows and unicorns? Get your head out of the clouds, little girl! There aren't many men like Oliver Parkerson."

No, there isn't. And Oliver deserves a woman who will fall at his feet. One who won't dream of a singular kiss and has butterflies fill her stomach. I'm not that girl. I'm the one who thinks of him as a warm cup of milk—settling, steady, and reliable.

That was appealing, and I would've been happy with that had I never taken a sip of another drink after him. One that sent fire through my veins and an ache in my chest.

One that was similar to one I tasted before, only that one

damn near destroyed my life.

Daddy leans forward, facing my mother. "She isn't a little girl anymore. Devney has made mistakes, but we aren't saints either. It's time to let go."

"Mistakes? Is that what we're calling her choice?" My mother rails and gets to her feet. "Yes, I have made mistakes, but I'm not the one who slept with my married professor and had to deal with the fallout of that."

Finally. *Finally,* she's said the damn words. "Yes, I slept with my married professor, Mom. What a shameful whore I am, right? Not that he took advantage of a nineteen-year-old girl, *lied* to me, *used* me, and then discarded me, right? It was *my* fault. It had to be me because I'm just a complete disgrace in your eyes."

"I taught you better!" she yells as she turns her back on me.

"I was *young*! I believed him, and I am the one who was hurt by it all!"

"Lily," Dad says, but she glares at him.

"I am not the one who is wrong here. I've done my best for her! All the headaches this family has endured because she couldn't be the girl I raised."

She must get pains in her neck from having to look so far down from the pedestal she's perched on. "I am that girl. I believe in all the values and beliefs that I always have. I loved him, and I thought he loved me. He lied to me about being married. He swore he was going to quit the university and marry me. All of that tore me apart, but the worst has been how you've treated me since then. I wasn't proud of what I did. I was mortified and ashamed, but you've spent the last six years since I finished school, making me relive it. I transferred schools. I moved farther away from him and my mistakes. Why can't you just see my side?"

"You act as though we can just move on from it all."

"What the hell have you had to suffer from?"

"The lies!" she yells.

Right. The fact that when she walks into church on Sundays, she has to pretend that I'm the perfect child. God forbid.

"You think that the women you're so close to don't have skeletons in their closets? Aren't forgiveness and acceptance covered in the sermons you listen to on Sunday mornings while you all sit around and discuss the ways you're going to save the town?"

My mother huffs and looks away.

Dad shakes his head. "This has to stop."

Mom's eyes meet mine. "If you want forgiveness, you have to atone for your mistakes, which you clearly haven't done. You've just blamed the situation on your professor like you weren't involved."

"I don't blame solely him! I just say the reality. I was a freaking sheltered teenager who was desperate for my first boyfriend and he paid me attention, made me think I was special!"

"You always were special, Devney," she says with a hint of sadness. "We all knew it, but you were so wrapped up in the Arrowood boys and running around with them that you didn't date."

The doe-eyed girl who left Sugarloaf at seventeen had no idea about the world. I was so accustomed to things being one way, and then there was this whole other life that was before me. No one to tell me what I wanted or not to do something. I felt free and alive. Options that never seemed possible were before me and a man who never would've looked my way in Pennsylvania was showering me with attention.

Christopher was charming beyond measure and I was gullible to a fault.

"We will never agree on this, Mom. You'll never stop seeing me as the whore in it, and I will never forgive you for not just understanding."

She turns away, swiping at her face. "I don't think you're a whore." I hear her voice crack.

"Well, you damn sure make me feel like one."

She shakes her head, shoulders slumped as her voice carries through the room. "Regardless of whether he was married or not, you were sleeping with a professor. You knew better." When she turns, I see the sadness replaced with disgust and any chance of a conversation where we might have found common ground is gone. She continues, "A man who was close to your father's age. It was wrong. You knew, he knew, and so did the school. I can't even imagine if you had gone to a local university."

"Yes, then the shame would've been public," I say with a laugh.

"It was public enough." Mom rubs her eyes and sighs. "You could've had a fresh start with Oliver. He is a good man, one who was able to overlook your transgressions and love you. Now, what? You stay in this house until we die and continue to waste your life away?"

I think about the current status of things, and they're not great, but I'm not wasting anything. I have a good job where I help people, friends who support me, and my family, all of whom I love, especially my nephew. Things aren't perfect, but my mother continues to make things worse. I am so tired.

I'm over it all.

"I understand that you feel that way, and I'm going to go."

Dad takes a step to me. "Go where?"

"Away from here, where I'm clearly not wanted."

Dad's eyes volley between Mom and me. "What are you saying?"

"I'd rather be homeless and sleep in my car than go through this anymore. I'm sorry that I've disappointed you." I look to my mother, who keeps her back turned. "I'm sorry that the pain you've suffered has been so great. You're not the one who lived it, but what the hell do I know? I'm going."

I head to my room, tears streaming down my face as I pack whatever I can, and then get the fuck out of here.

eight

"What's one truth about an arrow?" I ask myself as I sit at the end of the driveway to Sean's house.

I've been here for ten minutes, trying to get the tears to cease, but they won't. For years, I've bottled up my past, forced it to stay contained, but now it's all in the open. I loved a liar. A married, cheating, stupid liar.

The worst part was, I had to leave school after I was put before the disciplinary board, and he had nothing happen. His wife probably never found out, his job wasn't ruined. I've never told anyone outside of my family, and I know, showing up at Sean's door, I won't be able to lie to him.

I think about his mother and what she would think. Truth? I don't know the truth anymore. I may not have been an Arrowood sibling, but I had my own saying.

"I don't need an arrow thing like you do," I tell Sean as

I'm standing on the back of his bike.

"Say it or I'll dump you off."

I roll my eyes. He wouldn't dare because I would kick his ass. I don't care that I'm a girl, I'm not afraid of him. "You do it, and you die."

"Why are you always so annoying?"

"Because you hate it."

"I'm going to take the pegs off if you don't say it, and my mom won't give you any cookies."

He might just do that, and I love the cookies Mrs. A makes. She puts extra chocolate chips in. "Fine," I whine. "Forget the last arrow because only the next shot counts."

"Was that so hard?"

"No, but I don't know why you want me to have a saying like you and your brothers."

"Because you're my best friend, Devney."

"And you're mine. You will always be too."

Sean looks back at me from over his shoulder. "Good. We never look back."

How much I wish that were the case. We were too young to know that the past defines the future. Every action has a reaction, and once they're set in motion, they aren't easy to stop. I will never be able to fully forget that relationship.

Now I have to find a way to go forward and forget the last mistake.

When I park the car, Sean is coming out of the small, white farmhouse that looks like the farm built itself around it.

"What's wrong?" His voice is full of worry.

I rush toward him, the tears coming harder than before. His strong arms wrap around me as he pulls me tight against him.

Right now, I feel so safe and yet so vulnerable. I don't want to tell him about Christopher. I don't want to say his name, but Sean is my safe place. He won't act like my family did, and I have to trust him. No, I want to trust him.

"I need a place to stay," I tell him first. "I left the house, and I have nowhere to go."

"You always have somewhere to go, you know that."

I knew he wouldn't turn me away. Yes, Sean and I are a little up in the air and I didn't want to impose, but . . . he's got me. Always.

"Thank you."

"What happened?" He takes my bag and then threads the fingers of his free hand through mine as we walk up the steps.

"My mother and I had a huge fight. A lot was said. Things that can't be taken back, and . . . I just can't stay there."

"You'll stay with me."

I release a shaky sigh. Maybe this is stupid. I should just go back or see if Jasper will let me stay a few nights. I can't stay there for too long, but a night or two would be fine. Damn it.

"Sean—" I start to say, but he puts his hand up.

"No, don't. You can argue about why this is a bad idea once you've stopped crying. For now, let's get your stuff inside. There are three empty bedrooms, and I have beer. We were friends long, long before we kissed, so let's just put all the other shit aside and be the Devney and Sean we've always been."

I'm not sure I have the strength to explain to him why there's no way to just put it aside, but I need my best friend. Sean was really the only person I wanted to run to, and I need a friend.

"Beer is good," I say as I resolve myself to staying.

We get inside, drop the bags in the entryway, and then head into the living room. I know this house as well as I know my own, but it's so different. Ellie and Connor did a lot of renovations, and the doom and gloom that had lived here is gone. There is fresh paint, the cabinets and floors have been refinished to a beautiful dark wood color, and the lighting paints everything in softer tones. It isn't just one thing they did, it's all of it together.

"I'll grab the beer, you make yourself comfortable."

I take a seat, looking around, forcing myself not to relive the argument with my mother. For so long, I've listened to her spew hatred at me, as though I weren't a nineteen-year-old girl with no self-esteem, looking to be more than just the best friend.

I've been unwilling to share the burden with anyone, even Sean because it felt like I failed. For so long, I was considered smart and strong, but I proved that I wasn't. I wanted to forget it, pretend it never happened, but my mother wouldn't let that happen. I know it wasn't my fault in a lot of ways. I can rationalize that, but I can't seem to stop myself from feeling like a fool.

Sean enters the living room and hands me a bottle. "Sit and we'll talk."

I follow the first command, plopping down on the new couch, rubbing my hand against the soft fabric. "I don't want to talk."

"Too bad."

I roll my eyes and take a long drink from the bottle. Part of me is afraid to tell him. Not because he'll give two shits about me dating a married man but because I've never told him. All this time, I've kept the years of my college experiences to myself.

When we spoke, it was about superficial stuff. Parties. Friends. Exams. Never relationships. Even though I didn't know Christopher was married, I knew starting a relationship with my professor was wrong. But to walk away from him seemed so impossible.

He was otherworldly. Smart, sophisticated, and bold. The spell he cast on me was intense and unbreakable. I wanted to be under it. I needed to hear every incantation and feel enchanted.

I was an idiot.

It wasn't magic, it was madness.

"Sean, there are things . . . things that you don't know about. Things that I'm not proud of, and my mother likes to throw them back in my face."

He leans back, arm draped over the back of the couch. "And you think I'd do that?"

I look up into his green eyes and shake my head. "No."

"Then why the secret, Shrimpy?"

"Because every girl has them."

He smiles, and his hand brushes the back of my neck. "I've got you, Devney. I won't let you fall. I never have, and I never plan to. So, trust me, and let me be here for you."

A tear forms, and I nod. Here we go. "My sophomore year of college, I started dating someone. He was . . . older and definitely off limits. There was this connection, and neither of us was able to stay away even though we knew we shouldn't."

"He was your professor." Sean guesses.

"Yes, and it went on for the entire year. We were—I was—in love."

"And he broke your heart."

I play with the paper on the bottle, unable to look at him. "I found out he was married. I was so stupid. I was the other woman, and I wasn't even really a woman. I was young, stupid, and willing to do whatever he asked. I'm the whore, just like my mother says I am, right?"

After I learned he was married, it all ended instantly. But

it ate at me. I wondered if there were nights she stayed up, waiting for him. Did she know about me? Did he care that he ruined everything for me?

I hated myself for not questioning him when he came up with excuses to break plans with me. It was just so easy to take his word as truth. Also, how would I have known he was lying? He was an adult, had a life, a job that was demanding, and everything always made sense.

But Jessica Wilkens deserved more than her husband fucking his students.

Sean shifts, and I feel his finger under my chin, lifting it to look at him. His emerald-green irises that are speckled with gold and rimmed with the thickest black watch me. "Did you know the entire time?"

"No."

"Did you actively seek this man out?"

"No."

His thumb brushes my chin. "And when you found out, did you walk away?"

"Yes."

I ran. I haven't allowed myself to go back to that time, and I won't, but that shame was so intense that I couldn't function.

I cried and was so horrified by the level of deception Christopher went to that I made myself sick. *Months* of lies and mistrust were around me, and I never saw it.

Of course, hindsight is twenty-twenty. I looked back at all the little signs, wanting to slap myself for being so gullible. I was so angry and disappointed in myself. Then, when I went to my family for help, I was met with more of the same emotions from them.

But Sean's eyes aren't filled with either of those.

No, he's looking at me with something else.

"Why didn't you tell me?"

"What was I going to say? Hey, buddy, I was sleeping with my married professor and got thrown out of school. Of course, it was all my fault, and I'm completely ashamed of myself."

He releases a heavy sigh. "How the hell was it your fault? He took advantage of you. He used his position of authority to get what he wanted. You have nothing to be ashamed of. Nothing. Do you hear me?"

A tear falls, and Sean wipes it away. For so long, I've wanted someone to say that to me. I've tried to see things from different angles, but all roads lead back to my being stupid, to it being my fault.

I knew that any personal relationship with my professor was wrong.

I knew that I could lose my scholarship and be tossed out of school.

There was not *one* benefit to having a relationship with him.

"Don't cry. You know I can't handle tears. I get all nervous and freak out. So, I'm begging. No. tears."

I smile and try not to laugh as the tears keep falling. "You're such a guy."

"Yeah. I definitely am."

I do what I can to stop crying, but there's such a sense of relief in my heart that it's useless.

"I wanted to talk to you, but it's been hard with us, Sean."

He leans back a little and takes a sip of his drink. "How?"

Our friendship has shifted a lot. I've missed my best friend, but he's been gone and, in a way, so have I. If I would've called him—he would've come. It wouldn't have mattered that he was in college in Maine, his ass would've been on a plane to Colorado and probably beat the shit out of Christopher. However, our dynamic changed when we both left Sugarloaf. Neither of us can deny it, whether we wish it were true or not.

"When we both left for college, we knew things would be different, but I wasn't prepared for how different they would be."

"We were across the country from each other."

"Yes, instead of across a few fields."

My heart aches with how much I missed him. "After the whole affair started, it was as though somewhere in the back of my mind I knew how wrong it was. If I told you, you'd have said it was, and I didn't want to hear it."

Sean nods. "Yeah, I would've."

"I didn't want to disappoint you, Sean. It was the first time I didn't have you to protect me and look at the choices I made."

"Dev—"

"No, please let me say this," I implore. "I had the equivalent of five brothers who wouldn't let anyone near me. Between Jasper, you, and your brothers, I had no chance of a guy in this town even trying to talk to me. You all made it out like they were too scared, but do you have a clue how intimidating you idiots were?" He grins, and I want to slap him. "Right, so I had the first taste of what it was like to date. I was in this new place, no protectors, and a man who was great with words. I was weak and stupid and . . . God, I'm mucking this all up. I'm saying that I didn't want you to ever think I wasn't good enough."

I don't know that anything I said even makes sense, but when I think about that time, I hate myself. The girl I was isn't who I wanted to be. Sean has put me on a pedestal and there's a part of me that wanted to remain there. Telling him wouldn't change anything.

Sean's fingers tangle with mine. "I wanted you to find someone who was good enough for you."

"I get that and I believe you, but I didn't believe it for

myself."

"I hate that you didn't trust me with this, Dev."

"I do too."

"Why him?"

How many times did I ask myself that question? A hundred. A million. Maybe more. The only thing I can come up with is an answer he won't like. "I think it's because I didn't learn during high school how to weed out the assholes."

"Newsflash. They were all assholes."

"Including you?" I ask with a raised brow.

"Especially me."

He can talk all that crap somewhere else. I know better. Sean has always been a good guy. When he was a kid, he wasn't chasing girls around. He was either at the ballfield or with me.

"Anyway, he knew what to say and how to search out naïve and stupid girls. I learned after my dismissal from school that I wasn't the first girl he was inappropriate with."

Sean releases a heavy sigh as his fingers tighten on the glass bottle. "If you tell me his name, I'll happily kill him."

I lean my head against his shoulder with a smile. "I love you for that." I sigh. "The point is, my mother thinks this is some flaw that I have. She has spent the last nine years reminding me of it."

He leans back on the couch, pulling me with him. I nestle against his chest, tuck my legs under my butt, and relax. The long, steady thumping of his heart fills my ears, and his musky scent calms me.

Sean is home. He's comfort and the sunshine that breaks through the clouds. He's laughter in the rain and the constant in a sea of uncertainty.

I've never had to wonder where I stand with him.

"Your mom is angry at herself, and she's never been good at dealing with that."

"No, but I'm tired of hearing it."

"I'm sorry I wasn't here for you."

I lift my head to meet his eyes. "You're here now."

He presses his lips to my forehead. "And even when I leave, I'm always here for you."

If nothing else, this time together will give me a friendship I've been desperately missing. And for that . . . I'm grateful.

nine

"L et's go, Austin!" I yell, clapping my hands as he gets up to bat.

"Sean sure draws a crowd," Hazel says as she bumps my shoulder.

I've been trying to focus on anything but him. It's as if there were some announcement for single and desperate women to come to the nine-year-old boys' winter league game.

"Who knew that off-season kids' baseball was so popular?" The sarcasm is thick in my voice. "It's really gross."

"What?"

"That!" I point at the five women with their hair done, makeup on, and breasts on display.

Hazel laughs. "He seems to be handling it well. Plus, he's been back a month, and they've kept their distance."

I glance back down at the gaggle of desperate housewives, and he's giving them one of those dazzling smiles. This is exactly why I could never think about dating him. It's part of his job to be charming. He excels at it, and I would never be able to handle knowing this is how he would spend nights away from me.

"Yes, he revels in it."

"I wouldn't go that far. I haven't seen him do anything flirtatious or encouraging. I'm saying he rebuffs them better than Jasper or any other man probably would."

I roll my eyes. "Desperate Denise is by far the pushiest." I watch her wrap her fingers around the metal fence, lifting one foot in the air as she giggles.

Hazel shifts to get a better look. "Really? I think Psycho Sara is pretty bad. She keeps pulling down her shirt to reveal more."

I laugh. "What about Clinger Karen? She really seems to be laying it on thick."

We both nod slowly as she shoves Denise aside to get closer. "Do they think he came back to Sugarloaf to get married like his brothers?"

"Maybe."

"I didn't think he had any interest in settling down," she says offhandedly. But I know my sister-in-law, and there's no innocence to her question. "I mean, I don't know anything about him other than what you've told me. He just hasn't had many relationships, has he?"

"No, Sean has always been married to the game."

"Do you think there's something that could change that?"

Now I stare at her with a smirk. "Are you trying to ask me something?"

"Obviously." Hazel slaps my arm playfully. "You told me about the kiss, and now you're living with him . . ."

"It's only been two weeks. Two. I'm not living with him, I'm just . . . getting my options straight and figuring out a plan."

"Did he kiss you again?"

I really don't want to answer this.

I turn back to where Austin is up to bat and focus there.

Hazel chuckles. "Avoid away, Dev, but you answered without answering."

"Yes, he kissed me again. The night he showed up on my doorstep, but it didn't mean anything. It was also the last time his lips will touch mine. See that?" I jerk my head toward the girls. "There is no way I want to toss my hat in that ring."

"Yeah you do. If I wasn't married, I'd be right next to them, and you could call me Hussy Hazel for all I cared."

I laugh under my breath and shake my head. "You're insane."

"Yes, but you are as well. You have feelings for him, and by the way he keeps looking up at you, I'd say they're reciprocal."

I don't have to tell Hazel all the reasons why letting my feelings make the choices is a bad thing, but perhaps she needs the reminder. "The last time I let my heart lead the way, I ended up broken."

"There is good that came from that experience, Devney."

"Yes, but also a lot of pain."

She takes my hand in hers. "Don't let the past dictate your future. If you and Sean can only be a bit of fun, then have that fun. You are going to be thirty this year, and you haven't allowed yourself to live. I'm not talking about your tepid relationship with Oliver or what happened when you were in college."

She's right, but I have my reasons, and we both know it. I like safety and consistency. I want to know that, at the end of the day, my little life won't be in upheaval and things will be as they should be.

"Oliver was safe."

It wouldn't be the same with Sean.

His life is not his own. He lives and dies by his schedule. And I get it.

It's how he makes a living.

"Yes, and safe can be boring. You have a limited amount of time to have some damn fun."

"And when he leaves?" I ask Hazel.

"You let him go."

"Just like that?"

She shrugs. "It sounds easy enough, right?"

"Sean kissed me and look what happened. Oliver left for Wyoming, I'm living in Sean's house because my mother and I finally had it out, and I have no plan. None. What the hell am I going to do, Hazel?"

"You're going to survive, and I pray that you have a little adventure doing it."

The sound of the ball against the metal bat causes both our heads to turn as Austin takes off. We get to our feet, cheering and yelling as he makes it safely to third and the team rushes out.

Austin hit the game-winning run.

They swarm him, bouncing around, and I can't help but smile. He's such a good kid, so warm and happy when he's playing baseball that it's clear this is where he belongs.

Once the celebration is over, Hazel and I make our way to where Jasper, Sean, and Austin are standing.

"Well, look at you, my sweet and wonderful boy!" Hazel says as she ruffles his hair.

"*Mom!*"

"What? I didn't kiss you."

Austin groans and ducks his head. "You're embarrassing me." He looks to Sean, and I giggle.

"So, you don't want Sean to see us kiss and hug you?"

His eyes widen with fear and I bite my upper lip to stop from giggling.

"One day," Sean breaks in, "you're going to hope that girls hug and kiss you after you win the game."

"Not anytime soon," Hazel warns.

"Right. Not until you're, like, thirty."

I can't resist the urge to tease him. "Which is what you're turning in . . . twelve days?"

Sean glares at me and then shrugs. "And you're right behind me."

"Umm, I'm nine months behind you, pumpkin."

He laughs. "Yes, but it's coming sooner than you think."

"I'm going to be ten!" Austin pipes in. "And then I'll go up to the older league."

"You know, you could probably be bumped up now," Sean encourages. "I think your skill level is much higher than any of the kids on the team now, and maybe even better than some on the next level."

Austin looks as if he might pass out from the praise. "Really?"

"Really."

Jasper puts his hands on Austin's shoulders. "All this takes time and patience, Austin. We want you to enjoy your childhood too. Baseball is great, but not many people make it to the major leagues like Sean."

Sean smiles and nods. "He's right. School comes first, but if you keep training and playing the way you are, I can see this being something you do for a long time."

I wonder if Sean sees how much Austin is like he was when

he was younger. He's played since he was six. All year, he was either playing or talking about baseball. He joined every league he could, practiced all the time, and made me learn how to pitch so he could have batting practice whenever he wanted since his mother refused to buy him a batting cage. I swear he slept with his glove most nights, which I know Austin does.

"You know, while I'm here, I'm going to see a friend who lives close this weekend. I'd love it if maybe you and a few friends would come with me," he offers.

"You want me and my friends to hang out with you?" Austin asks with eyes wide.

I have a sinking feeling this friend is also someone in baseball.

"Sure do. We'd probably even play ball for a bit."

He looks to Jasper and Hazel, who both smile and nod. "It's okay with us."

"Maybe your aunt Devney can come?" Sean adds.

"Oh. I don't know . . ."

Hazel moves closer. "That would be great, Sean. I know you're close with Devney and all, but we'd feel so much more comfortable if she went. You don't mind do you, Dev?"

I'm going to kill my sister-in-law. She doesn't care if I go, she just wants to force me to spend time with Sean. "I was going to look for apartments or something."

"Why?" Sean asks. "You're staying with me, why would you leave?"

"Because you're here for five more months, and . . . well, because."

Jasper's eyes narrow a bit. "You're living with him—in the main house?"

"No! I'm staying at his house until I find my own place, but I'm not living with anyone," I say with exasperation. This is just a small amount of the hell I've endured with the men in my life when I was in high school. They're so damn nosey and think I need protection. However, now it seems my brother wants to include Sean in that.

"Okay, but you're staying there—alone?"

I sigh and pray to the Gods to give me strength. "Jasper, I'm a grown woman and I'm not alone."

"No, you're instead staying in a house with a grown man."

Sean puffs up a small amount. "See? *He* sees it."

"Sees what?"

"That I'm a threat. You could fall for me."

I roll my eyes and look to my brother. "Then it's a good thing you're about to graciously offer to crash in the tiny house while I search for a place to live."

Sean nearly chokes on his drink. "I am?"

"Yes, it was so sweet of you to offer, and I appreciate you being such a great friend. I know my brother and father couldn't be happier about how kind you are. Of course, I offered to take the tiny house, but you just couldn't bear the idea of it."

"Quite the gentleman I am."

I grin. "Yes, you are. See, Jasper? It's all fine. I'm just staying at the house—alone. No need to worry."

Jasper looks at Sean and then back at me. "Right. No reason at all."

ten

"How the fuck did you live in this thing?" I ask as Declan hands me the keys with a smirk.

"Oh, it's fun."

"Fun my ass."

This . . .. won't last. There's not a chance in hell I'm letting a single opportunity to be around her pass. If she wants pretenses, that's what she'll get.

"And just why exactly are you staying in here?"

I drop the bag on the bed and attempt to turn around without banging into anything—and fail. "Devney is staying in the main house."

"And you can't stay with her?"

Declan leans against the counter, arms over his chest as he waits for an answer. "Her brother wasn't very happy when he found out she was crashing here, so she told him I was staying out here."

"So, you just did what she asked? Just like that?"

"Pretty much."

His smile is bright as he laughs. "I fucking knew it! I knew it."

"You knew nothing."

"The hell I didn't. You have finally pulled your head out of your ass and realized you're in love with her."

Jesus. He's insane. "No one said anything about being in love. I kissed her—twice. That's all. We kissed. There weren't any declarations or anything. I don't know what I feel, okay?"

"Now you kissed her again, and I'm going to assume you were sober. So, how was sober kissing?"

That second kiss was . . . I don't really have words to describe it. She was so perfect in my arms. It felt as though everything I denied was proven right. Her lips fit mine as though they were made for me. There was passion, tenderness, and need that flowed between us. I had been so worried that the next time we kissed, it would be almost familial. That was definitely not the case.

I could've kissed her all day.

I wanted to.

And now, knowing there is no Oliver and she's this close to me, I'm determined to share more with her, which is absolutely stupid.

"It was a kiss."

He chuckles. "It was a lot more than that, my brother."

Fucking Declan and all his knowing crap. "I'm glad you have it all figured out."

"Dude, if it was just a kiss, you would not be in this thing. You'd be in there, cuddled up on the couch with your best friend."

I flip him off. "I'm giving her space to work through her

issues."

"Oh, is that what you're calling yourself?"

"Declan, I'm going to beat the shit out of you if you don't shut up."

He laughs and heads to the door. "Yeah, you might try."

"Don't you have a wife and a baby to get back to?"

"I do, but this is so much more fun."

I groan. "Let's talk about you and the baby. How's that going?"

Declan looks like he wants to say something more about Devney, but he doesn't, which means I won't make Syd a widow today. "It's crazy, Sean. Like every fear I have is wrapped up in that one little body. I would do anything, fight anyone, slay dragons for him and fight every instinct I have if it would make his life better. I worry about everything. If he makes a new sound, I watch him to make sure it's fine. And don't even get me started on the whole breathing thing. I swear, I spend more time at night putting my finger under his nose than I do sleeping."

I clap him on the back with a grin. "You're his dad."

"I am, and it's scary as fuck!"

All along I knew he'd be a great dad. He's been a good brother. Always willing to protect the three of us and I'm glad he's happy. He has fought against it for so long, walked away from anything he needed to if it meant that we might have a better life.

My brother is an idiot at times, but his heart is always in the right place.

"And things with Syd?"

"I wish I had words to describe how I feel about her. It's like my heart has found its way back into my chest. I worry about everything with her too. She barely sleeps, works because she can't stop herself, and I feel like I have some sort of

PTSD after the hell she went through. Sydney is everything to me—they both are. I know that makes me sound like a fucking pussy, but I'm telling you, that loving her has been a gift to me. It's like all the dead, rotted parts of my soul have life again."

I smile, liking this side of my grumpy ass brother a lot more. "Who knew you had a poet's soul?"

He humphs. "I wouldn't go that far."

"I didn't say it was good poetry."

"I'll show you poetry, let's go out back so I can show you how to pump the water, if it doesn't freeze, and empty the composting toilet."

"Wait, I have to *empty* the toilet?"

He rubs his hands together and gives me a maniacal grin. "Oh, yeah, Devney better be worth all this, brother. You're in the shit now."

There's no question of whether she's worth it, she is. I just don't know how we would endure the possible fallout if it doesn't work.

It's colder than a monkey's ass in this stupid box on wheels. I roll out of the bed, taking the blankets with me, and crank the heat. There isn't much room or very many amenities in here, and I am going to have to find a way to get back in the main house—fast.

I put on sweatpants and pack a small bag so I can grab a shower. There's not a chance in hell I'm attempting it in here. Declan showed me all the things I need to do to make the house livable. I heard him, but I was not in the mood last night to go out to the generator and refill it, and I forgot to turn on the coil to keep things from freezing.

So, I will have no water, let alone hot water.

I toss on my jacket and sprint to the house.

"Dev?"

No answer.

Her car is still out front, so I know she's here. "Devney?" I try again, not wanting to scare her.

Maybe she's still asleep. Honestly, that would probably be best.

The door to her room is closed so I open the door quietly to see if she's asleep, but it's empty.

"Devney?" I call out again, but there's still no answer.

I open the other two bedroom doors, but there is no sign of her. What the hell? Did she suddenly take up running?

Whatever. I need to grab something out of my room. I walk down, and when I open it, I find her nestled in the bed, hair fanned out over the pillow I slept on, and my heart does a flip.

She's so beautiful.

And she's here, in my room, lying on the sheets I slept on before she tossed me out. I enter quietly, not wanting to wake her, and lean down, pressing my lips to her hair, inhaling the flowery scent.

Feeling a bit like a creeper, I head out and hear her voice. "Sean?"

Shit. "Hey, I called out, but you didn't answer."

"What are you doing here?" She sits up, letting the sheet pool around her hips and giving me a delicious view of her nipples through the tank top.

"Uh, I'm . . . I need to shower and there's no hot water at that thing you forced me to use as my living quarters."

Her eyes widen a bit. "Oh. I didn't . . . really? No water?"

I nod. "Yeah, so, I'm going to need to use my house."

She takes her lower lip between her teeth. "Right."

"Don't play at being apologetic now, Shrimpy. Not when you walked me into that corner so perfectly."

"Whatever. We both know the two of us living together isn't the best idea."

I peek at her chest once more, unable to stop myself. "Why is that?"

"Because you keep looking at me like . . . well . . . that!"

"What's that?" I push her.

"Like you want to climb in this bed with me."

She has no idea how right she is. "And that would be bad?"

Devney's eyes widen. "Yes! Yes, that would be bad."

"But, you *are* in my bed already."

Her brown eyes dart around as she slides from the bed, and I'm fucking done. She has on the shortest pair of shorts I've ever seen. I'm not even sure they are shorts, they look like underwear. She turns around to grab something and I wonder if my knees will give out. Across the back it says: kiss this.

Oh, sweetheart, just say the word.

She groans when she can't find whatever she's looking for, and I watch those long, toned legs make their way toward me. I run through every nasty bug, fish, and nasty smell I can to keep from embarrassing myself in front of her. "I can move out into that shed thing."

"Not a chance."

"Why not?"

"Because I'm not having you sleep in that while I'm in here. Either you come stay in it with me or you stay here."

Devney bites her lower lip. "I'll find a place right away."

"No. You'll stay here for as long as you want."

Her hand rests on her hip. "You're only here for five more

months."

"And?"

"And then you leave."

"Okay. You can stay in this house until we figure it out. Declan and Connor would never push you out, and Jacob will need adult supervision when he comes. It'll all work out."

She runs her fingers through her long brown hair, capturing it and bowing her back so her tits jut out toward me.

For fuck's sake.

I clear my throat and step back, there's no stopping my erection this time. "I need that shower now."

"I'll make breakfast."

I nod and start to head out, but then I stop. "Hey, Dev?"

"Yeah?"

I turn, letting my gaze roam her body once more before my mouth ruins the view. "Put some clothes on unless you're trying to kill me. If you are, then, you're succeeding."

I see the surprise flash in her eyes before she looks down. "Oh my God!" Her hands cover her chest, and I'm out the door before I end up making a complete ass of myself.

I take a quick shower, stepping in as soon as the water is on, hoping the cold will help—it doesn't.

In fact, it makes it worse because there, in my shower, are all of Devney's things. Her floral shampoo and vanilla body wash. Like a fool, I lift it to my nose, inhaling the scent at its strongest, wanting to see if it still clings to her at night.

Which then prompts me to want to do a lot more with her.

This is a fucking mess. One month here, and I'm lusting after her so hard that not even a cold shower will get rid of my raging hard-on. I'm far worse than I was trying to convince myself. Not only do I love Devney but also I want her. I need her. I have to see if what I'm feeling is even remotely reciprocated.

Sure, she kissed me. Yeah, she really seemed to like it, but is she on fire? Is that why she kicked me out into that cabin?

Only one way to find out.

And it starts now.

eleven

Sleeping in that bed was the mistake of a lifetime, but I was lonely. All I wanted was to feel close to him, and then I went and got myself caught by the man I'm trying to avoid.

However, I am a strong and determined woman. I will not bend to the masculine wiles that threaten to weaken me. I will not make the same mistake again, and Sean and I will go back into the friend zone. That's all there is to it.

I flip the pancakes once more before putting them on the plate and turning to head into the dining area.

Instead of being able to move, though. I'm a statue.

My bones are granite, and my heart has stopped.

There stands Sean . . . dripping . . . wet.

The rivulets of water fall down his chest in slow motion, slide over the planes and contours of his very, very toned body, and then catch on the towel slung around his waist.

My eyes trace the path each drop makes, wishing my fingers were on his skin, getting to feel my way down.

His deep rumble breaks my stare, and when I catch his eyes, I see the mischief. "Did you hear me?"

He spoke?

"No. Sorry, I was . . . thinking."

"About?"

Your body. "Food."

"Well, since that's what I asked . . . we're in luck."

There is no mistaking the humor in his voice. He knows damn well what he is doing and that I was definitely not thinking of food. I need to control this situation and put us back on common ground.

Only, I can't seem to stop watching the water cascading down his skin. "You're planning to eat breakfast in a towel?" I ask, my throat feeling a bit tighter on that last word.

"I usually eat breakfast naked."

"Naked?"

Sean grins. "I thought this was a good compromise."

Yeah, what a prince he is.

I close my eyes, release a sigh, and focus.

I can do this.

He's trying to rattle me, to get me to say how much I want him, or maybe even be tempted into doing something stupid instead of just thinking it. I remind myself again of how strong and non-attracted I am to this man. That's a lie. I am very attracted, but I am not interested. Yes, because interest leads to want, and want leads to bad choices and bad choices lead to lifelong regrets, which I already have plenty of.

Sean Arrowood will not be a regret because he won't be anything other than a friend.

"You can eat naked if you prefer. This is your house and all."

"You want me naked?"

My eyes lift to his. "I didn't say that. I just said that it's your house."

"I heard: Sean, get naked."

"You need your hearing checked."

And I need a lobotomy.

"I'll put that on the schedule." Sean takes a seat at the table, and I set the plate down and rush back into the kitchen for the bacon.

My skin tingles as I rest both hands on the counter. This is Sean. This is the guy who never showed any interest in me before. We've slept in the same bed a hundred times, and I never once imagined him naked.

Now, though. God, now, I can do nothing but imagine it. If that towel slipped just a bit, there would be no more wonder. There's a throb in my core as my mind starts to imagine what could've happened if I had walked over, pressed my hand against his hard chest, and let his body heat envelop me.

I grip the edge of the granite, holding on as I feel myself slipping away.

Then I feel a hand press against my back.

"Devney." Sean's voice is deep and gravelly.

I don't answer as my pulse spikes.

"Are you okay?"

No. I am definitely not okay. In fact, I'm so far on the other side of okay that I don't remember what it looks like.

His hand moves up my back and then squeezes when he reaches my shoulder.

"I'm fine."

"You're not."

I have to stop this. We need to create new boundaries, ones I didn't know we'd ever need, but this isn't working. I need a place to stay, at least for a little while longer, so I can't leave.

I turn to face him, feeling a pull to him so deep it makes my head swim. I open my lips to say all of it, but nothing comes out.

There is something in his eyes. The dark rim is wider and there's a hunger burning between us, growing warmer.

I clear my throat. "I have bacon."

His lips slowly spread into a grin. "Yeah?"

"Yes. Bacon. I made it."

"Good. I like bacon."

He moves closer, only I can't go anywhere because the small of my back is against the counter. Sean leans in, his one hand rests next to me, and the other snakes around to the plate that's behind me.

"Sean," I say as a warning.

But he plucks up a piece of bacon and pops it into his mouth. "*Mmm*." He groans, and my stomach drops. "It's good."

I blink rapidly, trying with all my might not to think about him making those sounds while doing something . . . else. "You should get dressed."

He looks down at the towel again and then back up at me. "Am I making you uncomfortable?"

If he means by making me want to do very non-friend-like things, then yes. There's not a chance in hell I'm going to say that, though. Sean will get way too much enjoyment off it.

"Not even a little."

For two weeks, I've managed to avoid all things sexual, but right now, I want to rip that towel off him and fuse my lips to his. He leans close, the bacon scent still on his lips, making me want to taste it—the bacon, not him.

"You know, your eye does this little twitchy thing when you lie. Right, here." His thumb grazes the corner of my left eye, and I force myself not to move.

Sean's lips glide into an easy smile as he reaches around for another piece of fatty goodness.

"Step back so I can bring the food you keep eating to the table."

He laughs once, taking a bite. "I give you two weeks."

"Two weeks?"

"Yup." He taps me on the nose with the bacon. "Two weeks until you finally admit you want to jump my bones and are no longer able to resist me."

Oh, he's a fool. I may want to jump his bones, but I have way more self-control than he does. "You're on."

He takes a step closer, the heat of his body pulling me into a very unsafe cocoon. "Don't you want to know the terms?"

I laugh with sarcasm. "Please, I don't need to know because I plan to win no matter what."

"I'll tell you anyway, just so you can't complain about the results. If you are able to last the two weeks, then I will stay in the tiny house and you're welcome to stay here until you want to leave."

"And if you win?"

"Well, if *you* end up losing, I'll be doing exactly what I want—naked. A whole lot of naked, sweetheart."

I try not to let that sink in. Sean basically admitted he wants to have sex with me. That really shouldn't surprise me since he's a guy—a very hot guy, and we've kissed twice, but still. After it's been back to friendship. It's been us. Devney Maxwell and Sean Arrowood. The strange girl who was a bit tomboy, a bit chic, and a lot awkward and the jock who every girl tried to kiss. This . . . could be a damn catastrophe. I am not ready to go there. Kissing is one thing, but sex—with Sean is a totally other level of something I'm not ready for.

"I won't lose."

He smirks. "So you say, but after we have that fantastic, mind-blowing sex, I am moving back in here . . . where I plan to have a lot more of that sex I just spoke of. And you and I will spend the remainder of my time here as a couple. We'll figure out what this is and what we need to do about it."

"I don't need to do anything."

"Well, I do. So, you only have to hold out for two weeks."

I release a heavy breath and raise my chin. "Deal."

Sean steps back. "Want to seal it with a kiss?"

I glare at him, but I'm slightly impressed by the cunningness he presents. I lean forward as though I'm going to do just that. Our mouths move closer and closer, and then I let out a small laugh, turning my head at the last second. "Nice try, Arrowood."

His lips touch my cheek, and I can feel his smile. "You won't even last four days."

"Challenge accepted."

Sean doesn't look the slightest bit worried. He turns and starts to head back toward the dining room, stops, and then drops his towel, giving me a view of his ass.

I am so going to lose.

twelve

Hadley bounces up and down as we wait for her present to be delivered. She's been using a horse that Declan got from Devney's family, but this is the one we've been waiting for.

"Daddy, can I name him whatever I want?"

Connor sighs. "Of course you can."

"I am so excited. I love my horse now, but this will give him a friend and you will be able to come riding with me and it'll be so fun. I've thought of so many names. I was thinking if I named him after Uncle Declan, he would love it. Do you think he would love it?"

"He's definitely a horse's ass," I say under my breath.

"That's for sure," Connor agrees before turning to Hadley. "Sweetheart, you can name him anything you want."

My baby brother being a father is still something I can't get over. Hadley is his world, and I'm truly happy for him. He seems to have it all. Two amazing kids and the life I always knew he'd fit into, even when he didn't.

Here I am, still figuring my shit out.

"Do you ever wonder how it is that you've ended up living in Sugarloaf with horses and a farm?" I ask him.

"Not even a little. I know exactly how."

"Ellie."

He nods.

"And me!" Hadley cuts in.

"Of course." Connor leans down and scoops his daughter up. "And your sister."

Hadley giggles and wraps her arms around his neck. "This has been the best month ever. I got a sister and a new horse!"

"Which do you like better?" I ask.

She tilts her head to the side. "I think the horse. Beth-anne cries—a lot. And she always has stuff coming out of her mouth."

"I get it, Squirt. I have two younger brothers, and each time one of them came along, I wished for a horse instead."

Connor rolls his eyes. "Younger siblings make things interesting."

I get close to her ear and whisper, "But older siblings can make them do things."

Her face lights up, and she whispers back. "Like what?"

"All kinds of chores, and you can usually blame them for the mess."

Connor huffs. "Don't even think about it."

I give her a wink, and she grins. "I like you, Uncle Sean."

"I like you more."

"But Uncle Declan got me a horse."

She has the Arrowood brothers wrapped around her tiny finger. Between the humble abode her father built her that masquerades as a tree house, the horses Declan got her, and the quad I got her for Christmas, she's set forever. Lord knows that when Jacob comes, he'll want to outdo us all. She'll probably end up with a boat.

"Well, he's pretty cool, but if it weren't for me, he wouldn't have the best horse ever, so that kind of means I got you a horse too."

Hadley looks up to Connor and then back to me. "I guess you're right. Are Devney and Austin coming?"

I nod. "Yeah, she went to get Austin and hang out with your mom. After we eat and the horse settles in a bit, they will be here so we can go on a ride."

She squeals and wraps her arms around me. "You're the best."

And I've won out over Declan. See, this is what happens when you have a baby and can't be here when your niece gets her present. It serves him right.

"Be sure you tell Uncle Declan that."

She grins. "I will! Where is your friend, though? I am so excited."

Zach Hennington called about twenty minutes ago to let me know he's close. It's been damn near fifteen years since I've seen him. I was in a summer camp and college kids came down to mentor. Zach was assigned to my group, and we instantly got along.

Even though he was six years older, we became friends, and when camp ended, Zach and I kept in touch. When it was time for me to pick a college, he helped me choose the best one that would get me a shot at the majors. And then, when he got called up, I was cheering him on. After an injury to his shoulder destroyed his career, he moved back home, but he seems happy.

"He should be here any minute."

Hadley watches the road and squeals when she sees something.

"Can I go by the fence?"

He nods.

As she runs off, Connor and I lazily make our way there as well. "How's Ellie doing?"

"Good. She's exhausted, but good. I appreciate Devney going over there so I could be here with Hadley."

I smile. "I'm sure she's happy to be there."

"What's that grin for?"

"I'm happy for you, Connor. You're living the dream! You've got a house, kids, a wife, and all that. Plus, you're starting the security business, I mean, it's all good things."

When I got here two months ago, my brother called to ask if I would invest in a company he was thinking of starting. One of his friends owns a security company and was looking to expand into some tech security, which is what Connor did when he was a SEAL. So, he's able to work from home, be with his wife and kids, and already has a contract. Declan, Jacob, and I all put money in and are silent partners.

Although, there probably won't be much silence between the four of us.

"Yeah, there has been a lot of changes in the last year. I'm doing the best I can, but there are days I feel like I can't keep up."

I look at Hadley, who is standing on the fence, waving at us. "She's worth it, though, right?"

Connor laughs. "You have no idea. Hadley and Bethanne are everything."

"You know, I love that you named her after mom."

"Well, it's only kind of. It's for both Ellie's mom and ours.

I'm glad we were able to honor them both." He releases a long sigh, and I know where his mind is.

"You know that they would be proud. Especially Mom. She would've loved seeing you with the life you've made here. And I think Ellie's mom would be too. You make her daughter really happy."

"Thanks, man. One day this guilt will go away. I just keep waiting for it to happen. Ellie doesn't blame any of us, but there's this part of me that wonders if she doesn't think about how her family was taken away by the accident that dad caused."

I know what he means. I wonder a lot if Ellie sees us and associates it with her parents' deaths. I hope not. "I don't know if the guilt ever will, but we'll find a way to live with it."

Connor nods. "In the meantime, we go on. By the way, how are things with you and Devney? I heard a story—"

I stop and glare at him. "What story?"

"Oh, that you keep sticking your tongue in her mouth."

It's true. "I'd like to stick a lot more there."

He laughs and then we start walking again. "You should tell her how you feel."

"I have."

"And what did you tell her?"

I sigh. "I told her that I want more, and she's reluctant."

"Why?" he asks as though I have a clue.

"I don't know, dude. She says it'll change us, which it will. She says that she can't lose me, which she won't."

He lifts his hand. "You can't promise that. If you guys end badly, there's that chance."

He's right. If I let myself love her and then we end things, I don't know how we'd go back to what we've always been.

"Maybe we're just feeling all this because I'm back and

she's here, you know? What if this is some penance for the past? If I let this go now, then we can go back to normal and not mess up what we have."

"Sean, you're the best of us. You really are, but you're a moron when it comes to Devney. You've lied to yourself for so long I doubt you even know what you feel."

I haven't lied to myself. They seem to have this belief that what we feel has been there the whole time, but it's not. I have always loved Devney, but it wasn't until she told me that Oliver was planning to propose that I realized I was in love with her.

All I saw was her in a white dress, standing at the altar, but it wasn't Oliver's hand she was holding—it was mine.

I knew, in that instant, that I felt something for her that I didn't really comprehend.

"I know I want to see what this is."

"And if you see that you want a life with her?"

I look up the drive, praying a car comes so I can end this.

He nudges me with his arm.

"Then I have to find a way to make her come to Florida with me. Unlike you and Declan, I have zero possibility of staying in Sugarloaf."

And that's really the big hurdle. Devney won't leave. I don't know why or what is keeping her here, but that's going to be one thing we are going to figure out.

"You know, the funny thing is that neither Declan or I did either, but when you find the one for you, it makes things that were impossible suddenly seem obtainable."

He might be right, but I don't have the same luxuries that they do.

"Maybe so, but no one is saying that Devney is the one for me."

Connor snorts under his breath. "And, yet, you aren't saying she isn't."

I let that settle over us as finally I see the dirt kick up on the driveway. We both walk silently toward Hadley, who is bouncing up and down. The truck stops, and Zach and another guy, who I'm assuming is his brother, emerge.

"Zach Hennington," I say with my hand extended.

"God, it's been forever."

"It sure has, but you look great—old, but good."

He rolls his eyes. "If I remember, you're not too far behind me."

"I'll be thirty this year, you're, what? Fifty now?"

The guy beside him laughs. "I like this dude."

Zach grins. "You would. This is my brother, Wyatt."

I shake his hand as well. "Great to meet you."

"You too, I hear you're a pretty awesome ballplayer?"

"I'd like to think I am. I learned a lot playing with your brother. He was an awesome pitcher and showed me the ropes."

Zach laughs. "A lot of good it did me."

"How is your arm?"

He rotates his shoulder and shrugs. "It's fine. I'm honestly over it all. I had my shot, it didn't work out, and now I'm back home and things are good."

"Good. You married yet? Family? Kids?"

Zach's smile mirrors the one that my idiot brothers wear. "Yeah, actually, during these last few months, things changed for me, and I'm with the girl I was in love with back in the day."

Her name was something like Devney's . . . I'm trying to recall . . .

"Presley," Wyatt offers. "They were together when they

were still in the womb and just got their shit straight."

My brother slaps his hand on my shoulder and chuckles. "Seems it's a ballplayer thing, huh?" Connor extends his hand to them each. "I'm his younger brother, Connor. My daughter is who you're making a very happy eight-year-old."

Said child can't take any more and is inching closer and closer to the horse trailer.

"You ready to see your horse?" Zach asks.

"Yes!" She rushes toward me, wrapping her arms around my waist. "I love you, Uncle Sean."

I hug her back, smiling because even though Declan bought the horse, I'm the hero who got it for her.

"I love you too!"

"All right, you all ready?" I ask as we're geared up for the ride.

Devney comes along the side of me on her horse and Austin trails behind her a bit. "We are."

He sits up a little taller and nods.

"I'm ready too!" Hadley practically bounces.

Zach is riding the new horse to show us his temperament before Hadley rides him. Connor is staying back with Wyatt, and I am going to make sure Hadley is happy. The best part is that I'm not on a horse—I have the quad. It's been far too long since I've ridden, and there's no way my first time back in the saddle is going to be in front of Devney.

I'm trying to woo her, which would be impossible to do if I'm busy falling off a horse.

"You're sure you don't mind spending a little more time

here? I know you have a long drive back," I ask Zach as he lifts himself into the saddle.

"Are you kidding? This is my job. Besides, I helped out with Presley's sons when they were learning how to ride. I'm happy to go since you're too scared to get on the horse."

Devney laughs. "He is a chicken."

"You said it, darlin'," he drawls and gives me a mischievous grin.

Devney smiles and turns to him. "We'll have to forgive him. But, I am curious, you said you helped teach your girlfriend's kids to ride?"

Zach grins. "I did."

"Like you taught me, Auntie," Austin says as he beams at Devney.

"And I loved every minute of it."

"I bet I can ride better than you," Hadley says to Austin, and I roll my eyes.

"Can not."

"Can too!"

"All right, you two," Dev says with exasperation. "You both ride great, and we're very excited to do this together. If someone is not excited, then they can ride on the quad with Sean, who is afraid. Do you want to be a chicken like him?"

I glare at her. "Funny."

She shrugs.

"Sean isn't scared," Austin defends. "He's a professional ballplayer and a catcher who has to worry about pitches coming at him so fast it could break his hand."

I smile at his obvious respect for my manliness. "Yup. What he said."

Devney shakes her head. "Anyway, this will be a lot of fun, but we need to get along."

The kids settle down, and we head out. The ride is nice, and I'm very happy to have my ass not on the horse. Devney, Zach, Austin, and Hadley ride out in front of me as we head out to the fields that run along the creek.

On our way back, we pass an old building that still haunts me, and I allow my quad to come to a stop.

They ride on, but I feel as though I've been transported.

That building holds a car.

A 1973 red Camaro that almost destroyed my life.

A life that I've tried to live and a past I've fought to forget.

But it's all there, waiting to show me that secrets can be buried or unearthed.

"Sean!" I hear Devney's voice as she rides toward me. I hit the gas and head her way. "You okay?"

"I'm fine," I say with a smile.

She eyes me curiously. "You sure?"

This is a story I plan to tell her, but not now and not here. "I'm good. Kids okay?"

"They're worse than we were at that age."

I laugh. "You know what they say about the thin line between love and hate."

Devney rolls her eyes. "We all know that you have always loved me."

"I also wanted to throat punch you several times a week. You were always so damn competitive. It was annoying."

She gives me a crooked smile. "Yes, so annoying because you always lost. Hey, Sean?"

"Yeah?"

"Race you!"

She takes off before she's even done throwing down the challenge, and once again, I'm chasing the girl who has always been too fast to catch.

thirteen

I fly through the cold air, letting it burn my face and lungs. I love the winter. The smell of snow and the freshness that lingers in the air.

My favorite thing in the world is riding Simba as the flakes flutter around me. The ground being covered with the promises of untouched land. It's beautiful and hopeful.

I hear the quad coming up behind me, and I lean into the gallop. "Come on, Simba," I urge him forward. I'm getting closer to where I left Zach and the kids, but I hear the motor of the quad getting louder behind me.

Damn it. I can't lose. Sean is a very sore loser, but he's an even worse winner. I will never live it down, and I'm sure he'll find a way to make me pay.

Just as I reach Zach and the kids, I push Simba just a bit faster, and I fly by them, a smile on my face and laughter in the air behind me.

I circle back around and the kids are both laughing. "You

beat him, Aunt Dev."

"I sure did."

"I bet I could beat you!" Hadley taunts Austin.

"No way. I'm a better rider. I've had a horse my whole life and you're a *girl*." Austin sneers the last word as though it's a curse.

Oh, these two are either going to fall madly in love or they're going to kill each other.

Hadley refuses to let the insult go. "You're a stupid boy, and you don't know how good I am on a horse. I'm the best there is, right, Uncle Sean? You think I can ride a horse better than Austin, don't you? All girls are better than boys."

I look at Sean, who appears to be struggling with this particular minefield. "Sean, what do you think? Are girls better than boys?"

"Umm."

"Don't answer that, buddy," Zach warns.

Sean starts to speak again and then stops. "I think we're all going to head back, right?"

"But it's so nice. And my horse is so happy," Hadley says with a pouty lip.

It is not nice, it's freaking freezing.

I clear my throat. "I wish we could, but Austin has his big tournament tomorrow and we can't be out too late. Not to mention, our fingers might fall off soon with this cold." Sean is coaching with Jasper tomorrow. Well, he's helping or whatever they're calling it.

"What game?" Zach asks.

"I play baseball like Sean does. I'm a catcher too."

"Really? Logan plays, but he's a pitcher. Like I was."

"How old is he?"

"He's almost eleven, and he has some real skill."

I smile. "Austin is the same with skill. He'll be ten in a few months, but this league is all twelve-year-old kids, and he was brought up to play with them."

Sean steps over to my horse and pats Simba on the neck. "He has some real talent even at this age."

"Sounds familiar, huh?" Zach asks.

God. Boys and their baseball. My entire childhood felt as if it revolved around Sean and what games were happening. If I wanted to be around him, it was the sacrifice I made. No one could've known that it would lead him to this life. "I remember all too well having to hang around the field if I wanted to see you. It was fun, since I loved watching you play."

"I loved you being there," he admits. "For a long time, I thought you were my good luck charm. I can't tell you how many times I've wished you were in the stadium on nights when nothing was going right. If I could've just seen you . . ."

My heart sputters as we stare at each other. He's saying things that I still don't understand. How is this the same boy who used to tell me I was dumb? Now he's saying he wished I were there when he was having a bad day. It's like two worlds colliding and throwing everything off balance.

When my world fell apart, I wanted him there with me, so at least I understand his sentiment.

Zach looks at Sean and then me. "Are you guys . . . together?"

"No."

"Soon," Sean says at the same time.

Zach chuckles. "Well, that clears it up."

Sean moves his hand up and down Simba's neck, all the while watching me. "See, I kissed her, which scared her. Devney wants things to stay as they are, but there's very little chance of that since I've decided we're going to do it again soon."

I gasp. "Really? You're such an ass. Yes, we kissed, but I felt *nothing*, and he can't handle that."

"Nothing, huh?"

I cross my arms over my chest and sit up in the saddle. "Nope."

"Then what was the second time when you were trying to climb me like a tree?"

Zach's head turns toward me.

I'm going to kill him. "I didn't try to climb you like a tree! I was trying to get you off me."

"By gripping my hair and holding my lips to yours?"

I look over to where Hadley and Austin are walking their horses and then glare at him, keeping my voice low. "You're a pig and you're delusional."

"I wish I had recorded this so you could see what I do," Zach says under his breath.

Well, I sure don't, but I can't say that. No, I need to spin this. "Only so that Sean could see that I don't have feelings for him, I don't want to kiss him again, and I have no intentions of there being anything more than friendship between us. I have one more week to prove it."

One week of not wishing I could shove him against the wall, mount him like a horse, and do dirty things to him. It's been absolute torture so far, and it doesn't help that Sean prances around the house naked any chance he can. But I've held out. I can keep doing it.

Maybe.

Sean looks to him with a raised brow as if to say: See. She's full of shit. "I'll go check on the kids, Shrimpy. You keep feeding yourself the bullshit you're shoveling."

I glare at him as he walks away whistling.

Such a gorgeous, irresistible, asshole.

I sigh and then turn back to Zach. "Sorry about that."

He laughs. "Don't be. You remind me a bit of me and Presley."

"Is that the girl you mentioned before?"

He nods. "About seventeen years ago, I walked away from her. It . . . it was the biggest mistake I'd ever made. We were together since high school and so in love with each other it seemed like there was nothing that could break us. She was my best friend."

"Sounds like Declan and Sydney," I muse. Zach's eyes narrow a bit. "Sorry, Declan is Sean's brother and they were high school sweethearts . . . yada, yada, yada."

Zach laughs softly. "You sound like my brother."

"He seems like a good guy."

"He is, but he feels that way when we talk about me and Presley. It's a tale as old as time, huh? Two people who get each other and need to get their heads on straight."

I look toward Sean. "Yeah, and sometimes they don't."

"The tragic stories end that way."

"Is this a tragic story?"

"Depends on your perspective," Zach replies.

Great. I really don't need another version of relationships gone bad between friends, even if this ends well, the middle part doesn't. This is what keeps me from sticking my tongue down his throat again. I would rather deal with a lifelong yearning than pain from acting on it.

"Tell me the perspective about you and your best friend."

Zach nods once. "Well, first, I broke us."

This is everything I fear.

"I see."

"But nothing that's ever broken is beyond repair. All you need is a bond, love, and a lot of fucking patience. She taught me that. We had to spend seventeen years figuring it all out before we could be what we are now. There's nothin' in this world I wouldn't do for her—for us. You see, that's the friendship. At the very core of it all, she is, and always has been, my best friend."

The way he speaks of her gives me a glimmer of hope that the friendship Sean and I have built is strong enough to withstand any storm.

"And you think that friendship is enough?"

Zach smiles, and his gaze moves toward Sean as he makes his way back over to us. "I think that, without it, there's not a chance in hell you could ever be more. He loves you, no matter what flaws you think you have. Hell, if I were to guess, I would say that he loves you more because of them."

That almost completely sums up how I feel about Sean. He can be moody and stupid and stubborn, but I love him to the ends of the earth. We have been through times of happiness and the darkest of days. I don't know if that means we can be more than just friends though. That's the big wild card.

Still, he bet me that I couldn't last two weeks, and there's not a shot in hell I'm going to win. Each day it's harder and harder to resist the pull to him. I want him. Not just like I always have, but as something much deeper and more meaningful. I don't have a lot of time to figure it out, which is what scares me. If it's just attraction, that can be dealt with. However, if there's more, I don't know that walking away from him is totally possible.

Time is what I need. One more week is what I have before our bet is over and he goes back to being nothing more.

"Well, no matter what, we have another week where I'll be just his best friend, nothing more."

His chuckle fills the cold air. "The lies we tell ourselves."

"What lies?" Sean asks as he comes to a stop beside us.

"Just talkin' with Devney about feelings."

Sean grins, mischief dancing in those green eyes. "Don't worry, Zach. She might try to deny it to herself, but I've always been able to see through it. She has feelings for me, she's just not ready to accept them."

"Good morning, sunshine."

I jump, turning around to find Sean standing in the kitchen doorway—shirtless.

"What is your aversion to clothing?"

He smirks. "I don't have one. I just know it makes you flustered when I'm wearing less of it."

It's been two days since Zach left, and since then, Sean's made it his mission to drive me insane. Last night, he said he needed to do laundry, which meant taking off everything he was wearing other than his underwear.

I really hoped that, by now, I would stop drooling over his incredible body, but it seems that the more I see it, the more I want it.

Which is really going to make the next five days of resisting him—hard.

Pun intended.

"I am not flustered," I deny and turn to finish making my sandwich.

"No?"

"Nope."

I hear his footsteps nearing closer, and my body goes rigid.

"Not even when I do this?"

His hands move from my wrist up my arms, leaving goose bumps in their wake. A shiver runs through me, and his low chuckle is right in my ear. Every part of me wants to turn in his arms, kiss him senseless, and get lost in his touch.

There is seriously something wrong with me.

I do not want that.

No. No. No. I want him to step back and go back to being my sarcastic asshole guy friend who I didn't have feelings for.

It's the no shirt thing. That's what it has to be. I'm struck down by abs.

Instead of sinking into his touch, I straighten my back and remind myself of the bet.

I will not cave with only five days remaining.

"Excuse me," I say with as much detachment as I can manage. "I believe that we need additional rules regarding this bet of yours."

The warmth of his breath slides against my neck, causing the hairs to prick. "What rules?"

I turn, pushing his chest to gain some space. "None of this. You can't just come up behind me and start to touch me. It's not fair."

Sean's lips turn into a cheeky smile. "I never said I'd fight fair."

"We're not fighting!"

"No, sweetheart, we aren't . . . you are. You're fighting this and me and what we could be."

I huff and shake my head. "No, I'm fighting *for* our friendship."

"And I'm fighting for *more*."

This is impossible. I can't do this with him because it will end in disaster and I've had enough of those.

"You don't know that we can be more. This could be . . . the end of us. It could be the nail in our coffin, and I'd rather never have that."

He takes a step back, running his fingers through his hair. "I don't know that any more than you do, but I'm not going to be afraid either."

I laugh once. "You have never loved a woman enough to know the fear of losing them."

Anger sparks in his eyes. "You think I don't know loss?"

"That's not what I said. You have lost people you love, but it's different when you give your heart away. Losing your mother isn't the same thing, and you know it."

"No, but I know what not having the courage to try feels like. When you told me that Oliver was going to propose, I thought I was going to fucking lose it. It was as if all the things in my life that I was so sure of suddenly weren't the same. I saw it all, Dev. I watched our entire lives play out like some movie." He steps closer. "You were there, in a white dress, on the arm of your daddy, but it wasn't me at the end of that damn aisle. No, it was Oliver, and I couldn't let it happen."

"Why not?"

Sean's hand lifts, pushing aside the strand of hair that fell from my ponytail. "Because it should be me waiting for you. It should be me on a beach, standing there with the ocean at my back as you walk toward me."

My eyes widen. "Why are we on a beach?"

He leans in, presses a soft kiss to my cheek as my entire body tingles. "Because that's the dream, right? It's what you told me a long time ago, and I've never forgotten. There are no rules in this because I'm not playing a game with you, and I'll use whatever means necessary to win your heart."

"And what if my heart isn't ready?"

"Then I'll wait for you, Devney. I'll wait until you realize that this isn't about a bet or anything other than us belonging together. I want us and you and everything that comes with that. I want to kiss you good night, wake up with you beside me, and love you the way you deserve. So, I'll wait for your heart to be ready because mine is ready enough for the both of us."

Sean turns, leaving me standing here, trying to come up with anything I can to deny that he just stole my heart from my chest, and I'll never get it back.

fourteen

"**S**o what you're saying is that he has feelings for you, you have feelings for him, but you won't date him?" Sydney asks as she stares at me. I came here for advice and to work through my thoughts because they're muddled as hell.

"I'm saying that Sean wants more."

"And you don't?"

"I don't know. On one hand I do. He's the best guy in the world."

"And the other?"

I sigh. "The other is that we know we won't last long distance. I worry his fame will be an issue and I'll be insanely jealous."

She fusses with Deacon in the playpen and then sits next to me on the couch. "You're scared and an idiot."

"I'm not being stupid. There's a lot at stake here."

"Yes, there is," she agrees. "There's also a lot at stake if you don't take a chance."

I groan and drop my head back. "I need a freaking life! I need something. Anything other than this. I miss you at work because it's slow and I can't even escape this damn roller coaster in my head."

She shrugs. "There is no escaping the Arrowood hell. I promise. I tried for years and I got myself knocked up and married."

"Can we talk about anything else?"

"No way, you're not going to get out of this. Tell me something, why are you here?"

My eyes narrow, and I study her for a second. "You asked me to drop off a couple of files."

"Not in my house here. I mean in Sugarloaf. Why are you still here? You're smart, pretty, and have a degree in architecture. I'm sure you could've found a job anywhere. Instead, you're my very overqualified office manager. I don't get it."

She wouldn't, and it isn't something I plan to explain because my reasons are my own. "I don't want to talk about it."

Sydney's hand touches mine. "I would never judge you."

It's funny, I remember my mother saying those same words when I called her. I didn't want to tell her the truth, but she kept saying how she loved me and wouldn't cast judgment. That's exactly what she did and *still* does.

"Look, a long time ago, I made some stupid choices and trusted someone I shouldn't have. It changed a lot about me and what I want."

"What do you want, Dev?"

There is so much empathy in her voice that I want to tell her all my secrets and finally unburden myself, but there's no way I can.

Too many lives are at stake.

Too many people would be hurt if I spoke it aloud.

"I want to be happy," I say with honesty. "I want to move on and have a life like you do."

"Meaning?"

I think about how broken she used to be and how, after only a few months, she's happier than I've ever known her to be. Sydney has everything she could want. "I want to be loved."

She squeezes my hand. "Then let Sean love you."

"And if this is all just a mistake?"

"Then you'll survive it. He'll leave and probably only visit when he's seeing his nieces and nephew. It'll suck, but you can endure it. It really won't be much different from before he came back, right?"

My heart begins to ache at the picture she just painted. Sean coming here and me trying to hide from him so it doesn't hurt. I don't want that.

"Except I'll know what it felt like to let him in the way you let Declan in."

Sydney leans back, biting her lower lip. "I know that it's hard. Believe me, I get it. I also know that no matter what the hell paths we got lost on, I was found by the man who was meant to walk beside me. Life is hard and love isn't easy. It's terrible at times." She laughs softly. "It's fear and excitement in one ball of emotions that I swear can roll you over."

"You're really selling me on this," I say with sarcasm.

She shrugs. "It's also the single most human desire. You and Sean already love each other. That won't change. I really believe that, no matter what happens if you were to date, you'd still maintain a relationship. You guys are . . . more than Declan and I were."

My brows raise in surprise. "What?"

"Yeah, Declan and I were high school sweethearts. We

were always a couple, never friends like you guys. So, when we lost us, we lost ourselves. You and Sean are stronger than that. You'd have challenges trying to become something together, but apart, you'd still be the same people. And that's just the worst case, Dev. There's a whole possibility of a beautiful and happy life if you guys do make it work. There would be holidays, family time, and nothing is as bonded as those boys so we'd always be close. I think you're going down the path where you've painted this terrible picture to keep yourself from accepting that you already know it's a foregone conclusion."

All of this is so confusing. "I just don't understand why it has to change."

"Let me ask you this, let's just say that you guys don't pursue this, and you never risk it, do you really think the friendship is going to be the same? You and Oliver are over, you're living with Sean . . . well, you're kind of living with him. And now, there's this . . . thing between you."

In my heart, I know she's right. When he leaves, I won't be the same and neither will our friendship. I know what it's like to feel his lips on mine, and I've heard the sounds he makes when I grip his hair. None of that can be erased.

"He makes it hard to think. When he's around, I battle with myself in a way that I haven't in years. That feeling, the unease and uncertainty, is what makes me want to run."

Sydney exhales slowly. "You've never told me much about your past, and that's fine, but I'm going to assume there was a guy and it went south. Whatever happened then isn't what's happening now."

"I know this."

"Do you?"

I want to say that I do. Punishing Sean for what Christopher did isn't fair, but it's the feelings that terrify me. I could fall in love with Sean in a way that would leave me utterly destroyed if we didn't work out.

"I know what the ending of this story is, Syd."

She rolls her eyes. "You should've listed psychic on your resume, it would've really helped with the cases."

"Ass."

"I'm serious, you know nothing. Nothing. None of us do when it comes to love or relationships. Look at Declan. He's the biggest idiot of them all. He *knew* what would happen. He *knew* that we could never work. He. Knew. *Nothing.*"

I laugh because she's one hundred percent right. "He knew he loved you enough not to want to hurt you."

"And wasn't that the biggest joke of it all. I love him enough to heal his broken parts. Sean and you aren't broken, Dev. You're working with an advantage already. There's no torrid past to muddle through. Nothing other than a chance. Take it because, if you don't, you're going to be the woman in the back of the church, watching the man you love marry another. And that would be the worst ending to a story that you could've altered."

"What movie do you want to watch tonight?" Sean asks as he plops onto the couch.

"I want something that will make me laugh, unlike the gore and blood you've made me endure lately."

He pops a piece of popcorn into his mouth and then grins. "Chicken."

"I'm not a chicken."

"Bet you had a nightmare last night."

I glare at him, partially because he's right and partially

because the stupid man is, once again, not wearing fucking clothes and sitting much too close.

"The only nightmare I'm having is you right now."

"Sweetheart, I'm a wet dream."

I swear to God. "You're a terror."

"You say terror, and I say angelic."

"If you're an angel then I'm a saint."

Sean grins. "And we know that's not possible."

"Oh please!" I scoff. "I'm far more holy than you are. I've gone to church every Sunday since . . . well, ever."

Sean leans back in the couch, tossing his heels onto the ottoman without a care in the world. "Women scream out to the heavens when they're with me. Want to see God, Dev?"

My jaw drops as I stare at him. "Are you a complete idiot?"

"What?"

What? I swear men are so stupid. I slap his chest. "First, you're telling me about the other women you've slept with, which is never a good idea when you're attempting to woo a girl. Second"—I drop my voice to mimic his—"'Want to see God, Dev?' Was that a pickup line? Or are you really that much of a jackass with an overinflated ego?"

Sean shifts forward so fast that I jerk back out of reflex. "First, I wasn't telling you about anything. I was merely making a joke, but if you're curious about whether I'm exaggerating, I'm more than happy to show you. Secondly, I'm not a jackass, and you know that. In fact, I'm quite desirable."

By the time he's done talking, I'm almost lying down and he is most definitely on top of me.

My heart is beating so hard it might bruise, and each breath feels like it could be my last. The heat of his body and the scent of his cologne are making every cell in my body come alive with want.

"Sean," I say as both a warning and a plea.

"What do you want, Devney?" His gaze flicks to my lips and then back to my eyes.

I want him to kiss me. *God, not again.*

I shake my head.

"Do you want my lips?"

Yes. I keep my mouth closed, unwilling to say anything that might lead to a mistake.

"Say the words," he urges. "Tell me that you want me."

The dizziness is so heavy that my mind and heart are warring with each other. I want him. He wants me. It should be such a simple thing, and yet, there is still something holding me back.

"I-I don't . . . I don't know."

"Close your eyes," he commands.

I close them, and my other senses heighten. "Now what?" I ask with my hands plastered to the sofa. I can't touch him. If I do, I know exactly what the hell I'll say.

"Feel." His voice is low and coaxing.

Seconds pass, the anxiety of what's to come next building inside me. The emotions stacking up like bricks with each tick of the clock.

Then, right as I'm about to open my eyes because I can't take any more, I feel his lips just graze mine. The kiss is so soft, so light, that I'm almost afraid it isn't real, but it is. He hovers there, our breaths mingling, growing faster as the ache inside me deepens.

I crave him.

I want this and us and whatever we could be.

I need his lips on mine more than I need anything else.

It's crazy and irresponsible to allow this, but I know I

won't stop it. I can't.

"Feel us," he urges. "Feel me."

My fingers lift of their own volition and the pads of my fingertips touch the taut skin of his back.

"Yes." Sean's voice is soft. "Like that. Feel me, Devney."

My back arches, needing the contact of his chest, which he's kept away. I run my hands up his spine slowly, trying to memorize every valley and peak. His lips move to my neck, kissing and softly sucking the sensitive skin.

"Sean," I say softly.

"Say the words. Say what you need from me. Anything you want, sweetheart, I'll give you."

I don't allow my head to enter. I just feel and tell him exactly what I want. "Kiss me."

He brings his lips back to mine, there's no softness this time. He kisses me like a man crazed and starving. Our mouths move together, and he finally lets his weight settle over me. There's no more tenderness in my touch as my nails score his back, trying to pull him tighter.

Everything in this moment is right.

Him. Us. The fact that we're doing this.

I let my hands wander across his body, feeling how strong he is as I revel in the fact that it's happening. Sean and I are kissing again. Instead of giving myself the million reasons why I shouldn't, I sink deeper into the moment.

"God, you're so beautiful," he says before going back to silence me with his lips.

Hearing those words from him does something to me. He's never lied to me. We've always told each other the ugly parts because we weren't worried the other would shy away. So, when he says it, I know it's what he means.

He pulls back, eyes blazing with desire as he struggles to

catch his breath. He leans down, forehead touching mine.

"Why did you stop?" I ask.

"Because if I didn't, you'd be naked and I'd be inside you."

I'm not sure if it's because I'm more turned on than I've ever been, but I'm not seeing a problem there.

I cup his cheek in my palm, appreciating that he pulled back knowing I most likely would regret it. "Thank you."

His eyes meet mine as he attempts to smile. "Don't thank me. I'm still lying on top of you with a raging hard-on, your lips are swollen, and I've never wanted anything more than this."

"Sean . . . you say that, but . . ."

"No, you don't get it. It's you, Devney. It's you and me, and I don't fucking know how it's taken me this long to see it, but we're supposed to be together. Somewhere along the way, we became more to each other."

I brush back the strand of hair that's fallen in his face. "I'm scared. I don't want to lose you."

He kisses me softly and then rolls to the side, pulling me so we face each other on the couch. My hands rest against his chest as his thumb grazes my hip. "I don't want to lose you either, but I can't pretend that I want to be just friends. For the first time, neither of us is with someone else. There's no complications or reasons to avoid this."

Oh, how wrong he is. "There are a ton of reasons."

"Like what?"

"You live in Tampa, and I live here. You're rich, and I'm living in your family's farmhouse because I don't have enough money to get my own place. You have a job you love, and I'm . . . well, I'm grateful that I have a job at all. You're famous, and I'm some small-town girl who would never be able to handle your life."

He releases a deep sigh. "Okay, take those apart. We live

apart. Well, you can move in with me, which then clears up the second issue about living in my family's farmhouse. As for the job, if you came to Tampa, there are plenty of places that could use an architect. In fact, Declan's buddy, Milo, runs a real estate company with his brother, and I'm sure you'd be a welcome addition to their team. As for the last of your list . . . you're a small-town girl who has a small-town guy who wants to help you through it."

I groan, my head falling forward to rest on his chest. I should've known he'd find a way to make me seem crazy. "We can't be more."

"We already are." His thumb tucks under my chin, and he tilts my face toward his. "I'm just waiting for you to see it. There's no going back to what we were, there are two choices in front of us. We can give into what we want or we can walk away, and I can't do that."

"What if it's not up to you?"

"It's up to the both of us. Now, let's watch the movie before I start kissing you again."

He maneuvers our bodies so that he's spooning me instead of us facing each other.

I look over my shoulder at him. "You know this doesn't mean I lost the bet. You kissed me."

Sean chuckles against my ear. "Fine. Either way, I'm winning it all—your heart, your body, and the words. If I don't, then our friendship isn't what I always thought it was."

I don't know what the hell he means by that. Our friendship has always been strong. If I don't sleep with him, it isn't because of a lack of want but because of an abundance of self-preservation. Cocky asshole. "So, you're saying either I give you what you want or we aren't friends?"

He kisses my neck and then settles back with his arm holding me tight. "No, sweetheart. I'm just saying that I want more, and I think you do too. Our friendship will never change."

And I know he's telling the truth.

There's a freedom in that.

In not having to wonder if this is a game or if he just wants to take advantage of me.

It's trust.

And trust is everything.

However, if it breaks, it can destroy beyond repair, and when I can no longer hide all my secrets, I'm not sure he'll ever forgive me.

fifteen

"**H**ow did you convince Ellie to date you?"

Beer shoots out of Connor's mouth as he stares at me. "I'm sorry, what?"

"I figure you had to do some SEAL-Jedi mind trick or something. No one would willingly date a loser like you, so what did you do?"

He rolls his eyes. "I was a good guy. I was there for her. I didn't convince her to do anything, she loved me instantly."

"Oh, sure, I believe that."

"Believe what you want, you're the one who is single, lusting after your best friend, while I'm married with two kids."

"I'm not lusting."

"Sure you're not," Connor says with a laugh.

I'm far past lusting. I'm fucking dying. This morning, Devney made breakfast in my old college shirt that barely reached the bottom of her ass. The underwear—or shorts as she said—did nothing to hide it either. I leaned against the counter, watching, praying for her to lift up just a bit higher so I could see more.

I can't get enough. I can't stay away. I sleep in that tiny house, doing everything I can to stop myself from going over and climbing in bed with her. Not that I would, but I think about it.

I want her, but she's fighting me, and there has to be a reason.

"I'm doing the best I can."

He tilts his head to the side. "And how's that going?"

"Fucking horrible."

Connor laughs and then leans back in his chair. "You know, I remember how hard it was, no pun intended, when Ellie and I were under the same roof. I wanted her so badly, but she was in pain and there was no way I was going to be 'that' guy."

"So what guy were you?"

"The patient kind. The one who dealt with it, knowing that when she was ready, she'd come around."

I shake my head and sigh. "I don't know what Devney is waiting for or coming around from."

Connor shrugs. "Does it matter?"

"Well, isn't this the saddest bunch of idiots I've ever seen," Declan says as he makes his way up the steps.

"Be nice," Sydney chides. "It's good to see you guys. Happy Birthday Eve, Sean."

Tonight is my fucking thirtieth birthday dinner, but my actual birthday isn't until tomorrow. My brothers and I haven't been around each other for a birthday like this in years. We would've been fine keeping to the tradition we've had, which is send a text or ignore it completely, but the women in our lives wouldn't hear of it.

Sydney, Ellie, and even Devney demanded that we act like brothers, which is what we thought we were doing all along. When we told them that, Sydney brought up Mom.

She struck low and it stung.

Now we're here, forcing a little family time before the big night.

"Thank you, Bean," I say as I kiss her cheek and then look at a very content looking Deacon in her arms. "It's good seeing you. And you, little man, are just the luckiest Arrowood alive." I touch his cheek and smile.

"He's such a good boy," Syd says.

"Nothing like his father then."

"Definitely not," Declan agrees. "Thank God."

We all laugh, and she pulls the blanket a little tighter. "Speaking of God, don't forget that Christmas dinner will be at our house this year and breakfast is at Connor's."

Christmas is soon, but after the fight that Declan and Connor had about it the other day, it makes me wonder what Syd did to get her way. "Are you sure? I thought that Ellie was hosting dinner," I say, knowing it'll make my sister-in-law's head explode.

"Watch it, Arrowood. Watch it."

"Seriously, are you trying to get me killed?" Dec asks.

"Just need some entertainment."

She points at all three of us. "I'm going in to see Ellie and Devney, you guys don't stay out here too long and get sick."

"Yes, Mom," I say sarcastically.

Syd leaves, and Connor hands Declan a beer. "Helps with the cold."

He laughs and pops it open. "And helps with being around you idiots."

Even though our father was an alcoholic and beat the shit

out of us, we forced ourselves to learn restraint. We drink, but we never get drunk. We fight, but we never get physical, and we loved, but never enough to get hurt. That last one seems to be a failing concept.

Declan and Connor love their wives past the point of sanity.

"Sean here wants to know how to get Devney to give it up."

"Yeah?" Dec asks. "Give up what?"

"Her heart," I say without pause.

I wait for the smart-ass comments to fly. These are my brothers, after all, and they are bound to make fun of me.

"Good answer," Connor says with a nod.

"What?"

Declan agrees as well. "He's right. It's the only answer that would've granted you support from us. We love Devney, and since you have no intention of staying here, it would be the two of us who had to deal with the aftermath of this shit. If you guys fail, we'll have to be here, see her in pain, and comfort her. In order to stay together, the only choice is for her to go with you."

"It won't fail."

Connor speaks up. "Did you guys discuss any of this?"

"Not really. I know that she doesn't want to do long distance."

"Did you ask her if leaving with you is an option?"

"It's not."

For some strange reason, Devney will not leave Sugarloaf. I don't get it. I've never really gotten it. She was happy, or seemed to be, so why she stayed wasn't my business. Now, though, I have to push her.

Her family treats her like shit, so it can't be them.

If it's fear of another man hurting her, then I have a very limited amount of time to prove that I'm different.

Declan's eyes narrow a bit as he thinks. He's a business-man and sees things very differently than the rest of us do. Connor was always very single-minded. He found what he wanted and went after it. When he called to tell me that he got accepted into BUDs, I wasn't surprised. The day he enlisted, he said he planned to be a SEAL, and so he did. Jacob is free spirited and artistic, which is why he excels as an actor. Each of us has our strengths, and together, we're a stronger unit.

"What are you thinking?" Connor asks after a minute.

"Just that of all the people who I thought would get out of Sugarloaf, Devney was at the top. She was smarter than every-one by half and had this drive. When she got a full ride to that college in Colorado, I don't think anyone was surprised."

"I definitely wasn't," I tell Dec.

"Right. That is why I'm confused."

"She has her brother and nephew," I say as a sort of expla-nation. "She and Jasper were always tight. Hell, he followed her out to Colorado at one point during college and lived there." Now that I think about it, he would have been out there around the same time as all the shit went down with her pro-fessor.

"Yeah, but . . . staying around for Jasper? Come on. The four of us know about being close with siblings, and I wouldn't stay around either of you fuckers," Connor scoffs.

"And yet here the three of us are now," I point out.

Declan and Connor both shrug. Maybe there's some other guy who Devney isn't telling me about and that's why she's staying. Although, that makes even less sense because she was with Oliver.

"Maybe her dad isn't doing well. She's always been close to him," Declan offers.

That could be. As much as she hates her mother, her father is the bright spot. If there's something going on with him that no one knows about, it would explain it.

"I don't know, maybe."

"Has she spoken to them since she left their house?" Connor asks.

I shake my head. "She debated it, but I don't think she has."

"That's a tough call."

The three of us have zero room to judge someone for cutting off contact with a parent. We walked away nine years ago without a backward glance on our father. Of course, he was a drunk who beat the fuck out of us.

"Do you think Dad would've apologized had any of us given him the chance to?"

Connor laughs once. "Not fucking likely. He felt that hitting us was a way to teach us to be men. Do you remember when he took the stick to Jacob?"

I clamp my jaw as the anger rolls through me. "Yes."

"Yeah, all because he cried when he broke his arm. So, Dear old Dad thought to take a fucking stick and beat him with it to, 'Give him something to cry about.' He felt we were weak and his beatings were a way to toughen us up."

Each time a slice of something other than pure hatred toward the man bubbled up, it's quickly tampered down. There was no goodness in him. Not after Mom died, at least. It was as if she took all the kindness that lived in him and buried it with her.

"He was a piece of shit."

I nod and then push the beer away. "And that's why I don't think he felt any remorse. If he did, he had plenty of opportunities to reach out to any of us. Instead, he fucked us by forcing us back here."

"So far, we've all done okay," Connor says. "I found Ellie, and Syd and Dec finally got their shit together. Look at you, Sean, you're finally admitting your feelings for Devney. I'm not saying I agree with the methods, but had it not gone down this way, our lives would be on different courses."

Declan laughs. "Yeah, you'd be living on my couch, trying to figure out what to do now that you're out of the navy."

He smirks and raises his beer. "That I would."

"Or with me, living it up on the beach."

"Another promising possibility."

I roll my eyes. "But look at you now."

"Yeah, I'm not pining after a girl, hoping my brother can give me some mind trick up his sleeve that I can use to get her. Instead, I've got the girl."

My middle finger raises in his direction.

Declan pipes in. "Me too, brother."

"Yes, you're all living it up."

"Well, whatever it is that is holding her back, you have to uncover it and do whatever you can to help her through it." Connor finally offers some advice worth a damn.

"Guys!" Ellie yells. "It's time to eat!"

Connor places his hand on my shoulder as he gets up. "Let's go inside so we can watch you go down in flames."

Who knows, maybe I need to start a fire to get her to burn. It's time to light the match by telling her the truth about my past and hoping she'll tell me whatever it is that she's holding back. We can let the past become ash and rise into our future if she'll just try.

sixteen

Dinner was fun. It was great being with the guys and my friends as we just enjoyed each other. And then there were the babies. God, they're so damn cute.

I held either Bethanne or Deacon in my arms at all times. I loved how they fit so comfortably in my arms, making their sweet little baby noises. Each minute more precious than the last. One day. One day, I'll have that.

One day, I'll hold a child, protect them, snuggle them, and get to inhale that soft scent until I have it committed to memory.

"You okay?" Sean's deep voice asks from the doorway of my bedroom. "I called your name, but you didn't answer."

"Yeah. Sorry. I was . . . daydreaming I guess." I grab the pajamas I was going to change into and toss them on the bed. No way in hell I'm going to undress right now.

"What is heavy on your mind?"

I give a reluctant smile. "Us."

"It's the same for me."

I look at Sean, wondering if the feeling we both have is a figment of our imaginations or the real thing. A part of me knows it's real. Each night, I find myself reaching for him. Not in the normal best-friend way that we've always been, but deeper. When we talked about the kids on the horseback ride, he watched me in a way I've never seen before.

Then, when we watch a movie, we sit a bit closer. Each time we're together, something else pulls at me, making me want more and more. These last few months have shown me that Sean *is* more. He's . . . everything. He's the guy who makes it all feel right.

"And what are you thinking?" I ask.

He steps closer. "That it's my birthday, and I have one wish."

My heart begins to race, and my breathing grows deeper. "Yeah?"

Sean nods as he takes another step closer. "Do you know what it is?"

The words don't come out, so I shake my head.

"You, Devney. I wished for you. I wished that you'd stop fighting and let me love you. I wished that you'd see how much I want you, in every way."

I close my eyes, feeling the sting of tears and pain in my heart. I can't do this to him. He will love me, and I will fall desperately in love with him. And in four months, he'll be gone, and I'll be here.

He'll never understand.

I'll have to tell him the truth about what makes me stay here, and I literally can't.

It's a secret that I have to take to my grave.

"I wish it could be, but I'll only hurt us."

"Why?"

I look into his emerald-green eyes, ones that have seen me through almost everything, and hate that I can't share this. "I can't go with you."

"Tell me why."

His hand brushes against my cheek, cupping it as his thumb sweeps a slow arch. "It's not my secret to tell."

"Do you think you're the only one with secrets, Dev? Do you know why I left so many years ago and vowed to never step foot in this town again?"

I release a deep breath, my hand resting on his chest. "Your dad."

"It wasn't just my dad."

"No?"

His eyes close and I feel the pain radiating from his body. "No."

I've never been stupid or naïve enough to think that he doesn't have secrets. We all do, I'm the worst offender, but there's been this . . . hope . . . that maybe Sean didn't. That he bared it all to me, and it was only my sins that needed to be confessed.

Obviously, that's not the case.

"We don't have to do this tonight," I offer. "It's your birthday in two hours, and I have a present for you."

He smiles softly, but there's a sense of determination in his eyes when he looks at me. "I've kept it for a long time, only talking to my brothers about it, and even then, we didn't discuss it really. See, the thing is, I want a life with you. I want to be the shoulder you cry on, like you've always been mine, but I've held back." I focus on my breathing, but it falters when his head rests against mine. "No more, Devney."

I stand in this cocoon of warmth and safety as the two of us lean into each other. Here, when it's just us two, it's almost as if the world around us can't break the relationship we're building. It's easy to believe all the worries are superficial, and I want to stay just like this.

When a storm would roll through, Sean would run to my house, climb through my window, and lay next to me, holding my hand as the thunder shook me to my core. I hated storms, and I feared him going through the fields while there was a chance he could be hurt, but he knew I was more afraid he wouldn't come, so he never failed me.

Now it seems as though the storm isn't outside. It's raging within this room.

I lift my head. "You know that nothing you say will ever change how I feel about you."

He laughs once. "I hope that's not the case."

"Why?"

"Because I want you to love me. Not as your best friend, but as something more. I don't know what happened that night we kissed, but it changed me. It changed how I see you and what I want in life. It's not lust. It's not some fleeting thing that will pass. It's you and me. I've got you, Devney, and I can't ever let you go."

"Oh, God," I say as my head falls to his chest. "You say stuff like that to me, and I don't know how to handle it. You're my best friend. You're the guy who has always been there, and if I lost you . . ."

"Then love me."

My heart begins to pound so hard I know he must hear it. "What?"

"If you don't want to lose me, then just love me."

"I do love you."

He pushes my hair back and smiles. "You won't ever lose

me, no matter what. Well, you won't if you still want me after all this. I want to tell you everything and let you choose. I don't want to wait a few days, weeks, or months for you to find any of this out and be disappointed."

I look up, a bit of fear filling me because he looks so worried. "Why would you think that? I was disappointed when I found out that it was you who ate the last cupcake at my birthday party when I was nine."

He smiles. "This is worse than stealing the last cupcake."

"Are you sure? I really love cupcakes."

Sean's tension drains just a bit. "I'm sure."

"Okay."

He releases me and then sits down on the bed. "It goes back to the night Connor graduated."

"I was in Colorado."

Sean nods. "I know. You stayed there that year. It was our sophomore year of college."

Yeah. That year I stayed away from everyone. "All I remember about that time was when you called me."

"I was so fucked up."

"I remember. I don't know that I've ever heard you so angry."

Sean called me the day after his brother's graduation, and I thought he'd be happy and tell me about all the fun the four of them had, but the conversation was nothing like that. He was . . . so not like himself. I wasn't sure what to make of it, I just knew that his father must've really taken the news of Connor leaving for the navy poorly.

He takes my hand in his, lacing our fingers together. "That night, it was the most out of control I've ever felt. My father got drunk, as usual. He was pissed at us, as usual. But this time, he got in a car, my car."

"Your car?"

His breath is long and steady. "He killed two people that night. He drove them off the road as my brother and I followed behind him. He destroyed a family."

"Sean . . ."

"No, see, he didn't even destroy mine," he continues. "It was the family of the people he killed who bore the pain of it all. The Arrowoods were far too fucked already. But this family, they didn't deserve any of it. He took my car, killed them, and then threatened to blame it on the four of us if we didn't keep our mouths shut. People in town knew my car . . ."

My other hand flies to my lips. Everyone knew Sean's car. It was loud because boys and their stupid mufflers. He also thought it was super cool to drive like an idiot.

"So he said he would pin it on you? I don't understand . . ."

"After he killed them, he left the scene, and there wasn't anything we could do. They were dead, and we needed to stop him from driving. The four of us left the scene to try to find him, and when we did, he was at the house, already passed out. The next morning, we told him he needed to turn himself in, he threatened us, and . . . I would've lost everything. We all would have. If he'd pinned it on us somehow, we would've never . . . I can't make excuses. We were wrong, and we should've fought back, but when I tell you that the four of us were horrified, you can't begin to understand it."

"But that family," I say, and instantly want to take the words back.

"They've forgiven us."

My eyes meet his. "What?"

"Here's where my story gets worse, it was Ellie's parents."

I get to my feet, hand clenching my stomach in horror. Ellie has talked about losing her parents and how terrible it was. It was what set her life on the course that landed her with an abusive husband.

"Please tell me this is some kind of joke. That you're fucking with me or something because . . ."

"It's not a joke. It's why the four of us left and never returned. We never spoke to my father again."

"I came and checked on him! I went with Sydney to your mother's grave and brought him eggs or helped with the cows. I didn't know that he did that! I thought that . . . I don't know, I thought you'd want me to make sure he was at least okay, but . . . God, he killed Ellie's parents!"

Sean gets to his feet. "You didn't know."

A tear slips from my lashes, gliding against my skin. "Why didn't you tell me?"

He brushes away the wetness under my eye. "Because I was ashamed. I hated him. Hated that we were weak. Hated that we were so afraid of what he'd do and how it would look. I couldn't tell you, Dev. But now, now that I want a future with you. Now that I see that I'm falling in love with you . . ."

Damn him. I grip his wrist, pulling it away. "Stop telling me you're falling in love with me."

"Stop pretending you're not feeling the same." I release a shaky breath and try to twist away, but he grabs me, pulling me to his chest. "Tell me I'm wrong."

"You're . . ."

He's not wrong.

He's so not wrong.

I'm so incredibly screwed.

"I'm what?"

The words are right there. They're so close I can taste them. I could tell him everything, confess that my feelings for him are so strong that it's scary. If I were brave like him, I would admit it and everything else. But I'm not brave. I'm a scared, broken liar.

Sean lifts my chin, forcing me to stare into those green eyes. "I'll say it to you, and then, if you feel the same, you don't have to speak, just kiss me. Okay?"

My heart is pounding. I open my mouth, but he puts a finger over it.

"Just kiss me if I'm the one for you because, Devney, you're the one for me."

seventeen

I wait for her to move. I don't so much as twitch a muscle as I pray she won't push me away.

I know she's scared. I see it in her coffee-colored eyes, but I will protect her. I'll do everything to make her see that I won't let her down.

Her chest rises and falls as she moves closer.

She lifts onto her toes, eyes never leaving mine, and touches her lips to mine.

All the burden of the past fades away and hope begins to spread. We have a lot to deal with, but right now, none of it matters. The only thing that exists is us.

My arms tighten as I take over the kiss. I need her. I need her to heal me, make me live again, because I've been only half alive.

"Devney." I sigh her name and then kiss her harder.

Her fingers tangle in my hair, clenching just a bit, but it

only turns me on more. Our tongues slide against each other in a battle of wills.

I have never wanted a woman as much as I want her right now.

We start to move backward toward the bed.

Her legs hit, stopping our progress so I bend forward and we tumble down.

She laughs, and the sound does something in my heart. Devney is in my arms, and in my bed. It's something I've thought about while also trying not to think about at the same time. This was something that I didn't want to consider because she was off limits.

I was such a fool to let this much time stand between us.

I run my hand against her soft skin. "You're so beautiful."

"You make me feel that way when you look at me."

I hate the person who ever made her think otherwise. "You've always been breathtaking." I cup her face, staring down into those eyes that hold me captive. "Always."

"Kiss me. Please."

And I do.

My lips meet hers, and we become lost in each other. I hold myself up as she lifts to meet me, kissing me as much as I'm kissing her.

I want to touch her, feel her, be inside her so badly that I have to fight to keep control.

She doesn't deserve some barely holding on guy, I need this to be good for her.

Moving quickly, I change our positions so that she straddles me. Her grin grows as she looks down at me.

"Why are you smiling?" I ask.

"Because it's you and we're really doing this."

"Yeah, we are. If you're going to back out or regret this, I'm begging you to do it now. Before I've seen you, touched you, and tasted you."

My chest rises and falls a little harder. "What if it's you who regrets it?"

"Not a fucking chance of that."

She leans down, her brown hair creating a veil around us. "Are you sure?"

"Positive."

Devney kisses me, and I thank God she does. I don't want to talk about backing out or regrets. I want passion and a lot of clothes coming off.

As if she can read my mind, she sits back up and removes her shirt.

"Take the bra off," I tell her.

Her hands shake a bit, and her lower lip is nestled between her teeth, but she does it. The bra falls away, and I see her for the first time.

Jesus.

Wow.

Yeah.

Fuck.

I can only think in one-word bursts as I stare at her. How many times have I envisioned this? My fantasy was in no way close to the real thing.

She pulls her brown hair to the side, allowing me a full view. "You're stunning." I lift my hands, fingers grazing the underside of her breasts. "A man could die just looking at you."

"Sean . . ."

"No," I say without room to rebuke me. "You're what men fantasize about. What they close their eyes and wish for." My fingers circle her nipples, and her eyes close. "I will never see anything in this world more beautiful than you."

Her hands grip my wrist, bringing them up higher. "Touch me."

I cup both breasts, kneading them, memorizing the weight of them. I want more. "Come closer to me, sweetheart, and let me kiss you."

Devney's hands land on each side of my neck, the weighted globes dangle in front of me. I lift one to my lips, licking around the nipple and flicking it with my tongue. The moan that comes from her is low and throaty. I do the same to the other before taking it into my mouth and sucking hard. I continue with different pressure and movement, and when her back bows, I suck harder and then flip her onto her back.

I'm ravenous for more. I want to taste her skin, engrain her scent into my memory. More than anything, I plan to make her scream.

I pull off the shorts she was wearing, toss them across the room, and rip my shirt off.

She watches, tongue sliding across her lip as she gets her fill.

"Like what you see?"

She blushes just a bit. "You know you're hot. Don't even pretend you don't."

Yeah, I've heard it before, but for some reason, I've never put much stock in it. I'm rich and famous and a conquest to most girls, but she doesn't see that. Hell, I don't think she even realizes how much money I have or my last contract amount. No, instead, she's tried to get me to agree to let her pay rent to live here. She's bought her own groceries, even when I've already stocked the house, and she never brings up my job.

To Devney, I'm not a paycheck or a free ride. I'm more than that, and her opinion means everything.

"It doesn't matter what other people think. I want to know

what you see."

She shifts to her side, so we're facing each other while her fingers move to my chest. "Well, I see the boy who rescued my dog when he fell in the well and I was too scared to go down. I see the boy who let me drive his red sports car when his brothers weren't even allowed to sit in it. I see the man who sat at my nephew's baseball practice two days ago, letting kids hound him for hours without once pushing someone away. I see the man I want. I see the man who, for some reason, wants me. And you're the one for me."

I can't fucking breathe. I cup her face and bring her mouth to mine. If I could pour myself into her right now, I would.

I would do anything to make her happy, and I'm going to love her so much that she has no choice but to leave with me at the end of this.

There won't be a way for her to walk away, not if I can show her what she means to me.

She's lying on her back, and my lips move to her neck, kissing my way down to where I really want to be. I take an extra few seconds to worship her breasts and then move lower. As the anticipation grows between us, her breathing becomes labored.

I remove her underwear, and damn near blow my load. She's naked, completely exposed and vulnerable to me, and yet, I feel so defenseless.

"I'm going to make you scream, sweetheart," I warn before I toss her legs over my shoulders and taste heaven.

Her fingers grip my hair as I drive her wild. Every technique I've ever tried, I do now. My sole focus is to give her as much pleasure as I can. My tongue flicks her clit, and then I suck and lick over and over until she's writhing against my face.

"I can't . . . ." She pants.

I go harder, doing it again and again. I take her clit into

my mouth, biting down just enough for her fingers to tighten around the strands of my hair she's holding.

She's close.

I can feel it.

I work harder, inserting a finger into her heat, finger fucking her as I move my face, licking and sucking.

Her muscles clamp, and she lets out a yell as she loses control. I keep at it, wanting to make it last, and then I feel her body release.

Kissing my way back up her body, Devney shivers. "You look like an angel after you come."

She laughs softly. "You are a God for making that happen."

"I told you."

Devney rolls her eyes and then covers them with her arm. "Oh for the love of all that's holy."

"You said it, sweetheart."

She lifts her hands and touches my face. I lean in, kissing her softly, coaxing her to settle back into what we're doing here.

Her fingers slide down my body as her tongue tangles with mine. My abs tighten as her nails move against the skin and she pulls my boxer briefs down. "I want to see you, Sean."

I lift up, pulling them off and tossing them. My dick stands tall and proud for her. The slight worry in her eyes has my male ego puffing.

She reaches toward me, fingers gripping me for just a moment before she pumps up and down. I close my eyes. There has never been anything like the feel of her touching me this way.

"Devney." I say her name like a prayer.

"I want you." Her voice is husky and laced with desire.

"I want you. I need you."

"Then take me."

I slowly move down so I can kiss her. This time, it's soft and sweet. We kiss as though we have all the time in the world, and we do. I want her to know that this isn't just some fuck for me. She means something—*this* means something.

"Shit. I need a condom," I say and lean toward my night-stand, praying the box is there and one of my idiot brothers didn't take them. I find one and hold it up. "We're going to need more."

She smiles. "Yes, yes we will."

I roll it on and then line up. Our eyes stay connected as I guide myself into her. She watches me with trust as I sink deeper.

Never has it felt this good.

In all the years, I have never been so connected to anyone like this.

Her legs wrap around me and her hands hold on to my biceps as I push deeper, not stopping until I'm all the way in.

"It feels so good."

I nod. "You have no idea."

She moves her fingertip across my cheek. "Make love to me, Sean. Make me yours."

"You've always been mine, sweetheart, and you always will be."

And then I move, and my ability to speak is gone.

eighteen

The sound of his heartbeat in my ear is the same, and yet, it's different. It's as though there's a new rhythm and everything I've known is no longer true.

Sean Arrowood and I are together. Like, together-together. We're a couple, I guess. We haven't exactly talked about it or mentioned anything since we made love. God, even thinking the words "made love" in relation to Sean feels unnatural. When we were doing it, though, it was right and perfect.

"What are you thinking?" he asks as his hand traces my spine.

"That this is surreal."

"Do you regret it?"

I don't hear fear in his voice, but I sense the tightness in his body. I lift my head, resting my chin on my hand. "Not at all. You?"

"Not a chance."

"Good."

He smiles. "Good."

"Still, you don't think it's weird?"

His hand stills, and I feel his shrug. "Yes and no. If you asked my brothers, they would say this was a foregone conclusion. Not the sex tonight," he adds on quickly, "but that we'd be together. They've known I have been in love with you for a lot longer than I did."

The words that fall so easily from his mouth feel like a sledgehammer hitting me. "You love me?"

Sean jerks up a little, lifting me with him. "I've always loved you, Dev."

"No, I know that," I say, swatting him with my hand. "I get that. I'm saying that you *love* me. You're *in* love with me?"

"Do you feel nothing but brotherly love for me?"

I jerk back a bit. "Of course not. I love you. I've always loved you."

And then it hits me.

I've always loved him in a way that was different from how I loved Declan, Jacob, or Connor. Always more than I loved someone who was just a friend. There was this twinge or a niggling feeling that would bother me when he talked about a girl he liked. I would get jealous but then brush it off as if it were silly for me to think she would take him from me.

I never considered the possibility of being anything other than that. If I had, I would have had to admit that I wanted him.

My eyes meet his, and I let out a soft breath. "I love you."

Sean brushes his thumb across my lips. "Say it again."

"I love you. I love you as something more than a brother or a friend. I think I've always loved you."

He brings his lips to mine in the most sweet and tender kiss I've ever had.

"Come snuggle with me," Sean encourages. "I need to hold you."

We settle back down, and I am nicely tucked into his side, both of us facing each other. "This is nice."

"This is right."

My cheeks are going to hurt from the amount of smiling I'm doing tonight. I look over at the clock and see what time it is. "Sean?"

"Yeah?"

"Happy Birthday."

He looks down at me with so much affection I could cry. "You're the best gift I've ever gotten."

I laugh once. "Better than the bat I got you?"

I saved up for months to get him this bat he wanted. It was aluminum and had some special thing on it or something. He talked about it nonstop, but there was no way his father would ever get it for him, so I did. The look on his face when he opened it was worth every second I spent doing extra chores.

"You are definitely better than any bat in the world."

"Hmm," I say and move my fingers up his chest. "I'm glad to hear that baseball equipment doesn't do it for you anymore."

"No, but I bet you'd like to see my equipment."

"Oh yeah?"

He wiggles his brows with a grin. "Most definitely."

"I swear, you can turn any conversation dirty."

"It's a skill."

"One you've honed well."

"I'd like to hone something else."

I roll my eyes and gently slap his chest. "We should get some rest."

"Rest wasn't what I had in mind."

I sigh, thinking about how exhausted I was going to be tomorrow. For his birthday, we are going to celebrate in style. And by style, I mean I'm going to teach him about the cows. We're bundling up at five AM and heading out to move the cattle to another pasture. His farmhands have done great with running things, but Sean needs to know enough to guide them.

"Yes, well, we are going to be riding for hours, moving the cows, and I need to make sure you understand why all of this matters."

He laughs. "I don't care."

"And that's the problem. You need to help your brothers with this. Connor has done great with repairing things, well, sort of fixing things, and making the farm nice for you and Jacob to sell, Declan has been funding most of it—"

"I did too!"

I sigh. "I said most of it. My point is, you have the task of the cows, and you have a little under four months to figure it out."

I don't let that number stick in my head. I force myself not to focus on the time we have left because he's here now.

"Fine." He pulls me just a bit tighter. "I need a drink of water. Are you hungry?" My stomach growls, and I drop my head to his chest. "I guess that answers that."

Sean scoots out, and I clutch the covers to my chest as I watch his nearly perfect butt march out of the room without any modesty.

"Get chips!" I yell. "And cookies! Maybe some cake we brought back too!"

My head falls back to the pillow, and I sigh.

Is this all real? It has to be because there's a very distinct ache in my lower extremities, and my skin has the tiny prickly feeling you only get after some really fantastic sex. And it was. There's not a chance in hell my mind would be that vivid. I touch my lips, remembering the words he spoke, wishing I could memorize them.

He told me of my beauty, how he cared for me, how he wanted more and needed me.

After a few more seconds, I turn to see him standing in the doorway, leaning casually—buck naked—just watching me.

"What?" I ask, feeling self-conscious.

"You."

"Me?"

He nods and then walks over. "You were thinking of us, weren't you?"

The heat that fills my cheeks is enough to make me wonder if my face is on fire. "Why do you ask that?"

"Because you had this soft look in your eyes and you kept smiling." Sean places the bowl down and then climbs on the bed, pulling the sheet off me. "You were thinking about us and what we shared, weren't you?"

His eyes roam my body and I nod. "I was."

"And you were happy."

"I am."

He leans down, his lips hovering above mine. "I am too."

I run my fingers through his thick, brown hair and gaze into his green eyes. "Good."

"Are you still hungry?"

"Not for food."

He smirks as though he knew that was going to be the answer. "Me either."

There's something heavy and hot around me. I roll my head to the side, searching for the coolness, but I can't go anywhere.

"And just where do you think you're going?" a very deep male voice I know all too well asks.

All of that was real.

Yeah, no dream. Just one hell of an amazing night. "Hi."

His nose presses into my hair. "Morning. I think I could get used to waking up like this."

My arm wraps around his middle, and I moan as his hand wanders down my back. "Me too."

"I know you wanted to get up early to go out, but I much prefer this."

I laugh. "You make a terrible farmer."

"That's because I'm not a farmer."

"Good thing you're good at baseball."

"I'm still not sure how you talked me into working today."

I lift my head to look into his eyes. "What would you normally do today?"

He tucks both hands behind his head and sighs. "I would wake up much later than this, turn on ESPN as I got my coffee, and then go for a run."

"A run? In the winter?"

"It's Florida, sweetheart, we don't really have winter like this."

Okay, he has a point there. "Then what?"

"Shower, meet some of the guys for lunch, which is around the time you usually call me."

Every year, I call him at the exact minute he was born. It's been our thing since we were kids, and no matter what is going on in our lives, we've always stuck to it.

"Well, this year, I don't have to call you."

He smiles. "No you don't."

"Instead, I can kiss you at 1:08."

"I'm looking forward to it."

"I'm glad."

I lean in closer and kiss him. "Now, I have a present for you and then we need to get out to the pasture."

Sean grins, and there is a devilish gleam in his eyes. "A present?"

"Close your eyes."

He does.

I slip out of the bed, grab the item from under the bed, and then place it across his lap before sitting beside him. "Okay, open them."

There sits an aluminum bat, complete with scuffmarks from being used for years, tape around the bottom that he put on it when the grip started to wear, and the initials S.A. carved on the bottom. He stares at it, turning it over while shaking his head.

"Dev?"

"A long time ago, a girl met a boy, and she gave him a bat. That boy became a man who was strong and wonderful, and somewhere along the way, she fell in love with him. When he left for college, he didn't take the bat with him, but she did."

"You kept this?"

I wipe away the tear that forms and nod. "The last night we had together before we both left, I saw it in the corner of your room. I can't remember the last time you had actually used that bat since you had so many of them, but you had it there." I point to the area.

"I couldn't get rid of it."

"Why?"

He comes closer, his thumb slides against my cheek. "I

think you know why."

I do. It was more than a gift to him. It was the first gift I ever really got him, and he loved the thought behind it and how much it meant for me to give him something from my heart. It meant something to both of us—a sign of love and affection. Maybe all that time I was hoping for this. Maybe we've been fighting something and it just wasn't the right time.

"And that's why I took it."

"You've held on to this for nine years."

"It was yours," I say by way of explanation, hoping he understands.

Sean presses his lips to mine. "I've held on to you for twenty years, and, Dev, I'm never going to let you go."

We kiss again, him rolling on top of me, his weight blanketing me from the cold in the air. I hold on to him as the kiss deepens.

I could see this being my new normal. The picture of the future becomes clearer. Sean and I living like this, laughing, and becoming something more than I ever dreamed of. But what happens when the picture fades or tears as our lives become complicated? I worry that this isn't going to last. There are things that I'm not ready to share with him, and after everything he's told me, I don't know if we'll endure my secret being exposed.

nineteen

"Okay, so you're saying that I need to get a new foreman?" I ask Zach as we talk over all the crap that Devney pointed out to me on the farm the other day.

There are issues with the fences, which is why we had a loss of livestock. The cows aren't being moved properly, and she saw some issues in the actual dairy milking area.

I swear, fucking cows.

This isn't something the four of us wanted. Ever. I didn't dream of taking over my father's farm. No, I wanted to burn it down.

Since two of the four of us have kept a share of the land, we might as well make the most of the assets we plan to sell. No one is going to come in here and take a smaller lot and substandard cows.

"I'm saying you have issues. Also, remember, I own a horse ranch, not a dairy farm. The information I'm givin' you is just farm knowledge." Zach's Southern accent thickens on the end. "If you have those kinds of issues, then it's the foreman's head that needs to roll. Wyatt has been running Presley's farm for years, and if he pulled half this shit, he would be out of work by now."

"So, the foreman does what?"

Zach laughs. "Sean, you're in way over your head, buddy."

"No shit. Devney took me out two days ago, and I still don't know where to start."

"I'd start by marryin' her and then fixing the farm."

I chuckle. "It's not that easy."

"The hell it's not."

"If it were, why haven't you married Presley?" I ask, tossing it back in his face.

He releases a heavy sigh. "It's not for lack of tryin'."

I laugh, imagining him begging the same stupid way I was to get her to open up. Women, they're all a pain in the ass, but I wouldn't have it any other way. "Well, I'll let you know if I have it any easier."

"Fair enough."

"Let's talk about the farm since that is fixable . . ."

For the next hour, Zach and I make a list of things that he would do if he were me. It's long, and I'm not sure I can even accomplish half of it, but I'm going to try. The first thing is to get a new foreman on board, then I need to hire extra help and talk to our distributors.

We need to lower costs, fix the farm, and produce more . . . sounds like absolute hell.

I take a walk down to my brother's house and catch him just as he's exiting the barn.

"Hey."

"Hey." Connor smiles. "What's going on?"

I fill him in on everything I've learned, and he nods along, not making a comment until I'm done.

"Sounds like a lot of work."

"Yeah, and you're the one who wants this, tell me why."

Connor sits on a bale of hay and motions for me to do the same. "This farm may be filled with horrible shit for the four of us, but it doesn't have to be the legacy the land leaves."

"Meaning?"

"Meaning that Declan and I have families of our own in Sugarloaf, and I'm hoping you and Jacob follow suit. We can do better than our father. We can make this place thrive and not because we need the money but because I think the four of us need it. And I think it's what Mom would've wanted."

I give myself a few seconds to let that sink in before reacting. This land holds a lot of memories, most bad, but he's right about Mom. She would've wanted more for us. Even though we suffered here, there was good.

There was love.

And there was forgiveness.

"Is that what you want?" I ask my brother.

"I don't know. I've been trying for the last year to figure out what I want to do about this place. I don't need the farm to function to live. I have a very affordable mortgage, the land cost me nothing, and I have my company that is already doing well. Ellie's job is great, so it's not financial, but then I think of Hadley, Bethanne, and Deacon. I want them to have something when we're gone."

"It'll be a lot of work, Connor. It's not something I can just do in a day. This is going to take a fuckton of time and effort. It's firing and hiring people who won't be able to fix all the problems in three and a half months."

He nods. "I know. And you can't stay here. I get that."

"Do you?"

The thing I worry about is that they'll try to trap me here in some way. I want to sell my land. I have zero fucking desire to stay in Sugarloaf. My life is in Florida. My job is there, so even if I wanted to stay, I wouldn't have the luxury of doing it like Connor and Declan did.

"Of course I do." He gets to his feet. "I'm not asking for you to stay here and become a dairy farmer. I'm just asking you to do what you *volunteered* to handle. I got dealt the first hand and had to renovate everything, which I'm still doing, Declan is handling the real estate piece, you have the cows, and Jacob is going to pick up whatever is left."

"Relax, asshat. I'm just making sure that no one has any grand ideas of me moving in."

Connor lets out a low laugh. "I'm not counting anything out. Although, if it really happened, we might all kill each other."

"It's possible."

"Declan is already annoying the fuck out of me and constantly asking about the start-up and if I'm reinvesting into the business correctly."

I can't say I'm not enjoying that he's irritating him. "Good."

He flips me off. "Silent partners who don't know how to be silent. Both of you."

"Hey, I didn't say a word." I raise my hands.

"No, but you sent an email."

Yes, and it was so fun since it was a coordinated effort after Declan talked to him. Sometimes, the only entertainment we have is to pick on the weakest link. Jacob isn't here, therefore, it's Connor.

"I was merely asking about the status of my investment."

"The hell you were. You sent me an email outlining the things I need to think about, including giving you and Declan a larger role in a company that you said you would be *silent* in!"

I shrug. "It's business, not brotherhood."

Connor looks away, muttering under his breath. "Ellie said that you and Devney are together now, how's that going?"

"None of your business."

He raises one brow. "Really? Like you give a shit about boundaries in my life?"

"Touché."

"Devney and I are together, we're figuring things out, and I'm happy."

"I'm happy for you. Truly. Devney is a good person who has always been there for us. Don't fuck it up."

"Because you're the authority on women?"

Connor laughs. "I'm happily married with two kids. I'd say I'm winning on the woman front."

"Maybe so, but this weekend, I have big plans for us . . ."

"And what might that be?"

My grin is wide as I pulled a few strings to make this possible. "You'll find out later, but let's just say that your crown is about to be knocked off your head."

"Where are we going?" Devney asks as I hold her hand in the car. We're driving to the Allentown airport. Only, I'm not telling her that.

"Don't worry about it."

"You're being vague."

"I'm being romantic."

She laughs. "Oh, well, you're doing great then."

"Sarcasm is not welcome in this car."

Devney leans over and kisses my cheek. "I apologize, oh romantic one, I've never been on this side of your charms and was unsure of what it was."

"Uh-huh. Keep talking shit, you're going to be blown away by my take on how to woo my girl."

She pulls her dress down a bit and shifts. "Is that so? You know, you told me to wear a dress and bring something comfy for later, but nothing else. I'm not good with surprises."

That is exactly why I've told her nothing. It's fun to keep her guessing. I called Sydney a few days ago to get a little insight. Dev and I are best friends, but there are things that chicks only tell other chicks. So, I needed to be stealthy. Of course, Syd was more than willing to help me out.

Now, it's time to impress her.

I have a feeling that no one she's dated has ever taken time to think about her and only her.

I plan to change that.

"Well, I'm good at giving them," I say without feeling the slightest bit guilty.

We turn into the airport, and she looks around. "What? Why are we here?"

"Patience, sweetheart." I can feel her eyes on me as I park and slide from the car so I can open her door for her. "Ready?"

She looks up at me with a million questions in those brown eyes. "What are you up to, Arrowood?"

I extend my free hand. "I've missed my mark so many times before, but I've finally hit the bull's-eye with you, Devney. Let me give you my winnings."

Her smile is slow as she places her hand in mine.

The biting chill slices through us while we jog over to the building.

"Mr. Arrowood." The man behind the counter comes around. "I'm Thomas, and I'll be your pilot."

"Nice to meet you, this is Devney Maxwell, my girlfriend."

Her eyes meet mine as I casually give her the moniker we hadn't actually agreed on. She leans into my side, and I hold her tight. We don't have to say anything, the moment is loud enough for us both.

"Nice to meet you both. Your plane is ready as soon as you are."

"We're ready."

Devney looks up at me. "Where are we going?"

"To dinner."

"On a plane?" her tone rises in alarm.

"Yes and no. Come on, time is wasting."

She shakes her head but follows.

We climb on board and her jaw drops. There is a sofa on the right side where we can both sit or seats on the other with a table between.

"We're eating on a plane?"

I laugh. "No, we'll be at our destination before it's time to eat."

She glances back at me and gives me a smile that makes my heart stop. "Where do I sit?"

Is the answer *on my face* too much? Probably.

"Next to me," I say and pull her to the couch.

"Sean, this is . . . this is a lot."

I'm sure it seems that way, but in my life, it isn't. I make millions of dollars a season, have friends who make just as much, and we do impulsive shit like this sometimes. Baseball has given me a lot of privileges, and I've worked very hard not to abuse them. I don't drive my car like an asshole. I don't use my name to get things that others can't. After each game, I sign a ball for any kid I see because that's what we should do.

I play for them.

Without my fans, I would be nothing, and I don't forget that.

Tonight, I decided that, for her, I wanted to be extravagant. Devney dated a guy in college who never took her out. Then she was with Oliver, whose idea of a date was the bar in Sugarloaf. She should have the world at her feet, and if I can be the man to give it to her, I will.

I cup her face, moving my thumb gently over her lips. "This is a favor from a friend. It's his plane, he owed me, and I cashed it in. The thing is, even if he hadn't paid up, there's nothing in this world I won't do to make you happy. I want to make you smile, give you things, shower you with affection, and spoil you. Not because you ask for it, but because you don't ask. I'm not worried that you love me for my money or because I play ball. In fact, I think you'd rather neither of those were true."

Her cheek warms under my touch. "I hate that you're rich and famous, but I love you."

"And I love you. So, you're going to have to accept that I have three months left to make you so hopelessly in love with me that you'll come to Florida with me. I am going to use every resource I have, so be ready, Devney, because I'm going to win."

No matter what the cost, I can't lose.

twenty

"You brought me to New Orleans for dinner?" I stare out the window as we drive through the French Quarter in a sleek black sedan.

God, he's really going big.

"There's a restaurant here that has the best seafood I've ever had. My buddy owns it, so we're going to eat, and then you're going to have the best beignet this city has to offer."

I watch as the lights and people pass by. It's amazing, and the city is alive in a way I've only ever dreamed of being able to see. New Orleans is a city that has always fascinated me for no other reason than it seemed magical.

"It's so pretty."

"It's a fun place. There's a lot of history and culture packed in these streets."

I squeeze his hand. "Thank you. Thank you for caring and thinking of this. It's a little . . . much . . . but it means the world to me."

He smiles and pulls me close. His lips touch mine, and I melt into him. One touch is all it takes for me to forget the world around me. Sean robs the very breath from my body, but it only allows me to breathe deeper. It's crazy how much I've fallen for him in such a short time. Once it started, it was as effortless as it was inevitable.

"I told you I was good at wooing," he says before leaning back.

Yeah, yeah, yeah, he did, and he was right. I'm not going to admit that, though.

"So, dinner?"

"And then dessert."

"Will we make it back tonight?" I didn't pack a bag, because I didn't know that I might need it.

"Yes, as soon as we're done, we'll call the pilot and head back."

"Good because we have Austin's tournament next week, and he's expecting you at practice tomorrow."

"I know. I talked to Jasper yesterday about the team. They're really improving. I'm looking forward to the tournament."

"Me too. He's so sweet when he plays."

He smiles. "There's nothing stronger than a boy's love for the game. Especially when he's good at it."

"I remember."

"Anyway, this tournament is a big deal, and I wouldn't miss his practice for the world. I know how much those kids look forward to playing around scouts, and in that league, this one matters most."

I love that he cares so much. I love that he is thinking of Austin and the kids on that team as though they were his. He was so damn adorable at practice when he started running around with them, showing them all his moves.

The car stops in front of an old building that has the most intricate carvings on the front. When we step out and the warm air hits us, I'm glad I wore this dress. Back in Pennsylvania, I was cold in it, but here, the night is almost balmy. People are out with just a light jacket instead of the full-blown snow gear we would be wearing had we been home.

"This place is beautiful," I say, taking in the view. My heel catches on a crack in the road, but Sean holds me steady. There's so much to take in at once that I feel breathless. The buildings are painted in vibrant colors with green plants hanging from the balconies. The neon lights make everything seem alive and warm.

There's music all around, trumpets and horns as people dance and laugh on the sidewalks.

It's nothing like home.

"It's one of my favorite cities."

I can see why.

"You know, I've always loved the idea of the South. People seem nicer, the pace of life is slower, and it's always warm. I don't know, it's just that I could see myself enjoying this version of winter instead of the crap we deal with."

Sean's eyes dance with joy. "You like the milder weather?"

Oh, please. He isn't fooling me with that. I've always loved summer. "You know I do."

"Florida is warm." His hand moves up to my neck, playing with the hair on the back. "It's sunny, we have Mickey, and lots of other very attractive qualities."

"Like bugs?"

He laughs. "I was thinking that it has me . . ."

Yes, he is a very attractive thing that would make me want to go, but there are reasons for why my leaving Sugarloaf isn't going to happen.

"You also have alligators."

He rolls his eyes. "I've yet to see one just roaming around the complex. We have a gated community."

"You lie. Those damn things are everywhere."

"I'll protect you. No alligators come near me. I'm a repellent."

I want to focus on this and not the deep conversation I know is coming so I laugh. "Good. At least I don't have to worry about you being eaten."

Sean opens the door, and immediately someone rushes forward, arms wide and his smile wider. "Sean!"

I step to the side as Sean and the man embrace. "François, it's good to see you."

"You as well, my friend." His Parisian accent is thick.

"François, this beautiful woman—who is much too good for me—is Devney."

I extend my hand to shake, but he brings it to his lips and kisses my knuckles. "It is so lovely to meet you."

"You as well."

"François and I met a few years back when he was . . ." Sean stops himself, but François steps in.

"Dating one of his teammates who was a horrible lover."

I giggle. "I see."

Sean shakes his head. "Anyway, when he opened this place, I came to support him. You're about to find out why this is the best food in all of New Orleans."

François clears his throat. "All of the world, my friend."

"Did I mention how humble he is?"

I laugh. "I look forward to dinner, more than ever."

"*Fabuleux*! Come."

We follow him to a small table that is right in front of the window, giving us a street view, and he pours us both a glass of wine, and then it's just us.

"What do you think?" Sean asks.

"It's beautiful, and he's hilarious."

"He's a great guy. But enough about him and everything else." Sean lifts his glass. "Tonight is about us."

I do the same, and the delicate glasses clink. "To us."

We both take a sip, still staring at each other over the rims. He looks at me as though I'm every reason he draws breath. Here we sit in a small restaurant after flying on a private jet. Nothing seems real, but if it's a dream, I really hope I never wake up.

"Here, take a bite."

I close my lips around the fried dough and moan in delight. "Whoa."

"Right."

"It's amazing."

"You have some sugar," Sean says, but when I lift my hand, he swats it down. "I'll get it." He brings his lips to mine in a sweet kiss that has nothing to do with the dessert.

After a minute, I pull back with a grin. "I think you got it."

"I had to be thorough."

Dinner was great, we talked about his plans with baseball, some of his friends, and how much I like working for Sydney. I could see the questions in his eyes, but thankfully, he didn't push me.

The evening has been nothing short of magical.

"Before we head back to the airport, I wanted us to walk for a bit."

A few people are standing around, whispering and staring at Sean. "Is this normal?" I ask.

"What?"

I jerk my head toward the crowd. "They're all staring."

He shrugs. "Yeah. You get used to it after a while. I'm young, been in the papers, and apparently, am a very eligible bachelor."

Oh my God. "So, it's because you're hot?"

"You have to stop complimenting me, Shrimpy. If you don't, I'm going to ravish you right in front of all these people, and we'll be in the papers."

I push him away, unsure if he's joking. "Stop."

"I find you irresistible when you tell me how hot I am."

"I didn't say you're hot."

He tilts his head to the side. "No? Because if I remember you said: 'It's because you're hot.'"

"There was a question mark on the end."

"I didn't hear that."

I really do love him in spite of his ego, which is the size of Texas. "You are a total asshat."

"But a hot one. Say it." He nudges me.

"You're okay."

"Just okay? I think you can do better than that." He moves closer to me, the mischievous grin solidly on his lips. "Don't make me devour you here on the street, sweetheart."

"Fine. You're very attractive." I take a step back, knowing it won't make a difference.

"Better, but not quite there."

I try to retreat, but he is faster and grabs me in his arms. He holds me close, and my hands rest on his shoulders. "You're perfect."

Sean's playfulness fades away as his hands snake up my back. "No, you are. You're perfect for me, and now everyone will see it."

And then he kisses me, right there in the middle of the street without a care in the world that people are watching.

twenty-one

"God, how can I be so exhausted and still function?" Syd asks as she shuffles out of her office. "I swear, I am so over this postpartum shit."

"It's been almost three months."

"Three months of total crap!" she says as she grabs a folder off my desk. "I'm ready to come back to work and sleep through the night."

She's nuts. Most mothers want more time at home, but she's begging to go back to work. "You know there's something wrong with you, right?"

"Yes, apparently, I'm missing some part to my brain that says rest and snuggle your baby. Declan points this out daily." Syd sighs and sinks down next to me. "How is the workload going? Is Troy handling it well?"

Troy is the replacement lawyer who has been filling in on the cases she couldn't postpone. He's rarely in the office since he lives almost an hour away, and he seems nice, doesn't ask for much, and continues to say how much I'm helping.

"He's doing fine."

"I saw he won the case against Mr. Dreyfus."

"I know Mrs. Dreyfus was very happy."

They are in their late eighties, and about a year ago, she decided she wanted a divorce. It was strange since the Dreyfus' seemed to be the cutest and happiest couple in Sugarloaf, but apparently, he wasn't a faithful husband. After his dalliance, and God only knows what exactly he was able to dally, with Mrs. Kutcher, who is also married, Mrs. Dreyfus wanted out. So, she came to Sydney, who tried very hard to get them to reconcile. When that was unsuccessful, Syd handled the divorce case. Mrs. Dreyfus is now happy with Mr. Kutcher.

It was very big drama in Sugarloaf.

"I still feel like I ruined Christmas or the Easter Bunny."

"Why?"

"Because they were the cute couple who handed out full-size candy bars for Halloween, and she baked cookies for your birthday, and he was the sweet old man who taught damn near the entire town how to change a tire. They were supposed to *die* together, not . . . date their neighbor."

I smile at Syd's obvious despair. "You did right by Mrs. Dreyfus."

"What if she marries old man Kutcher? Will we just swap their names? Oh, God." She tosses her arm over her eyes. "I can't think about this."

"It's disturbing."

"Very."

"Well, as one of your best friends, I forbid you to ever sleep with my boyfriend or Ellie's husband."

Sydney's eyes widen. "Stop! Not only is that a hundred ways of fucked up but also it's gross. They're . . . ewww!"

the one for me | 177

I laugh. "Well, it's the same as them."

"At least none of us would change our names," she tacks on.

"Yes, that makes it better."

We both burst out into a fit of giggles. "I needed this. Hey, how was your big date?"

"It was good. I mean, really good. Do you know when it's so good that you worry?"

She chuckles and shakes her head. "Not really. Not at that point, at least. Let's remember what the last year was like for me."

"And look at you now."

"Yeah, after I nearly died!"

"No one said men were very smart," I remind her.

"True, but, if I can give you some advice?"

I nod.

"Don't overthink it. You guys have something that might feel too good to be true, but it only feels that way because it's right."

The last three months have been like a whirlwind. I mean, just this week, he literally whisked me away on a private jet, took me to dinner in a city that I've dreamed of visiting, and has been perfect in every way.

My phone rings, and I glance down at the number. "It's my dad."

Syd places her hand on my wrist. "You should take it." Then she stands and walks into her office.

She knows I haven't talked to him or my mom since I walked out of their house, but this is the first time she's given me her opinion on what I should do.

My mother may be horrible, but she wasn't always that way. I've seen a family fall apart, and I don't want to be that way with her.

"Hello, Daddy," I answer, feeling nervous.

"Hi, Devney. It's been a long time since I've heard your voice."

I have no idea why he's calling, but he reached out, so I should give him a chance. Plus, I miss him. "I know. I'm sorry I haven't called."

He sighs. "We have all been stubborn."

That is very true. "How are you and Mom?"

"We're doing okay. You?"

"I'm good."

Dad goes silent for a minute. "Are you staying with Sean?"

I know my brother already told him I was. "I am, but you knew that, didn't you?"

"Yes, Jasper told me the day you left. I'm glad you have a safe place to stay."

I lean back in my chair and sigh. "Daddy, you know Sean wouldn't let me be homeless. Or Jasper. Or Sydney."

He chuckles. "I guess I did. I wouldn't let you be out there and not ask around."

"I know. Did you call just to catch up?"

"No, I called because I would like you and your mother to sit down and talk this out. I love you both, and this is destroying me, honey. I know you guys have a lot of things in your past, but this has to stop."

It couldn't have been easy for him to say all that. We've gone through a lot as a family, and Dad had some health scares the last few years. He just wants his family to heal and go back to the way things were. I just don't know if that's possible. My mother is the one with the issues. Not me. I've forgiven myself for my mistakes. She is still holding on to it and making it impossible to move on. Still, for him, I'll do as he asks.

"All right, Daddy. Sean and I can come by the house this weekend after Austin's tournament."

I can hear the long sigh through the line. "Thank you, my sweet girl."

"Don't thank me yet," I say with a small laugh.

"Are you and Sean . . ."

"Together?" I ask, knowing that's what he's hinting at. "Yes, we are."

"It's about damn time the boy got his head out of his ass."

"Dad!"

"What? You're the best girl in the world, Devney Jane Maxwell. I've always hoped that the two of you would find your way together."

Well, now I've heard it all. "You're like the tenth person to say it."

"Which goes to show you just how long we've all been waiting."

I smile. "I'll be by late Saturday."

"All right."

"I love you, Daddy."

"I love you most."

When I hang up the phone, I feel a bit lighter than I have in a long time. It's all going to be okay. Somehow, someway, we will figure it out. If I can patch this up with my mother, then maybe I won't feel guilty about going to Florida with Sean. Maybe I can start to live my own life and not have to keep trying to make up for the past. I might have a future with the man I'm completely head over heels in love with. But first, I need to get his Christmas present.

"It'll take some work to get it the way you want it."

I look at the car, the exact one that he had when we were kids. "But you can do it?"

Jasper almost looks offended at the question. "Of course I can, it's just not a lot of time . . ."

"I need this."

"Why the hell do you want *this* car? I mean, it's beautiful. It really is. I can't believe how nice this Camaro is."

"Because Sean needs to have the perfect gift. Especially after the trip he just took me on."

It has to be this car. It isn't the same color, but it's the same make and model of the one Sean used to drive.

Jasper grumbles a bit as he runs his hand over the hood. "A private plane. The guy is making the rest of us look bad."

I laugh. "Hazel has no complaints with you."

"I wouldn't go that far, Shrimpy. I'm just housebroken and she doesn't want to start over."

"You are a bit of a dog."

He shakes his head. "You're a pain in the ass."

"This is true, but will you fix it up for me? Make sure it's perfect?"

Jasper lets out a very long sigh. "I guess. The things I do for my little sister."

I give him a big squeeze and smile. "You're the best big brother in the world."

"I know. Now, let me get you a fair price."

We talk to the owner, who is a much older gentleman who

has had the car for a long time and barely drives it. He comes down on the price so far that Jasper almost chokes. And even though I've just blown all my apartment money, I'm beyond happy.

Sean needs to heal and I want to be his balm.

"You'll follow me back in my car, okay?" Jasper says as he takes the keys to Sean's new car.

"Deal."

The ride takes about two hours, I'm jamming out to my brother's tunes, loving that no matter how old he is, he'll always love classic rock. Zepplin, Guns & Roses, and Warrant CDs still sit in the console because my brother refuses to use his phone to stream music, not that his car is updated enough for it. He still drives the car he got when Austin was born. It's old, reliable, and as he says . . . free.

We pull into the back where his shop is and he gets it up on the lift.

"Did it drive nice?"

"It was a good ride. Nothing smoked or made too many odd noises. It's actually criminal what you just got this car for."

"He was really nice."

He nods. "And you being pretty and smiling a lot didn't hurt."

I slap his arm. "That wasn't why."

"Okay."

"Whatever the reason was, he's going to be so happy!"

Jasper laughs and then nudges me. "He better be! You just got the man a gift from the mechanical gods."

He's so stupid. Boys and their cars. "Sean is always appreciative."

"He better be."

"Spoken like a big brother."

Jasper smiles and leans against the workbench with his arms across his chest. "Are you happy, Dev?"

I nod.

"You know that if anything goes bad, you always have a place here."

I love him. "I know."

"There's nothing that we wouldn't do for you."

I walk toward him, place my hand on his arm. "I know."

Jasper has always been there for me. I love him, trust him, and as surly as he gets about men in my life, I know that he loves Sean. Still, he was never this . . . protective before.

"Why weren't you this way when I was dating Oliver?"

"Because I knew that Oliver wasn't forever."

I jerk back at that one. "What?"

"He was nice and all, but he wasn't right for you. Still, he was harmless."

"And you think Sean will hurt me?"

"Fuck no," Jasper says with a laugh. "I think he'd cut his arm off before he'd do that, but he'll take your heart and . . ."

I don't need him to finish that sentence. We don't lie to each other, and the writing is on the wall about what will happen when Sean leaves.

"And me?"

His one shoulder rises and then falls subtly. "He's the one, isn't he?"

"I think he is." I shake my head. "No, I know he is."

"What does it mean for you?"

My heart aches at the idea of Sean going without me. To be apart from him after knowing what it's like to have him is . . . impossible.

"It means that I love him and I can't live without him."

Jasper's eyes fill with understanding as he stares at me. "You should go with him, Devney. You should open yourself up to him and tell him everything."

My chest tightens at the idea of doing that. "You think I should tell him the whole story?"

He nods. "If you love him. You give him all your burdens, Sis. You've been carrying it all on your own, it's time to allow yourself to be happy. Love him and go to Florida where you can start fresh."

"But what about everything here?"

"We'll always be here. We're not going anywhere, but you, Dev, you should be going places. You deserve happiness and love and a life."

My lower lip trembles as I stare at my brother. "I'll miss you and Hazel and Austin so much."

He pulls me close. "We'll miss you too, but now we have an excuse to go to Florida, right?"

I nod, giving him one last squeeze. Jasper has always been here for me. We grew up very close and have maintained that relationship. I hate the idea of not being around him, Hazel, and Austin. There is nothing in the world like being an aunt. I get to enjoy him, be his friend, all the while his parents do the hard stuff.

"I don't want to tell Austin."

Jasper releases me, his shoulders dropping a touch. "He won't take it well. You're his best friend."

"I know."

His brown eyes fill with warmth and compassion. "Still, you should go. You deserve your own family. One where you can love a man who is good to you and raise a child who will get to see how amazing you are."

A tear falls down my cheek. "Thank you, Jasper."

He winks. "Don't mention it. Now, let's get to work on this car."

twenty-two

"Honey, I'm home!" I call out as I open the door.

"That's something I could get used to. You coming home to me every day." Sean's smiling face greets me as I enter the house.

"My thoughts exactly."

His arms wrap around my waist, and he pulls me close. "You have a good day?"

"Yeah, Syd came to the office, I had an interesting phone call, and then I picked up pizza."

"A phone call?" Sean asks.

"My dad."

"And?"

I play with one of the buttons on the front of his Henley. "He wants us to come and talk with my mother."

"What does your mom want?"

I shrug. "World peace."

Sean lets out a throaty chuckle. "Yeah, I don't believe that."

"I don't know, but Dad asked, and I have never really been good at saying no to him."

His thumb rubs the area on my lower back. "I'll do whatever you want. If you'd like to talk to her, then you should."

"Does anyone ever want to talk to her? No. But I think it's been long enough, and if we're going to keep dating, I'd like to have my parents' blessing."

On the ride home from Jasper's, I thought a lot about the call and what it all means. My mother and I used to be close. She believed in me, and I lost that. I made mistakes, but to her, they've been unforgivable. I'm tired of trying to make life easier for everyone else. The mistakes were made, the damage was done, and we've all found ways to go on with our lives, it's time she does too.

"I've lived with not having said my piece for a long time. There are so many things I wish I had said to my father. I know it wouldn't have changed anything, but it might have made me feel better about myself and the choices I made. I'm glad you're going to say what you need to."

My hand lifts to his cheek. "I love you, Sean Arrowood. You and your brothers have done beautiful things. You've done everything right. I know that you wish you could've said something, but he would've never heard you."

"I love you too. I know that. So, I live to make my mother proud."

"She would be. I know this in the very depths of my soul."

All she ever wanted was for them to be close with each other and to be kind to others.

He gives me a kiss and then smiles. "I think she would be too, which is why I think that you should make amends with yours. Life is too short, and regret is the burden for the survivor. I would hate to see anything happen to your mother and you end up having to carry that or vice versa."

I agree with him.

"You're right."

Sean grins. "Say that again."

"Not likely."

"Why? It's easy, you just say, Sean, you're right . . . as usual."

"Sean, you're an idiot," I reply.

"Not quite correct, but I'll let it slide this time."

I roll my eyes. "How magnanimous of you."

"Now, since you're in a giving mood, let's talk about the future since you brought it up." My heart quickens, and I take a step back, but he grips my wrist before I can get too far. "Don't do that, don't pull away."

"I'm not."

"You are." He tilts his head to the side and watches me. "I know you, Dev. I get that this is all scary to you and that you've stayed in this town for some reason. However, things are changing, and I can't do what my brothers did and stay. I would if I could."

"I know that, and I'm not asking you to."

"Then, what do you want? Do you want us to do this long distance? I will if that's the only way I can have you, but after knowing what it's like to wake up next to you . . ." His voice lowers, and he moves an inch closer. "To be able to pull you close and bury my face in your neck at night or to make love to you in the morning isn't something I want to go without. I want us to have dinner together and to go on dates. I want to be able to come home to you, but I can't do that if you're here."

I want all of those things too, but I also know that when the season is in full swing, he's never home. Before I tell Sean where my heart is, I need all the information. "What about during the season? What do I do then?"

Sean pulls me to the couch, and we both sit.

"What do you want to do?"

I sigh and entwine our fingers, needing to feel bonded to him. "I need to work."

"Well, if we're together, you really don't."

"I will never be okay with that," I say quickly. "I have always supported myself, and I'm not starting our relationship off with me taking anything from you."

"Devney," Sean says softly, "it's not you taking, it's me giving."

"And that's great, but I can't be your trophy girlfriend. I won't."

He smiles. "All right. I'll do whatever I can to find you a job you want."

Now for the point I know he's going to argue. "During the season, I'd like to come up here as much as I can. I want to see my friends and family. I don't want to be stuck in Florida where I don't know anyone."

"Okay . . . I'd like you to come out to some games." I nod. That isn't really a concession.

"Done." This is going to be the part that Sean pushes back on, but I have to do it. "But I don't want us to tell anyone about this until three weeks before you leave."

I love him and have every intention of going. We are the real thing. I know, without a doubt, that he's the one for me. I've never felt this way about anyone else. There's always been a feeling in the back of my mind that said it wasn't right and that isn't here with us. Still, I need time. I need to be sure. I don't want to make a rash decision and this *new* relationship with him is very young.

"What?" He jerks back. "Are you kidding me?"

"No," I say as I tighten my grip on our hands. "Listen to me, we've been a couple for what? A few weeks? A month?"

"And we've been friends for an eternity."

"Yes, but this is different, and you know it. I want us to date without everyone giving us their unwanted advice. I love you. I want to be with you more than anything, which is why we need this time together without any added pressure from our friends or families."

Sean is my forever, and I want it to stay that way.

"I don't need the next three months to know it won't change." His voice is sure, and there isn't any doubt in his eyes.

"I know what I want, Sean, but I don't think us making such a life-changing decision when we are blissfully happy is a good choice. We're going to fight because you're an idiot. You're going to get mad at me because I can be a slob. Right now, we're in this perfect oblivion. Telling them is just going to add on more . . . things. I don't want more things. I just want you and us and what we're doing now."

"You want to fight?" Sean asks with a smirk.

He's such a dumbass. "No, my point is that we will. I know that I want to go with you. I know that this is what you want. But it's too early to make a choice like me moving to Florida with you. So, let's just act like we haven't made that decision, okay?"

He sighs. "So you know this is what you want? I know this is what I want, but we're just going to keep it quiet."

"Basically, yes."

"Sounds dumb."

I need to make this make sense. "I spent the last ten years listening to how my rash decisions caused the downfall of my life. I fear that this could be one of those again. We don't have to rush into a decision right now."

"No, but . . ."

I lift my hand. "All I'm asking is to spend the next nine weeks living together and figuring our life out. Then, three weeks before it's time, we'll announce our decision together. I'd rather us keep this to ourselves for a while. If nothing changes, then no one gets hurt."

Sean leans back, pulling me with him so I'm resting on his chest. "All right. We won't make anything official until then, but we're going to plan it. We're going to discuss how things will be when you come with me. Which really means, no matter what happens, I can't live without you. Okay?"

I smile and cuddle in closer. "I can live with that."

"Good, because I can't live without you. So, focus on my wonderful qualities and forgive my weaknesses."

I laugh and look up into those beautiful green eyes. "I'll try."

"Good, now try not to kiss me."

There's not a chance in that.

twenty-three

"All right, Austin, I want you to shift your weight back and forth and be ready to pop up at any moment."

He nods quickly and then drops into position. "I'm ready."

"When I throw this ball, I want you to pop up and throw down to second. The tag needs to be low and accurate."

When his brown eyes lock on to mine, there's nothing but determination in them. "I got it."

I turn to the runner, give him a nod to indicate he's to take off as soon as the ball leaves my hand, and then check on the shortstop.

Everyone is ready.

I lift my leg and let the pitch go.

Austin is fast as he grabs the ball, which I threw wide on purpose, and when he lobs it toward second, it flies from his hand like a bullet. It ends up a little too low, and the runner is safe.

"I don't know what happened!" he yells. "I threw it just like you said to."

Poor kid. "It's fine. We'll do it until it works. I know throwing this way is new, we just need your muscle memory to kick in."

I hate the way he looks away, but then I hear the breath leave his nose and he gets back into a squat. This is the attitude I had as a kid. I would work and work until I couldn't take much more. My legs would be sore and my arm would be on fire, but I wouldn't care.

"Do you know that, when I was your age, I would sit like that to read or even eat dinner?"

Austin grins. "I do too! Mom yells at me to sit at the table, but I know that I need to be ready on the balls of my feet."

"It's a catcher's life. It also leads to bad knees and sore joints. Do you make sure to ice and rub them down?"

He shakes his head. "I don't always remember."

"Make sure you do, I know it's stupid and you're young so you think it's no big deal, but when you get to be my age, it sucks."

I'm one of the younger catchers in the league, and I don't know how the hell I'll feel in ten years. I do a lot of massage, ice therapy, scraping, cupping—hell, anything they can try to give me relief. After the first year in the major league, I remember there was one day after a double header that I could barely stand the next day.

It's tough on our bodies, and if I were smarter when I was a kid, maybe it wouldn't be so hard now.

"So, ice my knees?"

"Yes, and stretch. It'll give you a lot more strength later on."

"Whatever you say, Sean. I'll do it. I just want to play ball forever."

This is the part of my job that I love. Looking at the kids who are going to one day replace me. I think about how I looked up to my idols who are now the people giving me advice about how to stay in the game. It's a weird sort of brotherhood, but one that I cherish.

If it weren't for the greats who came before me, I wouldn't be here today.

"All right, you ready to try again?"

"Let's do this."

For the next hour, we keep at it. Going over and over them until he feels comfortable. As a catcher, I want to protect his knees and his shoulder, those are the two most common injuries, and the way he was throwing before could cause tears or strain. The way I had him correct it is a bit strange, but it will lessen the burden on his muscles.

Finally, he throws a rocket that hits the target perfectly.

"I did it!" Austin's joy is overwhelming.

"You did amazing. That was a perfect throw."

His four teammates who stayed to run drills rush over to him, patting him on the back and laughing. The boys celebrate as I look around, parents are clapping and starting to come down off the bleachers, but I keep looking until I see a smile that makes my heart stop.

Devney has a grin on her face as she makes her way toward me.

"God, you're gorgeous," I say when she's before me.

"You're biased."

"Maybe so, but that doesn't make it less true."

Her head shakes as she looks over at her nephew. "I told Jasper I'd have him home an hour ago, but I didn't want to pull him away."

"I'm glad you didn't. He did great, and I wanted him to have this down before the tournament in a few days."

Devney smiles as Austin and the other kids chase each other around the bases. "Well, you are a hero for teaching it to him, Sean Arrowood."

"Then are you my prize?"

She laughs softly. "You think you deserve one?"

"Don't all heroes?"

"Maybe."

"If we're putting in requests, then I totally want you."

Devney leans in, kissing my cheek. "You already have me."

Thank God for miracles. "And tonight, I really plan to have you."

"I like the sound of that."

Oh, me too. I am going to have her in so many ways.

"How about we get Austin home so I can have my prize?"

"Deal."

We get Austin in the car and head to his house. The three of us talk about the tournament, which we have to leave for at five in the morning because it's freaking two hours away.

"Are you going to ride with us, Aunt Devney?"

She looks over at me, and I shrug. "We can if you have room."

"Yes! We'll make room. We can leave Mom home if we need to."

I laugh. "Dude, never leave your mother behind. She's the one who brings food and plans for things. If you're going to leave someone behind, it should never be her."

He nods emphatically and then his head tilts. "Who do we leave then?"

"Your aunt. Always leave her."

"Hey!" She slaps my chest. "Never leave me. I'm mission essential."

"Really?" I counter. "What do you bring to the crew?"

Devney sits up a bit straighter. "Well, I'm good in a crisis, so you don't have to worry about what to do. I have the ability to build things, so if survival is an issue, I can make a shelter. Then there's the fact that I am very funny, which helps the time go by."

I glance back at Austin. "Are you buying any of this?"

"Not the funny part."

Her jaw falls slack. "You guys are mean."

"Sweetheart, we're asking you to sell us on why we should bring you, not why you would be good in an apocalypse."

"And why should we bring *you*?" she asks with her arms crossed over her chest.

"Because he's Sean Arrowood! The greatest catcher of all time!" Austin informs her with a lot of gusto.

"Exactly."

"And that means what if we are talking about value in an emergency situation? Is he going to catch the snowballs that fly at us?"

Austin laughs. "No!"

"Well, I'm not convinced that he shouldn't be left behind. He has very few skills, and I would know because of the number of times I had to save him when we were kids. He's definitely not funny. I can't remember the last time he made me laugh, unless you count the times I laughed *at* him. We know he can't plan because he said he needed his mother to pack him snacks, and can you guess who does it for him now?" Her eyes lift and she points to herself. "I mean, if we're talking about anyone we should leave behind, it's very clear who the choice is."

I love this woman. I love her humor, her heart, and how hard she's trying to sell me down the river right now. Austin shakes his head as though the idea is inconceivable, which to a nine-year-old baseball enthusiast, it is.

"I can't leave him behind, Aunt Devney."

"And why not?"

His eyes widen as his voice drops. "Because he's Sean *Arrowood*."

"I know, but I vote him out of the car."

"You don't get a vote," I inform her.

"And why not?"

I smile at her as I park the car. "Because I would never leave you anywhere. I'd stay back if it meant you got a spot."

"Well, now you ruined my fight. How can I even think of leaving you when you say sweet things like that?"

I wink and then turn to Austin. "And that's why you'd never leave me. I'm a charmer."

They both burst out laughing. Devney rolls her eyes. "Go inside, buddy. I'll see you early Saturday morning."

"Love you, Auntie."

"Love you more."

"Thanks, Sean. I'll see you tomorrow at practice."

I give him a fist bump. "You got it, man."

He rushes to where Hazel is standing in the doorway, waiting for him. We wave to her, and then Austin gives an enthusiastic wave back.

"He really looks up to you," Devney says as we watch Hazel slide Austin's gear bag off his shoulder.

"Austin is a great kid with a lot of skill. If he sticks to it, I'm telling you, he's really got potential."

She leans her head back, tilting it so she can look at me. "I hope he finds whatever makes him happy. If it's baseball, then so be it, but I hope he finds a passion in school too. I worry that he'll be one of the guys who barely makes it. It'll destroy him."

She's talking about Isaac Withers. I played college ball with him, and he had it all . . . talent, discipline, and ambition, but he never could get through the minor leagues. They make next to nothing, travel, train, and never see their families. It took a huge toll on him, and he took his life a year ago.

Devney came.

She was there, holding my hand as I struggled with the loss. Isaac had just gotten married and had a baby on the way.

I take her hand in mine. "He has so much time to figure it out and he has people who love him and will guide him."

"I hope so."

"Even if he doesn't play ball forever, sports are such a huge part of kids' lives, and he will never forget how it felt to be on the field. Still, I would never encourage him if I didn't think he couldn't make it."

She gives me a sad smile. "I hope we never have to have that conversation in a few years."

In a few years. The words rattle around in my head and I try not to make too much of it. We have been friends for so damn long that it could mean anything, but I really fucking hope it's more. I want the rest of our lives to be this way.

I will give up everything if it means I end up with her.

My biggest worry is that she'll change her mind last minute. She'll want to stay here and therefore, I am making alternate plans in my head. I haven't said it to her, but if it's the only option, then I retire from baseball. I have more than enough money for us to live the rest of our lives without having to worry. Yes, there will be huge penalties that I'll have to pay back and it won't be the life I promised, but if Devney chooses not to come with me, then I'll have no other choice.

It isn't what I want, and it would be the stupidest choice I make, but I can't lose her.

I kiss the top of her hand. "I hope not either."

"Now," Devney draws the word out, "about that prize . . ."

twenty-four

N ever has anything felt so good. "Sean," I moan as his tongue swipes against my clit again.

He does it again, and everything turns tight and tingly. I could wake up this way every day and never have a single thing to complain about.

A few hours ago, we made love. It was soft, sweet, and filled me with so much happiness I could burst. We fell asleep in each other's arms, and what I thought was an erotic dream, turned out to be Sean spreading my legs and bringing me to climax in my sleep.

There is no light in the room other than the slivers of moonlight that filter through the window. I can't see him, but I feel him everywhere.

"Please, baby, I can't take much more," I say between heavy breaths.

"Let's see if that's true."

My eyes close, and I focus on the immense pleasure. Sean brings me higher, so much so that I can see the peak, but then he stops, kissing the inside of my thigh.

I force myself not to complain since the last time I did, he made me wait longer.

I don't want to wait.

Thankfully, he doesn't. He goes back in, licking harder, his tongue making circles that drive the build faster than he had before. It's like a train, barreling toward me so fast that it won't be able to stop before it runs me over.

My heart races, and every muscle in my body goes taught. Everything feels uncomfortable and twitchy before his finger slides deeply into me, and I fall apart.

I scream his name, back arching off the bed as I get swept away by the most intense pleasure I've ever felt.

And then he's over me, sliding into me, pushing at a pace that is hard and unrelenting. I love it. I love his power, his strength, and the fierce way he's giving himself to me.

I take it, wanting him to give me everything he is.

"Sean!" I yell as he pounds harder.

"I love you."

"I love you."

"God, I need you," he grunts.

"You have me."

Sean grabs my hips and tilts my body so he can reach deeper. My fingers grip his shoulders, needing to hold on because I feel like I'm falling apart. It's too much. The pressure, wild and chaotic, begins to build again.

"I can't do this again." My voice is strained as I fight off another orgasm. My body is already too spent. It'll kill me.

He thrusts his hips forward harder as his finger finds my clit. "Yes, you can."

The musky scent of our lovemaking fills the room, and he pushes harder. "Please, it's too much."

"It's never enough, Devney. Never. I need you. Give yourself to me, let me catch you."

The deep need in his voice has me relinquishing my tenuous control, and he increases the pressure and starts to move again.

One.

Two.

Three more pumps of his hips, and I'm gone. I fall apart, unable to hold on to reality any longer. My head thrashes from side to side, fingernails digging and scoring the flesh on his back, needing him to anchor me to this world.

Sean yells as he follows in his own release, and then he collapses on top of me, leaving us as a tangled mess of arms and legs and heavy breaths.

"That was . . ." I say as I pant.

"Yes."

"Yes?"

"It was." Sean's head turns to me as his hand finds its way to the tangle of hair at the nape of my neck. "I can't let you go, Devney."

I nestle into his chest as his arms tighten. "I don't want you to."

"Good."

"We need sleep," I tell him. "We have to be at Jasper's in two hours."

He releases a deep sigh, tucking us under the heavy blankets. "It's been snowing for hours. There's no chance they're having it."

I look out the window, seeing the falling flakes. "I love snow—as long as I'm inside and by the fire."

202 | CORINNE MICHAELS

Sean chuckles. "I remember."

"You think it'll be cancelled?"

"Weather report says five to ten inches. They should cancel it."

I nod, the warmth taking any wakefulness from my body. "Good."

His lips press against the top of my head. "Sleep. We'll wake up in two hours and make sure."

Sleep is good.

My eyes close, and I fall asleep with a smile on my lips as I imagine the rest of my life with this man.

My eyes open, and it's bright in the room. "Morning. Shit!" I try to move, but Sean's arms are clamped around me. "We slept in!"

He releases me and moves to rub his eyes. "I thought we said it was cancelled."

I reach over to find my phone, but it isn't on the night-stand. Damn it. I left it in my purse. "You said it should be cancelled." I grab the blanket off the bed and wrap it around myself. It's freaking freezing in here.

I rush out to find my phone, only to see that I have five missed calls and six text messages. I open them and read the first two.

Jasper: Hey, Austin is asking if you're coming?

Jasper: If you can't, that's fine, just let me know.

Then I read the next when it switches to my sister-in-law.

Hazel: We're getting on the road, let us know if you're riding with Sean since you didn't show up this morning.

Hazel: Please let us know you're okay. We are pulling into the tournament now.

My heart is breaking. I would've been there. I should be, and I'm not.

Jasper: This isn't like you, and I'm hoping you're okay. We are here and the first game is starting, but roads are pretty bad, so don't come unless you have four-wheel drive. I'll handle Austin.

Tears fill my eyes as I see the last message.

Austin: I guess you're not coming.

"Hey." Sean's voice causes me to look up. "Are you crying?" The second he reaches me, he's pulling me in his arms. "It's okay."

"No, it's not. I've never missed a tournament. Never. I've been at each one, and he was so excited to play for you."

Sean rubs my back and then pulls back a bit. "We can go now. It's not even eight. We'll make at least two games."

"Jasper said the roads are bad."

"We can take Connor's truck. He put snow tires on it yesterday."

I release a sigh, warring with myself on if we should go or

not. "You sure?"

"Yes. Let's get ready, I'll call my brother and get his truck, we'll head there. We won't let Austin down, and I wanted to be there for him too. I swear I set an alarm, but we'll go and see as much as we can. Okay?"

I nod. "Okay."

He kisses me and then lets go. "You get in the shower, and I'll take care of everything else."

This means everything to me. That in the middle of a snowstorm, he knows that what I really want is to go. Austin is everything to me, and I need to be there for him. I want him to know that no matter what, I will always have his back.

Just like Sean has mine.

I grab my phone and shoot a text off to Jasper.

Me: We're coming. We slept in, but tell Austin we're on our way!

twenty-five

How we got to this tournament in one piece is beyond me. Even with the plowing, sanding, and salt, the roads were slick. I wanted to turn back at least two times, but I remembered the look of despair on Devney's face and the tears in her eyes, and I couldn't force myself to.

Thank God we have Connor's truck and I was fortunate to get behind a plow on the highway.

Getting home is going to be another story.

We both get out and head inside.

"You made it!" Hazel says as she pulls Devney in for a hug.

"Barely," I say, my hands still shaking a bit.

"I know, I can't believe they didn't cancel this, but there are only two boys who didn't come. Two. Out of all the teams. It's the last tournament before Christmas, so I guess they were determined to play."

Yeah, because they knew who they would be playing in front of. Up on the bleachers that separate the ballfields are the scouts. They have their tablets and phones out, taking notes and doing whatever it is they do.

I remember it all too well. I also remember begging for rides to games and tournaments I knew they'd be scouting.

Devney takes my hand in hers. "We're sorry, we slept in."

Hazel looks down to our entwined fingers and grins. "I see."

"It's my fault," I attempt to smooth over any awkwardness. "I must've forgot to set an alarm."

"And my phone was in the living room," Dev says before I can say more.

"It's hard to hear the phone when there are other things on your mind." Hazel's grin says it all.

"And she's pretty loud when she's occupied," I tack on.

Devney slaps my chest. "Sean!"

"I didn't say it in front of your brother."

Hazel tilts her head with a grin. "And I wouldn't if I were you. I would hate to see your pretty face messed up or my husband thrown in jail."

I chuckle and pull Devney to my side. "She's worth any pain I have to endure."

"Awww," Hazel says with her hands clasped in front of her. "You guys are so cute. I'm so happy you are together and in this blissful state. Truly, it's about damn time."

The number of times we're going to have to hear this is going to be exponential.

"Well, I love her. I always have, and now, I just have to convince her that life outside of Sugarloaf is worth it."

Hazel's eyes widen as she glances at Devney. "You're thinking about leaving?"

"I'm thinking about my future and what that looks like, you understand, right?"

She smiles. "Of course I do. It's time you find your own path. Jasper and I have always wanted you to have your future. I know what has kept you here, and I love you so much for it, but . . . I want you to live *your* life."

I have no freaking clue what they're talking about, but I feel awkward standing here. "I'm going to check on the team."

They both nod.

All right, then. I sneak off and go down to the dugout. "Hey," Jasper says, clapping my hand.

"Hey, sorry we missed you this morning. It was a late start."

"My sister has always been lazy in the mornings. I'm used to it. Glad you guys made it, though, the weather is no joke."

I shudder a little. "We had a few close calls."

"I'm sure."

"We should probably get a hotel close to here," I suggest.

There's no way in hell we're driving back if the roads are going to be like that.

Jasper shrugs. "The snow should stop in the next hour or so, and if they salt the roads, it should be fine. We're trapped in here for at least the next seven hours."

That's true. "We'll play it by ear."

"Sean!" Austin spots me and barrels my way. "You're here!"

"We are. Sorry that we're late, but we had to get my brother's truck."

"It's cool. I knew Aunt Devney wouldn't miss it."

I smile at his ultimate trust in her. "No, she would have walked if she had to."

"She's always at my games."

"Is she your lucky charm?"

He purses his lips. "I don't think so."

"All ballplayers have something that brings them luck. You have to figure out what it is and always have it near you."

His eyes widen. "What's yours?"

I reach into my back pocket and pull out a picture. "This has been with me at every game, practice, tournament, and tryout."

Austin takes the very worn photo and looks at it. "Who is this?"

"That," I say as I point to the first person in the photo, "is my mother. She died when I was about your age. This person"—I point to the kid to the left of my mom—"is my brother Declan, and I'm next to him." I move to the other people. "That's Jacob, who is an actor."

"Your brother is the new superhero, isn't he?"

"He is."

Jacob was cast in a role last year that has changed his life. He went from starring in some low-budget films to being a new box-office phenomenon, and his producer, Noah Frazier, says it's going to be the role of a lifetime. He is the lead in the newest superhero action movies that will span at least fifteen films. All the heroes will intertwine, and the first movie, which was released four months ago, is looking to be the highest-grossing film of the year.

"That's so cool. Your whole family is! You have a brother who was a SEAL and apparently a huge hero because Hadley never shuts up about him. You're a famous baseball player. Your other brother owns all of New York, and then one is a superhero!"

I laugh because, to a nine-year-old boy, it would seem that way. "Well, they are pretty cool, but you see that person right there?"

Austin looks over his shoulder, getting a closer look.

"That is my good luck person. She's why I carry this pho-to."

Austin squints and then his eyes lighten with awareness. "That's Aunt Devney!"

"It is. We were all together that day, and this photo is all of the people I love most. They're who are always there for me, make me play harder so I make them proud, and give me strength when I need it. So, they're my lucky item, and even if I can't have them at the game physically, they're always with me."

He looks over at Jasper and then at me. "My parents and Aunt Devney are mine."

"We're lucky to have people like that, right?"

His head bobs up and down. "Mom, Dad, and Aunt Devney are always there. They love me more than anything."

Jasper puts his hand on Austin's shoulder. "Your nana and pop, too."

"But they don't come to my games like you guys do."

"True," Jasper relents as Austin's teammates call his name. After he's out of range, Jasper turns to me. "Thanks for that."

"For what?"

"Giving him something to hold on to. You know the ins and outs of this while I'm just fumbling along. I built cars when I was his age, sports were never my thing. Devney prob-ably knows more about it than Hazel and I combined."

Dev hated sports as a kid. I'm sure some part of her still does, but she was always with me and had to learn or be bored. "I'm just happy to be here for the kids. I know how hard it is at their age to have big dreams. If there's anything I can do to help, I want to do it."

"The trick you taught him with his arm, he's been at it every day. He made me clean out a part of the barn so he could put a pitch-back in there, he does exactly what you told him, and he's been at it for at least an hour a day."

That's the kind of spirit that will take him places. "He's got a great shot at playing long-term if he keeps at it."

"You can tell at his age?"

"He is playing at a level much higher than he should be. I know it's hard to understand, but most kids can't throw like he does or hit the ball as far. He has natural skill and ability. If he hones it, he'll go far."

Jasper smiles and then claps me on the back. "You're a good man, Sean. Thank you."

"Happy to do it."

"However, if you hurt my sister, I'll break your knees."

I want to laugh, but I don't doubt for a second that he wouldn't make good on that threat. If God had given my mother a daughter, my brothers and I would've protected her, threatened any man who came near her, and would've done a lot worse if they'd hurt her. Devney was sort of our sister growing up, and I understand the point he's making. He loves his sister, saw her hurt by a man before, and he doesn't want to see her go through it again.

My back straightens, and I look him in the eyes. "I love her. I will never hurt her intentionally, and if by some stupidity, I do something to break her heart, you won't have to find me to fulfill your promise."

Jasper nods once. "Like I said, you're a good man, and I hope that never happens."

"I do too. She's everything to me."

He looks toward where Hazel and Devney are sitting. "She's given me the world, and I owe her everything."

I turn to him, trying to decipher if he's talking about

Devney or Hazel, but before I can ask, the game is called to start and baseball becomes everyone's focus.

twenty-six

We're heading toward the hotel after a huge argument about the road conditions. It is *not* that bad, but my boyfriend is taking no chances. Even though everyone but him wanted to head home, he called a place and got two rooms, insisting we stay the night.

"I know you're pissed, but it's not the end of the world."

"I never said it was," I reply with my arms crossed. "We just were supposed to go to my parents' tonight and talk to them. It's only two, the roads are clear, and we're going to a hotel for no reason."

He sighs, running his hand down his face. "Why is going there so important?"

Because I wanted to talk about more than just my parents.

It's time to tell Sean everything about my past. He deserves to know, and I'm finally ready to tell him.

"Because I wanted to talk to you before we go there."

"So, why can't you do that now? It's just us, sweetheart."

"It just . . . I can't do it in a hotel or in the car."

"Why not?"

"I don't really have a great reason, but . . . I want us to be alone and in our home. Where the walls aren't down."

"You're starting to scare me. What is this about?"

Yeah, this is not going to be how it spills out of my mouth, but I need to let him know the truth to some extent. "You asked me a while back what I wasn't telling you."

"Right."

"The thing is, I trust you. I always have, but I didn't trust myself. I wasn't able to tell you certain things because I was too scared to, but I love you in a way I didn't know was possible. I want to talk about the whole part of my past. I just can't do it in a hotel."

Sean takes my hand in his. "Is it really that important we do this tonight?"

"It is, but I'm scared," I confess.

He sighs and pulls over into the gas station. "Scared of me?"

"No! No, not that."

"Then what?" he asks after I stay quiet for a few seconds.

How do I explain to him what I'm afraid of? It isn't that I think he won't understand, because he will. He won't blame me for any of it. What Christopher did to me was horrible and no one faults me for it—well, no one other than my mother.

Still, I have kept this secret, made it my talisman to the past, and fought hard to prevent anyone from finding out.

I look into his eyes, which are filled with concern. "Devney . . ."

"I'm scared of saying the words."

Jasper's car pulls up next to us, and Sean curses under his breath. The window rolls down, and my brother's voice breaks the silence. "You guys okay?"

"We're fine. Are you comfortable driving back or do you want to stay at the hotel?"

"Roads seem to be okay. I'd rather get back. The horses need to be fed, and I have to check on the tarp we put on the roof of the barn."

Sean looks out at the road and then back. "All right. Devney wants to head back too. She was planning to see your parents."

"Well, that's reason enough to avoid going," he jokes.

I lean over. "It's about everything, Jas. It's time."

A few weeks ago, he said it was time, and he's right. Sean is the first person I've loved enough to even want to tell. It never even occurred to me to tell Oliver, which showed me just how much Sean means to me.

Sean looks from Jasper back to me. "Time?"

Jasper smiles. "It's not a bad thing. I'm glad she's finally going to open up to you."

"Well, I guess I am too." Sean then shakes his head.

I hate that we're being deliberately obtuse, but I wasn't lying when I said I couldn't do it now. There are things you tell someone in a car and then there are things you don't. This falls in the latter category.

"Okay." Jasper clears his throat. "We're going to stop for something to eat, but we'll call you when we get home."

"Sounds good." Sean rolls the window up, and we wave to them as we pull back onto the road. "We'll head back to our house first to talk and then go to your parents."

"All right."

The car ride back is tense and quiet. Sean's focus is on the road and mine on my feelings. One hour feels like an entire day, and I have a knot the size of Texas in my stomach that grows more each mile we get closer.

For so many years, I prevented myself from feeling this way about Sean, and it was so stupid of me. I should've seen how amazing he is and how perfect we are for each other. I love him so much more than I ever knew was possible.

We get to the entrance of the driveway, and Sean puts the car in park.

He stares up at the sign, hands tight on the wheel.

"What's one truth about an arrow?" I say what I know he both needs to hear and hates at the same time.

"Just because you don't hit the bull's-eye, it doesn't mean the other shots don't count."

There's an edge to his voice, one that sounds a bit like dread. I put it there, but it's me who is feeling it more than he can ever know.

Sean turns to me, his eyes full of questions. "What's one truth about an arrow, Dev?"

God, how fitting my truth is. My hand lifts to wipe away the worry lines between his brows. "Forget the last arrow because only the next shot counts."

"Whatever is in your past is just that . . . the last arrow."

How I wish that were true. "Sean . . ."

"No, I just need to say this before you tell me whatever it is." He pauses, and I nod. "I love you. Whatever you have to say to me won't change that. I know there's more to the story of your ex. You wouldn't have been living the way you have been if there wasn't. I can't promise I won't be mad, but not at you—for you. Understand?"

My heart is pounding, and a tear falls down my cheek. He says that, but will he still feel that way after I tell him? Will he still love me? God, I hope so because losing him will be impossible to live through.

Here I am, for the first time, in love with the right person at the right time, and the secrets I've kept might change the way he sees things. I've lied to him for so long.

"I hope you mean that."

He leans in and kisses my lips softly. "I've got you, Devney. I've always had you, and I'll have you still."

It's as though he has some code to my heart. He dials into whatever I need and is able to give it to me.

"Let's go inside and talk."

As we get to the end of the drive, my phone rings. I look down and see my mother's number. I can't do this now. If I talk to her, I will never get through this part with Sean and it's imperative we talk first.

"Who is it?"

"My mother."

I move to drop my phone into my bag but the ringer blares again.

"It's my father's number this time," I say to Sean.

"Answer it."

"I'll call them later."

I silence the phone, and we exit the car, but then Sean's phone rings.

We both glance at each other as we trudge through the snow and get on the porch. He looks down. "It's your father."

"Why would they call you?"

"I have no idea. I'm going to take it."

"Okay." It's clearly important if my mother has called me a few times and my dad is calling him.

He swipes the phone to answer. "Hello?"

I watch as he moves toward the door. "Yes. Okay." He stops moving, and his back goes straight. "Where?" I step closer to him, trying to hear, but Sean walks to the other side of the porch. "How long?" Dread starts to fill my body as he moves farther from me and actively avoids looking in my direction. "We're on our way."

"Sean?" My voice is shaky. "What happened?"

When Sean spins to look at me, there's a bleakness in his eyes, and I know something has happened. Something that has him terrified. My body trembles, and it has nothing to do with the cold. "There's been an accident."

twenty-seven

I don't remember how I got here. Just that Sean drove, and neither of us spoke. I could feel him looking at me, taste the worry in the cab of the truck, but I wasn't aware of anything else. Nothing but the passage of time.

Sixty-three minutes since he said the words that left me numb and terrified.

"There was an accident."

I hear it over and over in my head and try to wrap my mind around the rest of it.

"Who?"

"Jasper. The car hit ice and flipped several times. We have to go."

"Are they okay?"

"I don't know. Get in the car, we'll be there as soon as we can."

And here we are.

"Are you Ms. Maxwell?" the police officer asks as we enter the room.

"Yes."

"I'm Deputy Reston. I was at the scene of the accident."

My heart begins to pound as I stare up at him and Sean's hand presses against my back. "What can you tell us?"

The deputy looks at Sean for a second and says, "The car hit black ice, the driver lost control, and the damage is extensive. The passenger was ejected from the vehicle, we found her about ten feet from the car."

Oh my God. My hand flies to my mouth as I feel my knees buckle. "What about the boy?" I ask, my voice breaking at the end.

"He was conscious when we found him. We were able to extricate him, all the while talking and keeping him calm. He did sustain injury and is currently in surgery, but it wasn't life-threatening."

I'm only slightly aware that Sean's arms around me are the only things keeping me standing. "What about Jasper, the driver?"

"Both the driver and the passenger were . . . they were in critical condition when we got to the car. The driver was pinned, and we had to cut him out. I don't know more than that."

Sean pulls me to his chest. "I see, but the boy was okay?"

"Yes, Mr. Arrowood, I was talking to him as we got him out of the car." Tears fall, and I lean against Sean, needing his strength more than ever. "The accident could've happened hours before another motorist came upon it and was able to call for help, but we did everything we could."

Sean rubs my back, my head starting to feel fuzzy and unable to think anymore.

"Thank you."

"If you need anything," the deputy leaves the statement open.

"We appreciate it."

He leaves, and Sean guides me over to the couch on the side of the room and crouches in front of me. "It couldn't have been hours, Dev, because we had just gotten home."

I nod. "Right."

"It's a good thing. Be positive."

"Sure."

Sean's finger swipes a tear. "I'm going to check to see if there are any updates. I love you."

"I love you."

I can't think. Everything feels like it's too much. My brother and sister-in-law are fighting for their lives, and I can't do anything. I would give anything for this to be a bad dream. I sit, feeling so alone in my terror. I can't lose them. They mean everything to me, and I have so many things to say to them.

The waiting room is cold and quiet. There's a television up in the corner, but I have no idea what's playing. I close my eyes and do something I haven't done in a long time, I pray.

God, if you're listening, please help my family. Please don't take them from me. I know I've disappointed you. I haven't done what I should, but if you can just give me this, I swear I'll do better. You have to save them. They're the very best of us. Jasper needs to be there to watch Austin grow. Hazel has to hug him more. Please. Please. I beg you, don't let them die. Not because I didn't want to stay in the hotel. Not because I was selfish.

"Sweetheart." Sean takes my hand in his, and I do my best to focus on him. "You're shaking."

I hadn't noticed. I don't feel much, other than dread. I can't lose them. I can't . . . live through it.

"Did the nurses say anything?"

"No. Just what we know. Surgery and no updates yet. The doctors will be out as soon as they can."

He pulls me to his side, rubbing his hand up and down my arm, trying to warm me. "I did this," I say the words that have been my companion the last few hours.

"What?"

My stomach flips and bile rises in my throat. "I made us drive. You wanted to stay the night, and I didn't. I wanted us to talk, and I was selfish."

"Devney, no."

"Yes. If something happens to them . . ."

He shifts so he's squatting in front of me. "You didn't do this. It was ice. The roads seemed fine and your brother and I both made judgment calls. Don't put this on yourself."

I don't see how I can do that. I feel responsible. Jasper would've followed us back to the hotel, but I didn't want to go so he said it was fine to drive.

Sean pushes back the hair that fell in my face. "No matter what happens, this wasn't your fault, and when they pull through, they'll tell you the same."

I wish I had his level of faith.

"Devney!" My mother's voice is loud as she rushes in. "Did you hear anything?"

I shake my head. "Nothing yet. They're all in surgery. Austin's injuries are not life-threatening, but Jasper and Hazel are. Other than that, we're just waiting."

"Oh, how can this happen?" She flutters around the room, nervous energy rolling off her in waves. "Why? Why is this happening?"

I get to my feet and pull her tight. I can't imagine what she must be feeling. No matter the issues we have, I don't want her to suffer. "I'm sorry, Mom. We just have to be strong."

She wipes at her eyes. "I know, sweetheart. I'm sorry. I just . . . he never should have gone to that stupid tournament. Baseball!" Her hands fly in the air. "All because of baseball. I swear, I could scream. He's my son. He's . . . they're my . . . I can't lose them over a game!"

Me too, but the need to defend Jasper rises in me. "Jasper and everyone else felt the roads were okay."

She sinks down into the chair. "If that were true, we wouldn't be here."

"I know."

Sean gives me a soft smile and then looks to my mother. "Mrs. Maxwell, what can I get you? Are you thirsty?"

"You sweet man, nothing. I just need my son, daughter, and grandson to be okay. That's all."

"I'll get you some tea, and you both can sit." His voice is placating, but it does the trick. "This has to be incredibly hard for you."

Mom moves beside me and takes my hand in hers. "They'll be okay, won't they?"

I look up, tears blurring her face. "They have to be."

A moment of understanding passes between us, and the fights, barbs, and anger disappear. She's my mother again. The woman who held me when I was scared, read me stories each night, and helped me learn to love. "Mom . . ."

She pulls me to her chest. "Shh, it'll be okay, Devney. It'll be okay. We're strong, and we will get through this. They'll need help, but we can handle it."

My mother rocks me as I fall apart. I cry for my brother, his wife, and Austin. I think about the long road ahead of them and how much I need them. They are my family and they saved me when I was breaking.

Throughout everything that happened, Hazel and Jasper were who held me together. Their love, understanding, and friendship is why I stay in Sugarloaf. I owe them more than I can ever repay.

Sean returns with a cup of coffee for me and tea for my mom. Another few minutes pass and my father comes in.

"Any news?"

We all shake our heads. "Nothing yet."

Dad comes to me, kisses the top of my head, sits so he can hold my mother's hand, and we talk about the accident.

Sean relays the information clearly and with far more authority than I ever could. I would be on the ground in tears if it weren't for Sean's arm that's tight around me.

"It'll be okay," he tells me again.

"You don't know that."

He lifts my chin so his eyes pierce mine. "No matter what, it'll be okay. I'll be right here and I will love you through it."

My lips part to tell him the secret I've been keeping. He needs to know, now more than ever.

Just as I'm about to tell him, my mother grips my leg as she stands. I turn to look at what captured her attention and then we are all on our feet as a surgeon enters the room.

The four of us wait, holding our collective breaths as he walks over. "Are you the Maxwell family?"

"We are," my dad says, stepping forward.

"I'm Dr. Eacker," the surgeon says. "I operated on Austin. First, I want to say the surgery went well. His injuries were not critical, but we needed to set the fracture in his leg immediately. It required pins, which he'll need to have removed, but it could have been a lot worse. He'll need rehab, but I am expecting a full recovery. His other injuries were minor. There are some cuts and contusions, but he was very lucky. You'll be able to see him once he's awake."

I could fall on my knees in gratitude. "Thank God."

"Any news on my son or daughter-in-law?" Mom asks.

"When I last checked, they were still in surgery. I'll see if I can get any updates."

My father pulls my mother and me into his embrace. I can feel the slight ebb of relief through the room. Austin will be okay.

He'll recover, and now we just need to hear good news about Jasper and Hazel.

The minutes tick by, but no one comes out. I watch the door, feeling anxious in my too-tight skin. The metallic taste in my mouth grows as fear does as well.

Twenty minutes pass.

Thirty minutes.

Then an hour and still no news.

"What is taking so long?" I ask to no one.

"I'm sure they're working and can't come update us," Dad says as he checks the door again.

Mom takes my hand in hers. "No news is good news."

Maybe, or it's about to be horrible news. Either way, my mind goes down a million paths of what-if. Each time I start to spin out, I try to refocus on the fact that Austin is well and maybe that means it wasn't too long before their car was found. I know every minute matters, and I have to hope that time was on our side.

My father paces while I seem to shrink into myself with every passing second I watch tick away on the clock. There is something soothing about watching the hand jump from second to second.

Every sixty seconds, it will move.

Every sixty minutes the small hand will follow.

It's the only thing concrete in this room right now.

We have no idea how bad my brother or sister-in-law's

injuries were or if they will survive. We don't know if they are fighting or giving up, but I have to believe, for Austin, they won't ever stop trying. They love him more than their own lives.

The big hand moves again, and I count.

One. Two. Three . . .

When I get to fifty-six, two surgeons enter the waiting room. Their eyes are cast down, fatigue clearly set in the slump of their shoulders, and dread fills me so heavily that I can't stand.

Their eyes meet ours, sweat beads on their foreheads, and they both look—dejected.

Everything seems to happen in slow motion. They stand in front of us, heads shaking back and forth, and one of the doctor's rests a hand on my father's shoulder. I watch my mother's legs give out, and Dad pulls her to him as a sob breaks. I take note of the way the doctor's lip quivers slightly as his regret saturates every molecule in the room.

I can hear the sound of the automatic door opening and closing as people exit.

All of it engrains itself in my mind.

Each detail becomes clearer as my world adjusts.

"We tried," the first doctor says. "They were in very bad condition, and we did everything we could."

The next one tries to console my mother. "The blood loss was too great, and the damage to Jasper's spleen was too extensive to repair. The brain damage that Hazel sustained during the ejection was severe."

My father continues to fall apart as I sit, unable to move or speak.

Mom's sobs are muffled against his chest as she holds on to him.

The worst has happened.

My brother is dead.

My sister-in-law is dead.

They're gone.

And then, the only thing that could snap me out of it comes rushing forward. "Austin!" I yell.

Sean is on his feet, trying to reach me as I rush out of the room. "Devney, stop."

"He needs me!" I say as the tears that I thought had dried up come back with a vengeance. "He needs me to be there. He can't be alone. He can't wake up alone!"

He takes my face in his hands. "Okay. We'll go, but . . ."

"No, he can't. He has to hear it from us. He's going to be so scared." The tears fall like rain.

"All right, just breathe, sweetheart. I promise, we'll be there."

"Oh, God!" I cry so hard I can barely draw in a breath as Sean pulls me against him.

My brother was a great man, one of my best friends, and now he's gone. I will never get to talk to my sister-in-law again but there are many things I wanted to say. I close my eyes, allowing the sadness to wash over me.

"Easy, love, I'm right here," Sean murmurs in my ear.

I cling to him as if he's all that's keeping me together. "I need you."

"You have me."

My eyes keep welling with tears that spill over before I can stop them. I wipe another set away and turn to the doctor. "I need to see Austin."

"Devney," Mom calls to me. "Please."

I force down all the emotion that is threatening to overtake me and force myself to remain strong. Austin needs me. He has to hear it, and he has to know that he has people around him who will be strong for him. He's just a boy who is about to find out that he's lost his parents.

Jasper, Hazel, and I discussed the possibility, like most parents do when they make their will.

I'm now his guardian.

"It has to be me, Mom."

Tears fall down her face, and she nods. We both know why.

"Of course, he should be awake very soon," the doctor says.

My heart is pounding, and my throat is closing. I don't know how I'll ever say the words to him. This was never supposed to happen, but it has, and I have to keep my promise to my brother.

Sean pulls me back to him, keeping me in his warmth. "Whatever you need, Devney, I'm here."

He says that without knowing that my entire life just changed in just a few hours. I have to make him understand that I am no longer free. Austin is all that matters.

"Sean . . ."

"You don't have to say anything."

"I do. I have to explain. When Jasper and Hazel drew up their will, they named me as Austin's sole guardian if something were to happen to them."

He releases a sigh and then touches my chin. "I figured. I'm Hadley and Bethanne's as well. I understand what this means."

"No." I sigh and step back. "You don't. You see, but you don't understand." Panic is building inside me as the enormity of the situation crashes into full color high definition. "You can't understand because you don't know why they chose me."

"Of course I do. You're his aunt."

I look into his green eyes, my vision hazy as the tears and

the truth spills out. "I'm his biological mother."

twenty-eight

H e hasn't said a word since I told him the truth a few
minutes ago. Right after I said it, the doctor led us
back to Austin's room. Now, we are standing in the
doorway, listening to the machines beep and watching the
frail-looking little boy in the bed sleep.

Austin's leg is wrapped and in a brace and elevated. The
recovery will be difficult, but I will do everything I can to
make this easier for him.

First, I have to break his heart and pray my love is strong
enough to help heal it.

"Are you going in?" Sean asks, the edge in his voice causes
me to shrink in a bit.

There were a million better ways today could've ended.
My brother could've stayed in the hotel, lived, and the pieces
would've fallen the right way in telling Sean about my . . . my
son.

But that didn't happen. Instead, I might have ruined everything.

I glance up at him, his thick lashes framing those incredible emerald-green eyes that are distant. "I didn't mean for this—"

"Not now. Not when he needs you."

We turn to where Austin lies. "We have to talk, though."

He nods. "We will, but right now, there are more important things than whatever you and I need to resolve."

I know I've hurt him. I can feel the tension growing between us. I've kept this from him for ten years, and I can only hope he'll understand once he knows the whole story.

First, I have to handle the situation at hand.

"He should be waking up soon," the nurse says softly as she approaches. "If you want to be at his side, it might help for him to see a familiar face."

Sean's hand touches my back, and I let him guide me into the room. Like the parting of the sea, we stand on each side of him. My chest hurts as I stare down at the little boy I love more than my own life.

"He doesn't deserve any of this. He should be riding his horse in the snow, throwing the ball with his father, and planning ways to get into trouble," Sean says as he pushes Austin's hair back.

"No, he doesn't deserve any of this."

His happiness and his chance at a good life are the reasons I've endured any of this. What I could give him at twenty was nothing like the life Jasper and Hazel provided. They were able to provide for him and raise him the way I wanted him to be raised.

There was never discord or unhappiness for him. Austin was loved and cared for in every way.

I was lucky that losing my son meant gaining a nephew who Hazel and Jasper loved like their own son. They wanted me to love him. They begged me to come back to Sugarloaf, be his auntie, and get to see him grow.

As hard as it was, I did it, and it was the greatest gift they ever gave me.

"Austin," I call his name with all the tenderness I possess. "It's okay, sweet boy." I run my hands through his hair and then trail them down his sweet face.

As much as I want to see his eyes, I don't. When he wakes, he'll have questions, and the answers aren't what I want to give.

There is no easy way to give anyone news like that. This has to be done very carefully.

I look over at Sean and his gaze meets mine. "He doesn't know, and we can't tell him."

He breathes through his nose and then looks down. "I wouldn't say anything. I'm just here for support."

I wonder how much a heart can break before it just gives up. I'm going to suffer more losses than I can bear today.

"I'm sorry, Sean." Before it's too late and everything becomes too muddied, I say it.

"I know."

"Do you?"

Sean nods.

"Do you know I love you?" I ask, my voice catching at the end.

He reaches out to where my hand rests on Austin's shoulder and twists our fingers together. "I know that too."

I hope that it's enough. I need him, and these next few months are going to be a test that neither of us is ready for. No couple just starting their lives together should have a tragedy like this.

We are strong, but I have no idea if we're strong enough.

There's so much we have to work through.

Austin moves a little and both of our gazes snap to his face. He releases a small moan, and I take his hand in mine. "It's okay, buddy."

After a few more seconds, he opens his eyes, and the brown with tinges of yellow meet mine. "Auntie?"

Tears run down my face as I'm swallowed in the relief from seeing him awake. "Hi, sweet boy."

I bring his small hand to my lips. He's okay. I know that everything else around us is bad, but right in this very second, I allow myself to feel joy that Austin isn't gone too.

He looks over at Sean.

"Hey, little man."

Austin's smile at seeing Sean makes my chest tight. "Where are Mom and Dad?"

Sean touches the top of his head. "What do you remember?"

He looks around. "I was on my phone and then . . ."

Austin gasps, and I grip his hand tighter. "It's okay, Austin."

"The accident. We were flying. I remember . . . I remember Dad yelling and then there were screams." Austin's body begins to tremble.

"Shhh," I try to soothe him. "You don't have to say anything, just breathe."

"Mom? Dad?"

A tear falls down my cheek, and I use every ounce of strength I have to hold myself together. "The accident was bad. I'm sorry, Austin. I'm so sorry. They tried, but they . . ."

"No!" he yells as he tries to yank his hand from my grip. "No! I need to see them! Dad was okay. He was talking to me."

A sob rips from his throat, and I want to scream and cry,

but I hold his hand tighter. "And he fought so hard." I wipe the tears that continue to fall.

"I know this is hard," Sean speaks through tears of his own. "I know how much you want to make this stop, and we wish we could too. Your parents loved you so much."

Austin cries harder, his fingers grip mine tighter. "I know you're hurting, and it's okay to cry and be angry," I tell him. "I'm here. Sean is here. Nana and Pop are here. We love you so much, and we will do anything we can."

He doesn't say anything as he sobs, turning his head from side to side. "Dad was talking . . . he said it would be okay . . ."

"And he wanted it to be," Sean replies.

"He said I had to fight. I had to be strong. He said once help came, we'd be fine. Why? Why isn't he okay?"

My chin trembles, and I feel so hollow. "I don't know. I don't know, and I wish it was okay. I wish he was standing here with us, telling you how right he was."

My brother must have fought until the end. He would never allow Austin to feel alone or scared if he could help it. I imagine my brother and Austin stuck in the crushed car, he can't move, but he tells him how brave he is and to stay strong. Jasper would've said or done anything to keep Austin from losing hope.

Austin cries and then grabs at his leg.

"Are you in pain?" Sean asks.

He nods, and I push the button for the nurse. She comes quickly with pain meds after we explain what's wrong.

"In a few seconds, this will help with the pain." Her eyes meet ours, sympathy clear on her face.

No matter the physical pain he's in, the emotional is much greater.

I kiss the top of Austin's head and murmur in his ear about how strong he is and how we're going to get through this.

He cries.

I cry.

And then, after a few more minutes, his eyes close and he drifts off.

Sean steps toward the window, his hand wiping down his face as he stares out.

"This kid will never be the same," he says without turning to me.

"No, none of us will."

"I lost my mother at his age, and it altered the course of my life. Everything changes when you lose a parent. *Everything.*"

Everything will change for us all. I move toward him, needing to touch him, to be held, to feel some sense of comfort that he gives, but before I can reach him, there's a knock on the door.

We turn to see my parents there. "Did he wake yet?" Dad asks.

"Yes. We told him."

Mom's hands cover her mouth, but I can still hear her muffled cry.

"We'd like to sit with him," Dad explains.

"Of course."

Sean and I walk out into the hall because we know there is nothing we can do inside that room so long as Austin is sleeping. I can feel the tension rolling off him and my very affectionate boyfriend seems miles away. I know he is hurt, and he has a right to be, but I did what I needed to do in order to protect my family and now I have to do it again.

twenty-nine

D o I touch her? Do I hold her hand? Does she want me near her? I ask myself a million questions as we make our way back to the waiting room. Until an hour ago, these weren't things I wondered about. I just knew.

I knew her.

I knew us.

And now, nothing makes sense.

"I'm his biological mother."

She can't be his mother. It doesn't . . . Jasper and Hazel . . .

We find an empty room and sit.

Her brown eyes, which are similar to Austin's, stare back at me. I never noticed it before. I wasn't looking to see the subtle similarities in the shape or color of their eyes. When we were in there, I started searching for more things that I missed. His nose is close to the same shape and their hair color is close.

"Please." Devney's voice is pleading. "Say something. I

know you're upset. I know this is all a shock and I . . ."

"He's your son?" I ask, just in case I misunderstood.

"Yes." She stands and steps toward me, eyes pleading for me to understand. "He's my biological child, but then no, because he's not my son. He was Jasper and Hazel's son."

"I see."

Hurt fills me. Call it selfish. Call it ridiculous, but it's there. The woman I love, who I bared my secrets to, didn't do the same. She didn't trust me, and I'm fucking hurt. There's not a secret in the world she could've told me that would have made me love her less, not even this. But she didn't tell me until she had no other choice.

I feel a sense of betrayal that I have no right to feel.

Devney moves even closer. "I'm sorry. It's what I wanted to talk about tonight. I had a plan to explain. I know that I kept it from you, and there were so many times I just wanted to talk to you about it, but to protect everyone, I couldn't."

"I told you everything." My voice is a bit terser than I want. I'm angry, but not for the reason she probably thinks. It's more that I had this belief that once I told her about the accident, we had no secrets. Nothing that was like this.

"I know. I should've told you, but I had to talk to Jasper first. It wasn't just about me or you. I never wanted for you to find out this way."

The pain in her eyes is too much to bear. Still, I need to hear this.

I keep my voice even and take her hand in mine. I don't know if I'm trying to comfort her or myself, but I have known her for over twenty years, and I love her to the depths of my soul. I can't watch her cry, not when I can see her trying to be brave. "I'm just confused, Dev. How did you carry a baby for nine months and never tell me? How could you keep this from me?"

"It wasn't easy. It was actually the hardest thing I've ever done. There were so many nights I picked up the phone to call you. I only managed to connect the call once, but I was so upset that I chickened out and had to lie about why I was so broken. Do you remember?"

I filter through, trying to recall a time when she was a mess ten years ago. "Was it when you said you wanted me to run away with you?"

She nods. "I begged you. I was so beyond broken. I just wanted someone who would make it better, and I called you."

Fuck. I was such a tool back then. I thought she was just homesick, and I remember trying to soothe her. "I didn't know . . ."

"It was meant to be that way. It was the night I decided that I had to give him to my brother. I was . . . I don't know, I just couldn't handle the emotions."

And for her, I have to deal with mine now. She's breaking, in a sea of pain and uncertainty, and I won't be the reason she falls further. I want her more than anything in this world, and I want her to trust me. "Will you tell me everything?"

Tears fall down her cheeks as she rushes into my arms. I hold her tightly, kissing the top of her head and inhaling all that is Devney.

I don't know how long we stay like this, but when she pulls back, I know it wasn't long enough.

She takes my hands in hers and then draws a deep breath. "When I was with Christopher, we had rules. We only met at my apartment or a hotel, we didn't go anywhere, which made sense at the time since our relationship was forbidden. But after about seven months, things were . . . different. I wasn't allowed to call on certain days or he would break plans with me at the last minute. It was just small things that made me uncomfortable. Then he changed his phone number for no reason, and there was this niggling feeling in my gut that wouldn't ease up. So, I followed him, and that's when I saw her. His wife. She was standing in their doorway, smiling at him, and he grabbed her by the waist and kissed her the same way he did when he saw me."

Rage burns through me as I imagine Devney sitting in her car watching this. A young woman, innocent and naïve enough to think that a relationship with her professor could work. Then she had to see firsthand just how slimy some men could be. "Go on," I urge.

"I was . . . well, I was crushed. All that time I thought he loved me was a lie. Every touch felt dirty. Every kiss was tainted by the fact that he was cheating on his wife and that I was the mistress. I wanted to die, Sean. I wanted . . . I thought about . . . I couldn't handle any of it. He came by the next morning, and I told him that I knew everything. He was beyond livid that I followed him." She laughs a little. "Yeah, angry at me for following him but not the fact that he had been lying to everyone. I remember thinking the whole thing was insane. We fought, and I called him out on every lie he'd ever told me. He kept saying I was crazy and I wasn't understanding, but I knew."

"He didn't deserve you, Devney."

"It didn't matter. I loved him and for a few moments, even after I found out, I hoped that maybe he'd choose me. That's the real sick part in this. I was so dependent on loving him that I wanted to break up a family—even if just for a few moments. I cried and threatened to kill myself." She looks back up at me, lips trembling and eyes glistening. My stomach twists at the idea of her even thinking of it.

"You were young."

"I was stupid and selfish and old enough to know better. It didn't matter, though, because he would never throw away his career for his side piece, and I think, all along, I knew that."

I've never wanted to go back in time. My past and things I've endured were horrible and belong in the past, but right now, I'd like to make this right for her. I should've been there. I should've known when she was distant and wouldn't talk. As her best friend, I should have seen the signs that there was something wrong.

"Anyway, three days after I said we were over, I found out I was pregnant." I want to comfort her, but she pulls away. "I don't think you can even begin to understand the level of pain I was in. I was hormonal, scared, angry, and everything in between. I was so beyond broken at that point. So, the night I took the test, I asked him to come by because it was urgent. Nothing could've prepared me for his response. He told me my options were to raise the baby however I want without his help or he'd pay for an abortion."

If I thought I was angry before, this is a whole new level. I want to kill him. Break his arms off and choke the life out of him. To do this to any girl is disgusting, but to her . . . unconscionable. Devney is everything beautiful in this world, and as a man, he should've been there for her.

"Dev . . ."

"No, let me say it, please," she implores. "I couldn't do it. Not because I didn't think about it. Not because I wanted a child but because I didn't, not with him and not like that. Two days after I found out I was pregnant, Jasper and Hazel lost their sixth baby. Six times they had tried to become parents and failed, and there I was, just turned twenty and pregnant with my married professor's child that he didn't want. My brother was sobbing to me. He was so distraught that he was failing her. It was the level of emotion I expected from Christopher. He should've been crying because he broke me, but he was with his wife." Devney wipes away her tears and releases another deep breath. "Hazel was in nursing school in Colorado, and I was going to ask her to take me to the clinic to end the pregnancy. Instead . . ."

I stare at her, wondering if she has a clue how selfless she is. "You gave them your child." A deep sob escapes her lips, and I hold her face in my hands. "Oh, sweetheart."

"I didn't give them *my* child. I gave them *their* son. A little boy with brown eyes who needed parents to love him. It was the most painful and beautiful day of my life. Hazel was in the room, holding my hand as tears flowed down both of our faces for different reasons. Here was my sister-in-law, trying to not be happy because she knew I was dying inside. She hugged me, thanked me, told me how selfless I was. It was the right choice, but felt so . . . wrong. But I loved Austin. I loved him so much and I handed him over because I knew I couldn't give him more than they could. We agreed they'd stay in Colorado while I transferred to a new school to finish my degree and we all came back with Austin as my nephew and a secret that only six people knew."

The breath comes from my chest hard and fast. "Jesus. I don't know what to say. Why didn't you tell me before this?"

"Because I was so ashamed. I always thought I was this tough girl who would never allow a man to hurt her, and then I saw my weakness. I didn't want you to ever see me that way."

"Sweetheart, I would never."

"I didn't believe it myself. I didn't ever want to see censure in your eyes. Even though you say you wouldn't, I didn't trust it."

"You didn't trust me."

"I wish I could say that's not true and that I did, but . . . I didn't. After time went by when we would talk, I couldn't bring myself to say it. Then, time passed and it became this secret that couldn't be exposed. Austin was growing and I needed to protect him."

I run my hands down my face. "I just wish you hadn't lied or kept it from me."

"I didn't want to lie, but the truth is that I am Austin's biological mother. This secret has haunted me and my family for a while." She looks toward the chair her mother occupied earlier.

"Your mom?"

"Yeah. She was so torn over it, but Jasper and Hazel needed Austin, and I needed them."

"Is that why you've been fighting so much?"

She huffs and shrugs. "It was a sin all the way around. She wanted me to keep him and take responsibility. The fact that I even considered an abortion was unforgivable in her eyes."

"And Austin doesn't know anything at all?"

"No. Jasper, Hazel, and I agreed that I would be exactly what I am, his aunt. I got to watch him grow, love him, and be there for him in a way that most people who give their child up never do. It was the hardest and most important thing I could do. From that day forward, I decided to consider him my nephew. I never, not once, let myself say *son*. It was the best thing for my own well-being and for Austin."

"What about now?"

She's his mother, but Austin doesn't know. She's his mother, and she is now faced with having to navigate an entirely new situation.

Her head tilts down as she rubs her thumb over my hand. "I don't know. When Austin was three months old, they created a will. One that spelled out what they wanted to happen. They want Austin to go to my care, and I am to raise him however I see fit, even though I'm alone and unsure of what any of it means."

"You're not alone."

She laughs once. "I am completely alone, Sean."

I know that she's drowning in grief, but it's the furthest thing from the truth. "I'm here."

Devney's eyes meet mine. "You've always been, but this is different."

"Why? Because you're making it be different?"

"This is an entirely new situation. We have no idea what's going to happen other than I am now raising a child. You can't tell me this doesn't change everything!" Devney lets out a few short breaths.

I run my fingers through my hair and step back. "It doesn't have to."

Her head shakes back and forth as she stares at me. "You want to instantly have a child in your life? Not only that, how can you even fathom that I could leave Sugarloaf now?"

"I don't know. I just know I can't lose you."

That's the only part of this that I can't allow. I can't go back to Florida and just live as though I've never known what it's like to love her. There's no other woman who will ever fill the void that she has. Devney is perfect for me. I'm perfect for her, and losing her is not an option. I'll find a way, I have to.

She wipes away a tear. "Things have changed for us. In one instant, it all became a new life. I can't ignore that, and you can't pretend that you're not going to have to go."

"I can take time off."

"And ruin your career? Come on, Sean. I can't let you do that any more than you can ask me to change my situation."

"So this is it?" I ask, feeling panic rising up. "You're quitting now? When we still have months to figure it out."

"I'm being realistic. I'm . . . I don't know."

I take her hands in mine, pulling them to my chest. "Nothing gets decided now, Dev. You promised we'd wait until three weeks before I leave."

I hold on to that sliver of hope. If she can adhere to that, then I have some time to figure out a plan.

"I don't know what is going to change in that time . . ."

"Maybe nothing. Maybe everything. All I know is that I

love you, and no matter where our relationship goes, I want to be here for you now. Will you let me?"

I wait, my heart pounding, and my breaths are coming in short bursts.

"As long as you promise that, no matter what the end result is, you'll accept it."

"I'll accept it." I lie through my teeth because there is only one acceptable end result, and that's the one where she and I end up together. I tell her what she needs to hear and promise to find a way to make it go my way.

I won't lose her. Not now, not ever.

thirty

My heart feels empty. That's all I can say as I sit here at the entrance to the driveway, knowing I will be going to a vacant house.

I had to leave Devney at the hospital so I could come home, grab some stuff, and bring it back. Now, I'm staring at the sign above, hating the name and this place.

I came back because I had to. I'll leave because I have no choice, and I'll once again regret the day I stepped foot back in Sugarloaf.

"Fuck the arrow. Fuck saying the truth!" I grip the steering wheel, anger pulsing through me. "Here's the truth, Mom. I'm going to lose the only person worth loving because of this fucking life that your piece-of-shit husband created for your boys."

Barreling down the driveway, I almost plow into the two cars parked by the house.

My nosey fucking brothers.

Not in the mood to deal with either of them, I throw open the car door and walk past them.

"Sean, stop!" Declan calls to me, and I flip him off.

"Hey, seriously, what is going on?"

I turn to stare at the both of them. Things are horrible. Things couldn't be going worse after being so incredibly good. "Everything is falling apart!"

"We came by to check on you and Devney. Sydney was on the phone with her, and I felt you might need a friend."

"And you're now a friend?" I ask with acid in my voice.

"I'd like to consider myself more since I'm your fucking brother." Declan crosses his arms over his chest and waits.

"I'm pissed."

"We see that."

"I'm really fucking upset. No, fuck that! I'm . . . I'm done!"

Connor steps closer. "I'm going to assume there's more than just Jasper and Hazel dying. You look like a train wreck, and it's better to talk to us, let us be your punching bag for the anger you got rolling around in your head."

When the hell did my younger brother become like this? If I weren't so close to losing my fucking mind, I might just be impressed.

I'm not sure how much to say. I don't know what Devney told anyone, and I won't betray her. So, I'll explain the facts and leave out the whole secret child part.

"Devney is going to be Austin's legal guardian. We had . . . plans."

"What plans?" Dec asks as he sits. Gone is the asshole attitude and in comes all the concern.

"We were going to go back to Florida together. At least, that was the goal. She and I were happy. So fucking happy that it was like the entire world made sense, and now, nothing does."

"Nothing is that bleak, brother."

I look at Declan and sigh. "Isn't it? What the hell choice does she have? She can't be like, sorry kid, I know your life is here, family, friends, and the remains of your parents, but I love this guy here so we're moving."

Connor nods. "You have to think of what's best for him now."

"I know that."

"I'm not saying you don't, Sean. Don't misinterpret what I'm saying." Connor claps his hand on my shoulder. "I'm empathizing with you. When Ellie . . . well, when things happened, it was the same issue for me. All of a sudden I had this little girl who I was responsible for. Hadley needed a hero, and so does Austin."

There lies the problem. "I'm not a fucking hero."

Declan shakes his head. "The hell you're not. You're more of a hero than any one of us—well, maybe not more than the actual war hero here, but still. Do you know how many kids look up to you? *Especially* to a kid like Austin. You're on the posters on their walls and the cards they trade."

Maybe that's the case, but I'm also the guy who wants nothing more than to wrap Devney up and take her away. That isn't the man he needs to look up to.

"I'm not . . ." I start, but I can't say it. The truth is, yes, I want to take her away and keep her, but I never would if it means having to hurt her or Austin that way. The last thing in the world I want is to cause her any heartache.

I want to be her salvation, not her destruction.

"You're not?" Dec urges.

"I'm not even sure what to do."

Connor releases a heavy breath. "You do the best you can. You give that kid stability and an outlet. You love Devney through it all."

They're missing the point. I can do all that, but the ending will still be the same. I can't rewrite the story. We all see the way it's going to go, and there is no happily ever after here. It's a fucking tragedy.

"And then I leave? How the fuck does that make sense? I love her. She loves me. I fall for the kid who has done nothing wrong and then get on a plane and head back to Florida? That makes things better?"

Both of my brothers look at me and then to the other. Declan is the one who speaks first. "You know, there's nothing saying that she won't go at the end. You have what? Just under three months to be the man she and Austin need."

My fingers pinch the bridge of my nose, and the weight resting on my shoulders gets heavier. "I'm glad you both have faith in me because I'm not so confident. I love Devney and the next three months are only going to make it harder to leave her. And you can't convince me that she'll ever choose me over Austin's welfare."

Declan huffs. "And you'd ever ask her to?"

"God no!"

"Exactly! So don't tell me that you're suddenly aware of what she'll do. You're not a mind reader, you're a guy, and a pretty dumb one at that."

I flip him off, and then Connor starts in.

"Listen, I thought I had all the answers with Ellie. I was so sure of what would happen and what I'd do if that happened, but the truth is, we know nothing. Declan definitely doesn't know a damn thing." I agree on that one. "My point is that, right now, you guys are going through a huge thing. Her brother and sister-in-law died, she's now the guardian of a nine-year-old who is sure to be pissed off about losing his parents and guilty as fuck because he lived when they didn't."

"Guilt?"

Connor laughs once. "Do you not remember how we felt when Mom died?"

Declan makes a low groan and then gets to his feet. "We were so sure we killed her."

I try to think back to that time, but it's like walking through fog. There is so much of my childhood that I fought hard to forget. Who the hell wants to remember losing their mother and then their father beating the shit out of them? No one.

The only memories I allowed myself were ones of Mom. The way she smelled like apples and cinnamon. How she always had fresh flowers on the table, and the way her voice got just a little softer when she smiled.

"I don't remember that," I admit.

"Well, I do," Declan says with an edge of sadness. "I was convinced it was something we did. Because angels don't get cancer. They don't get sick, and Dad was always calling us little demons before he actually believed it. I thought, we did this. We are evil so we had to be what made her sick."

I lean back as parts of that come back. "We didn't make Mom sick."

Dec sits next to me. "No shit, but at eleven, I couldn't wrap my head around that. Imagine how Austin will feel. It was his tournament they were coming home from. He's going to feel guilt, and he's going to need someone there who can understand that feeling."

"Also," Connor starts in, "Devney is a mess right now. She just lost her brother and her entire life has shifted. You shouldn't take to heart whatever she says for the next week or so. Let her work through what she's feeling, and then you guys can make a plan."

He's right. I know it, but by the way she was talking at the hospital, it was pretty clear that she has already decided this is the end. Fear can make you think and say things, but she isn't the type to change her mind once she's settled. Which is the part that has me so concerned.

thirty-one

"Where are you going to take him?" Mom asks as we wait outside Austin's room.

"What do you mean?"

"Are you taking him back to his house or to Sean's?"

I haven't gotten that far. Sydney came by earlier and got all the paperwork together that I have to sign, giving me full custody of Austin. I sat there, looking at it, trying to read it all through my tears, and then wrote my name on the line. It felt so impersonal and so final.

Here I am, a parent to the child I gave up.

I keep waiting for all of this to make sense, but it doesn't.

Austin is going to live with me, but I don't have a house. I'm going to have to be his mother—or rather, his aunt who is actually his mother only he doesn't know that.

Why does this all have to be so damn complicated?

"Well?" Mom presses.

"I don't know."

"Devney, you have to make these decisions."

I release a heavy breath and rub my temples. "I know. I wanted to see the paperwork to see what Jasper or Hazel wanted, but all it said was that I would make the best choices and they had no requests. So, I don't know where he will want to go. If he wants to go back to his house, I'll move in there. If he wants to go to Sean's and not be surrounded by all their things, I'll do that."

She looks to the window where the blinds are barely open. "He needs stability."

"I'm aware."

"He can come to us. I know why you're the one they chose, but your father and I can give him more."

I'm not doing this. "Mom. Stop."

Her eyes meet mine. "I'm only thinking of him."

"So am I."

"He should go to his house," she says as a last jab.

Normally, I would go back and forth until one of us relents, but I don't have the energy for it. None of us do.

Mom takes my hand in hers. "I'm sorry, Devney. I don't mean to snap at you. It's just that I'm losing it. It's been four days since I lost my son, and I feel so out of control." Her tears fall, and the ache in her voice breaks me.

"I'm so sorry, Mom."

"I just . . . I want to help. I have to *do* something or I'm going to go out of my mind. It hurts so much, and everything is out of my control. I can't fix this, and . . . ."

I squeeze just a bit. "I know. You are helping by being here. Austin needs you, me, and everyone in his life. I have to take things day by day and do whatever is best for him. I'm struggling too."

She releases her hold. "He smiled when I mentioned that Sean was coming this afternoon."

My heart sputters at the sound of his name. We've seen each other every day. He comes to the hospital every morning, brings us food, stays for a bit, and then does errands or something. After dinner, he usually comes back with a bag of things I might need before he and Austin talk baseball.

I want nothing more than to rush into his arms and have him hold me, but I keep pulling back a little each time.

Nothing is going to change.

We have to stop fooling ourselves that we'll have anything more than these six months. He is going to Florida, and I am going to raise Austin in Sugarloaf.

"Sean is good to him."

"And to you?"

I nod. "Exceedingly."

Mom goes quiet for a moment, and then her voice changes a bit. "I know I've been hard on you. I've made things difficult, and for that, I'll never forgive myself, but I have to tell you that if you let what you have slip away, you're a fool."

"I don't want to let it go."

Her gaze meets mine, and I see the tension set in her jaw. "Then don't."

"It's not that simple."

"That's where you're wrong. It is that simple. You love him, and he loves you. He's sitting at a hospital with your nephew each day. He's bringing him books, talking to him about sports, and giving that little boy a sense of normalcy. He's doing all of that as well as taking care of you."

I jerk back. "Taking care of me?"

My mother rolls her eyes. "Seriously, Devney, you have no idea. How many famous, wealthy men do you think would behave the way he is? Hell, how many men in general? Take out the other adjectives. Not many. Sean Arrowood has always been your rock, don't throw it into the river."

"I'm not."

"Then let him care for you. Allow Sean to show you the kind of husband he would be. This is his perfect opportunity to duck and run if he wants to, but all I've seen is a man who wants to help. You have no idea how hard being a parent is, but choosing to do it on your own . . . well, I can't imagine. It's why I was so hard on you. I was wrong. I thought that if you had raised Austin that it would've been kinder to you."

She says that, but her actions negate that. Right now I am not in the mood to argue with her. It's easier to let it go and pray that this . . . kinder version of my mother is here to stay. "And yet, here I am, raising Austin all on my own. It's ironic, isn't it?"

Mom's eyes fill with tears. "No, it's sad, and after all you went through to give him what you couldn't, it's . . . unfair. And yet, I can't help but wonder if this wasn't how it should've been."

"Me raising him?"

She nods and sniffs. "I know it's terrible, but I can't help but wonder if this wasn't the plan."

If she's even remotely considering that I was meant to care for Austin and that's why my brother and sister-in-law are dead, I might scream. "Mom . . ."

"No, listen, I think that you giving Austin up was the right choice—the only choice. You weren't ready, and Hazel and Jasper needed a child to love. It was the plan. It was impossible and difficult and right. But so is the fact that you will be there for him now. You and Sean can help him through this in a way that your father and I wouldn't be able to."

"We shouldn't have to. This should never have been how it went."

She nods and glances back through the blinds. "I shouldn't have to bury my son." Mom turns to me smiling softly. "And I'm glad you don't have to know what it's like to do it either. Trust your heart, Devney." She kisses my cheek and then walks out toward the nurses' station. I stand, stunned and unable to move because we just had a conversation that didn't end with an argument and she defended Sean.

I know that he's good to me, but he always has been.

I've never had to worry when he's around because Sean just . . . does.

It doesn't mean that things will be possible for us now. More than ever, I have to take this time to consider the future. We can't make life-changing decisions when nothing about our life is secure.

The nurse exits. "He's doing well. We'll have him ready for discharge early tomorrow."

"Thank you."

Trepidation fills my stomach, and there's a sick feeling in my throat. Tomorrow we have to go home and start this new journey, and I don't know how to navigate it. Austin and I have had the most amazing relationship because my place in his life has always been clear to him. I was his aunt. I was fun, took him places, bought him things, and was a comfort. Now, I'm a parent.

Jasper always joked that I got the good end of the deal, and I did. I was a part of his life in the best way. The dynamic has to change, and I wish I had him to tell me what to do.

But he's gone, and I have to figure it out. I'm not a little girl anymore, and they trusted me to raise him if they were gone.

I push open the door, and Austin looks up. "Are you feeling okay?" I ask.

"It hurts."

"It's going to."

His eyes well with tears. "I miss them."

"I do too," I say as I cup his face in my palm. "I miss them so much."

"The doctor said I can go home tomorrow."

"Yes, do you . . . do you know where you'd like to go?" My voice trembles. "I can move into your house so you don't have to leave."

He shakes his head quickly. "I don't want to go there."

"Why not?"

Austin wipes at his face. "Because they're not there."

Oh, my heart can only break so much more. "Do you want to go to Sean's?"

He turns to me, tearful eyes hopeful for the first time since he woke up from surgery. "Can we?"

"Of course you can," Sean's voice fills the room with authority. I turn to stare at him as he comes toward us. "If that's okay with your aunt."

Austin's eyes brighten. "I would really rather go to his house."

I also think this would've been the answer if I asked him two weeks ago. Still, I hear my mother's words in my head about trusting my heart.

"All right, but we're going to have to go back at some point." Like when Sean goes back to Florida.

"I know."

Sean rests a hand on my shoulder and squeezes. "We'll figure it out—together."

I try not to let myself feel the emotions, but they're impossible to ignore, so I lean my head against his chest and let his strength fill me.

He's got me, and he won't let me fall.

I smooth my hand down my black dress and wipe under my eyes again. Waterproof mascara my ass. The number of tears I've cried could fill the ocean.

"I will never see my parents again," Austin says as he stares at the caskets sitting over the holes.

Navigating this is just too much. I can't take away his pain. All I can do is hold his hand and try to help him through it. Last night, he fell asleep in my arms, wetting my shirt as he cried for my brother. I could do nothing else but hold him and cry alongside him. At some point, Sean came in, moved Austin, and carried me to our bed.

We all knew today would be hard, but it has been agony.

I brush back Austin's dark brown hair. "They loved you. So much."

He nods. "I just want them back, but they're gone."

"I know it's hard right now, but we will never let ourselves forget how wonderful they were. Okay? We will remember how much fun we had and how lucky we were to love them and be loved by them."

Austin sniffs. "I don't want to go back home, but I'm worried about the animals."

Sean squats so they're eye to eye. "Do you want to bring your horse to our barn? He would be with Hadley's, and we could keep a better eye on him?"

"Yes. I need him to know he's not alone."

There is so much pain in each syllable that it highlights his underlying message. He feels alone.

I go to say something, but Sean beats me to it.

"No one is alone in this, buddy. You have your aunt Devney, your grandparents, Hadley, me, and my brothers. We're all here for you, okay?"

Austin looks to me with unshed tears. "Can we go home now?"

"Yeah, we sure can."

Austin didn't want to use his crutches, so Sean offered to be his legs for the day. I swear, when I don't think I can love this man any more than I do, he does something like lift Austin into his arms to carry him.

"Would you like to come by today?" Mom asks when we get to the car.

"No thanks, Grandma."

"All right, but you'll come see me soon?"

Her eyes are puffy, and her nose is red. This has been a hard day for her. Jasper was her oldest, and now he's gone. I answer for him. "We'll be at the house for Christmas, Mom. Like always."

I watch her lip tremble as she nods, crumpling into my father's arms. "We'll see you then," he replies.

As we drive to Austin's house, Sean holds my hand as he and Austin talk about baseball a bit. All day long, he has found a way to be my anchor. His hand was in mine, his arm was wrapped around me, or his palm was pressed to the small of my back. I never had to worry because he was right there. Once we park, he squeezes gently and turns to Austin. "How about we check on the horses and grab a few more things?"

Austin looks out the window and then sighs. "Okay."

"Dev, can you go and get whatever Austin needs for a few more days while I take him down to the stable?"

I smile, grateful that he's going to keep him out of the way so I can get what we need.

The boys head out to the barn and I enter the house. It's funny how much a house is a home because of the people in it. Where we live is defined by those we share the space with, and right now, this place is empty.

Jasper and Hazel are gone, taking the warmth and love that lived here with them.

I move through the house, grabbing the dishes that were left on the counter and putting them in the cupboard. There are a few things left out, mail that is in the holder, Austin's backpack from before winter break started sitting in the cubby.

I grab it, pull it to my chest, and then sink to the floor. So many things I've never thought about. He'll have school, and I have no idea when they go back. I don't know his teacher's name or how to contact her.

The wall in front of me has a family photo of the three of them. My sister-in-law is smiling, and I swear it feels as though she can see me.

"I'm so not prepared for this," I tell her. "I know you thought I was the right one, but I gave him to you. I didn't plan to ever have to do this, Hazel, and you didn't prepare me. My role was clear, and . . . what do I do? Do I tell him who I am? Did you prepare him for if he ever found out? This wasn't supposed to happen."

But it did.

Austin is the one thing that has kept me here, and now, it's up to me to do right by him.

I look into Jasper's eyes, hoping that, if he can hear me, he'll believe this. "I will do everything I can to make you both proud. I know you thought I was stronger than I ever did, but Austin will never have to wonder if he's loved."

After another moment, I get up and go into his room to grab some clothes and things he'll need for the next week. I'm not sure how long the two of us will stay with Sean, but he doesn't seem to be in a hurry to be rid of us.

I toss two bags full of various clothes into the car and head out to the barn.

"Do you believe in Heaven?" Austin asks.

I stop, not trying to eavesdrop, but at the same time, not wanting to break up this moment.

"I do. I think my mother is up there."

"Do you think she knows my mom and dad?"

My hand clutches my throat as I wait for his answer.

"You know," Sean says with a lift in his voice, "I think my mom went and found them, since she knew your dad. I bet she is helping them with how much they miss you."

Austin is quiet for a second. "Because she misses you?"

"I'm sure she does. But I think our moms can watch us and make sure we're doing okay. There are probably times when they're here with us, even if we can't see them."

"I bet both our moms are here now."

"Yeah? Why do you say that?"

"Because they made sure we had Aunt Devney here."

A tear slides down my cheek.

"She's pretty great, and I think you're right. They knew that, with them gone, we'd need someone to love us both."

I lean against the barn wall and fight back the onslaught of tears. They have no idea how much I love them. How much I want to do right by them, and how absolutely terrified I am to lose one or the other.

"You know, Austin, I think our moms knew we'd need each other too," Sean says, his voice is soft and full of emotion. "You see, when I lost my mom, I was so sad, but I had my brothers. Declan, Jacob, and Connor helped me when I was sad or when things were bad."

"Did Aunt Devney?"

"She sure did. She was always there for me, just like she'll always be there for you. Just like I will always be there for you. If you need to talk or cry or throw the ball because you are so angry you can't take it, I'm here. I'm your friend, and friends always stick together. There will be days where it hurts and some days where it's not so bad. Don't ever be afraid to talk to me or your aunt if you need it, okay?"

"I'm glad you're my friend."

Sean chuckles. "I'm glad too."

And I am so beyond in love with this man that I have no idea what I'm going to do when he leaves.

thirty-two

"Are you going to eat?" I ask Austin as he sits on the couch.

"I'm not hungry."

I look at the bowl of spaghetti. "That's a shame. I cooked and I am a master at this dish."

He looks away from the television. "What is it?"

"Spaghetti."

"Even I can make pasta."

I shrug. "Listen, my skill set is pasta, sandwiches, and chicken nuggets."

Austin grins. "I like chicken nuggets."

"I'll make that tomorrow."

Devney is at work for the first time since the accident. I was adamant that she start getting back to normal—for both of them. It's been a week of us hunkering down, working through his feelings and avoiding anything heavy.

Austin is healing. Every part of him is a little hurt, and I'm doing my best to be here for him.

I bring over a bowl, and plop down next to him. "So, what are you watching?"

"I don't know."

I look at the screen to see a bunch of guys working on cars. My heart breaks because I'm sure this was something he did with his dad. "Mind if I watch?"

"Nope."

I swirl the spaghetti and take a bite as the mechanic rips out the seat from the back, tossing it. "What's he going to do now?"

"They'll rebuild the whole car. They take it all apart and then make it have every gadget possible."

"Cool. I had a tricked out car once."

He looks up at me. "Really?"

"Yup. It was beautiful. Had everything I wanted, and it was my favorite thing I ever bought."

Austin nods. "I was going to buy my first car and Dad said he'd fix it."

"I bet it would've been fun to do that with him."

"Yeah."

I take another bite, and Austin looks over at me. "Want some?"

He grabs the other bowl and eats a bit. We sit in silence as we watch the show. After a few minutes, we've finished lunch and he places the empty bowl down. The show goes on and I have to admit, it's really cool. I'm not much of a car guy, nothing like Jasper was, but the things they're doing to the car is crazy.

"You think they'll put the laptop in the console?" I ask.

"They always do the coolest stuff."

He's not wrong.

Once the show is over we discuss some of our favorite parts. It's fun just talking to him and seeing his spirits lift a little.

"I wish you could see the episode where they put a projector screen in the trunk."

I laugh. "For all the times I've needed it?"

"Dad said he'd do it so we could watch a movie anywhere we wanted. He used to take Mom out to the field in his convertible and look at the stars."

"I didn't know them that well because he was much older than me, but they seemed really happy."

He nods once. "They were. They laughed a lot and danced all the time. It was gross."

I nudge him softly. "It's what guys do when they love a girl."

The mood drops a bit as he looks down. "Did you hear me last night?"

Each night, Austin wakes us up screaming. His nightmares are horrible, and it's the same dream each time. This is the first time he's talked to me about it. "I did, but . . . there's no judgment here. I had nightmares for years after my mother died."

"Aunt Devney said that."

Of course she did. "She loves that she knows something I never told anyone." I nod and give him a small smile. "I tried to stop them. I thought if I could fall asleep later or earlier or sleep with something I loved it would stop, but it didn't. Not right away."

"I see the accident."

"Yeah?"

"The sounds are so loud, and I think it's happening."

This kid needs a break. I hate that he's dealing with so much at such a young age. "I want to reassure you that it's okay and the accident isn't happening, but you know that. What maybe you need to hear is that it will stop. One day, you won't have these dreams and you won't feel sad. I know it feels like it'll never happen, but time really does heal things. You'll walk again. You'll have a new routine and things will become . . . different, but steady. We'll be here to help you."

"But you're going to leave soon."

My stomach drops, and the new territory I thought I could navigate becomes filled with obstacles I can't avoid.

"The season starts soon, and I have training, but that's part of the game."

"Where will we go?"

"You and your aunt are welcome to stay here. No one is going to throw you out when I leave. Not to mention . . ." *I really want you both to come with me.* ". . . we still have time."

Austin moves his leg a little, wincing as he does. "I guess."

"We'll figure it out. I've been around for twenty years with your aunt and she hasn't been able to get rid of me yet, don't worry."

I say what might have been my famous last words because every outward indication says she wants me, but every warning bell in my head is going off.

He smiles and grabs the remote. "Should we watch another episode?"

I force myself to return his grin. "Yeah, let's do that."

"Are you still planning to come over for Christmas morning?"

Ellie asks as she places a cake on the table.

"The hell if I know."

She rolls her eyes. "I wasn't asking you." She turns to Devney.

Dev shrugs. "It was the plan, but now with Austin and my parents really needing to be around him, I'm not sure."

"I get it. You don't have to be here at a set time, but if you can, we'd love to have you."

We came by to get Austin out of the house and force him to be around someone other than us. Since the accident, he hasn't returned to school and since Christmas break starts tomorrow, Devney didn't want to push it.

Hadley brought his work home and has taken it upon herself to teach him everything he missed.

My niece is the perfect distraction for him.

"Thanks, we'll definitely think about it," Devney says smoothly.

Connor enters the room. "He looks good. He's using the crutches now?"

"Yeah. He's getting there."

"We broke enough bones to know that it takes time and patience that no kid has to heal."

He couldn't be more right. Declan broke his arm when we were kids and I broke about every finger in my hands because I was an idiot many times behind the plate.

"Yeah, there's a lot of healing that Austin needs, which we know as well."

"We all do," Devney says quietly.

My hand wraps around hers and gives it a squeeze. "I know, sweetheart."

"I'm sorry." She pulls her hand back and adjusts her shirt. "I shouldn't be like this. Today is just . . . weird. I don't know.

It's like it's hitting me all at once. It'll be Christmas, and . . . I have to do all these things. We don't have a tree or gifts to put under it. I need to do all of that."

Little does she know I already got him a few special gifts. Before I can say anything, my sister-in-law takes over.

Ellie sits beside her. "I can help. Whatever you need. Connor will go get you a tree and I can send him shopping if you want. He can get everything done while we handle the other stuff."

"Uhh," Connor mutters. "Huh?"

"Yeah, Connor, you can go. You're good at shopping and doing all that," I tack on, like the helpful brother I am.

"What the hell are you doing? She's your girlfriend."

"And your wife wants you to help."

"I want you to shut up," he says under his breath.

Ellie eyes him with a brow raised. "Are you saying you won't help your brother and Devney?"

"Of course not!" he says so quickly it's comical.

"Then why are you complaining?"

I sit here, shit-eating grin plastered on my face. "Yes, Connor, why are you complaining?"

He puts his hand on the back of my chair before flicking me when they look away. "Ouch!"

"What's wrong, Sean? Did you stub your toe?"

"I'm going to stub something."

Devney rolls her eyes and looks away. "Idiots."

"They really are," Ellie says without a pause.

"Yeah, well, you're both the idiots who have fallen in love with us so what does that make you?" Connor asks.

Devney answers first. "Bigger idiots."

"At least they know it," I say to him.

"True. If they were in denial, I'd be worried."

They go back to their conversation, and I follow my brother outside. "I really am an idiot," I say as the cold air hits us.

"Why?"

"I didn't think about a tree or making Christmas . . . more. I've been so worried about Devney and Austin that it slipped my mind."

He claps me on the shoulder. "Well, you have like three days, better make them count."

thirty-three

"What about this one?" I ask, pointing to a nice fat tree in the new row we had to check.

Devney tilts her head, eyeing it, and then shrugs. "I don't know, it doesn't feel like our tree."

"What the hell does our tree *feel* like?"

"I don't know, but that isn't it."

I swear she's trying to kill me. Not only have we been out in the freezing cold for an hour, but she also has no idea what kind of tree she likes.

"Dev, it's a tree."

Austin laughs from his very comfortable position on the quad. We put the trailer on the back and made him what looks like a bed back there. His leg is secure, and he's cocooned in blankets.

"Austin, isn't the tree the most important thing?"

He looks to me and then back at her. "Sure?"

274 | CORINNE MICHAELS

"See?" I yell. "The kid doesn't care. Does this tree look good?"

He shrugs. "I guess."

Devney slaps my chest. "See? He doesn't like it. He's just trying to be nice. Now, let's ride out and find the perfect tree."

"The perfect tree will be the one in our living room."

She huffs. "This matters."

"So does me having all my toes!"

Dev rolls her eyes. "Dramatic."

I'll give her dramatic. "Sweetheart, it's two days before Christmas and all the perfect trees were cut down three weeks ago. Now, we have a perfectly adequate tree right here, and since I still have enough feeling in my hands to cut it down, we should take it."

She walks over to the quad and climbs on. "Not the right one."

I groan, looking up at the sky. "You're killing me."

"You'll get over it."

I release a breath, causing the fog to surround me, blocking my face from her view as I resign myself to the fact that I am going to stay out here for however long she wants because that's what idiots do for the girl they love. They spend hours on a bare tree farm because she needs to make sure Austin has the tree she needs him to have.

Reality is that I'm not going to argue it.

I get on the quad in front of her and swear I can feel her smile behind me. Adorable little wench.

We ride for another ten minutes until she taps my shoulder. I pull over and try to wipe my nose, but it actually hurts. I wonder if snot can freeze. If so, mine has.

"Yes, my love?" I ask with a nice layer of sarcasm.

"This one."

She points to a tree that is leaning a bit to the left. "That's the perfect tree?"

There's no way that's the one she actually wants. "Yup."

Okay, it seems there is a way. "Dev, that tree is leaning."

"I know!" She smiles and bounces over to it. "It's a little lopsided and no one would ever want it, which is why we have to get it."

I'm . . . not really sure what to say. "How pray tell do you think we will get it in a stand?"

"I don't know, but it needs a home."

"And we are going to give it one?"

She nods. "What do you think, Austin?"

"It's crooked."

"Yes," I agree with him. "It is. And do you know what trees that need ornaments and lights should not be? Crooked."

He laughs. "Aunt Devney, I think we should get one that won't fall over."

Smart kid. "See, even he gets it."

She waves her hand and drags her fingertips over the branches. "It's a strong tree. It has good roots."

"It has a bad trunk."

I love her, but I am so lost. We have been searching for the perfect tree, and she wants to take one home that I'm going to have to get Connor to secure because I don't have a clue how I would do it.

"I want it," she says without apology.

You know, I'm too cold to care enough to argue. I'm freezing, my balls have shrunk up into my stomach, and we have an injured kid riding around as his insane aunt searches for a tree.

She wants this one, she's got it.

After blowing on my fingers for a good two minutes, I start

up the chainsaw and chop down the delipidated tree. We wrap a tarp around the branches and then hook the trunk up to the back so that we can haul it to the house.

When we get back, I help Austin inside before sparking a fire in the fireplace as Devney makes hot chocolate.

Now, I must tackle the tree.

I try. I really do. I get the tree into the stand, where it stands for a whole three seconds before tipping to the left. This happens three more times while Austin laughs nonstop. At least I can provide him with entertainment.

"Maybe if we cut a little more off the bottom it'll work?" Devney offers her very non-helpful advice.

"Sweetheart, we have to cut half of it off if you want that."

She sighs and stands there with her arms crossed over her chest, eyeing it. "Maybe we can build a special stand that counter-tilts."

"That's it," I say with exasperation. I'm not handy. I can't build it a special stand. She is about to have the next best option . . . my version of a special stand.

I head out to the barn and grab the water can and bring it in. Devney has settled on the couch next to Austin, and they watch me with a mix of humor and fear.

I put the bucket in the corner and shove the tree in there. It leans against the wall, bowed side out.

"This is the best you're going to get," I tell her.

Devney gets to her feet, a smile on her lips as she wraps her hands around my arm. "I love it."

"You love it?"

"Yup. It's perfect. It's there, standing tall, the perfect tree."

My eyes meet hers, wondering if she's been brainwashed by aliens, but I just see love. She really thinks it's great.

"Can we decorate it?" Austin asks.

"Of course, we'll just do the front." Devney kisses my cheek and then moves to the boxes of decorations, some of which came from the attic and others came from Austin's house.

She lifts the lid off one we took from Jasper and Hazel's and hands the ornament to Austin.

His eyes fill with tears, but there's a slight smile on his lips. "I made this one."

She nods. "I remember."

I find some space between them and squeeze in so I can see the ornament he's holding. The bruises and scrapes have started to heal and fade. He looks more like the little boy he was before the accident two weeks ago. "Can I see?" He hands it over, and I examine the photo of him, Jasper, Hazel, and Devney in the middle with crumpled green paper around it. "It's sort of like the photo I have, huh?"

"Do you think I can keep this one like you do?"

Her brown eyes widen and her lips part. "Like the one Sean has for his good luck charm?"

He nods.

I take the photo out that mirrors the one I keep with me. It has the people in my life that matter. "See, you're always with me. Always."

She lets her hair fall in front of her face, shielding me from seeing what I'm sure are tears. "That's so sweet."

Austin makes a gagging noise. "It's not sweet, it's luck."

"Well, I think it's both," she says, laughing and lifting her gaze back to us. "You want that photo as yours?"

Austin pauses, looks at the tree, and then shakes his head. "No, not this one."

"Why not?" I ask.

"It's missing people."

We both look to him. It's the group of people who matter.

"Who do you want in it?" Dev questions him.

"Sean."

In that moment, I know that Devney isn't the only one I don't want to go without, it's both of them.

Yesterday we finished last minute shopping and I got busy on planning the real surprise for Devney. Right now, I want to enjoy our first Christmas morning together.

I roll over and wrap my body around Devney, pulling her close. The clock says it's four in the morning. I need to get up and make sure the last of the presents are under the tree, and that the tree is still standing after I worked all night.

Earlier last night, I carried her to bed after she fell asleep in Austin's bed when putting him down. The poor kid has had the worst nightmares for the last three nights. He wails in his sleep, and Devney is beside herself as it seems to be getting worse. It did however allow me to work without fear of her noticing I was gone.

She nestles back, rubbing her ass against my cock, and I have to fight back the urge to make love to her.

I've been patient, taking my brothers' advice and letting her lead the way, but I miss her. I need to be close to her again, give her every reason to want us to continue, and I'm afraid she'll keep slipping away.

"Sean." Her voice is sleepy, but the rasp causes me to harden. "Merry Christmas."

"Merry Christmas, sweetheart."

She turns over so her hands are on my chest, and she leans

up to kiss me. "I love you."

This is the one thing I know hasn't changed. She looks at me with more love each day. I can see how hard this is for her. Maybe the right thing to do is to take the additional stress of deciding off the table and let her go, but I can't. I've lived a life without her, and I won't give her that out.

For years, I've abided by the vow to be alone, and now that I've broken it, there's no way to go back.

She's filled my world with colors that I've never seen before and muted tones aren't what I want to be surrounded with.

"I love you," I tell her.

"Make love to me," Devney pleads, her hands moving down my chest. "Please, I need you."

I take her face in my hands and kiss her softly. Our tongues move together in a perfect rhythm, taking and giving when the other shifts. My hands glide down her smooth skin, tracing every curve, committing each one to memory. I love how she feels. The way her body fits with mine so easily.

I kiss down to her throat as she lifts it to give me better access. She tastes like sunshine and smells of vanilla. Moving back up to her lips, I capture the moan that escapes as I cup her breasts. "You drive me crazy," I tell her. "I want you every moment of every day."

Her fingers slide through my hair before curling into fists so she can pull my face back to look at me. "You have no idea how much I want you."

"Show me."

Devney pushes me back, and I go easily, letting her take the lead. Her legs straddle me, and her heat settles against my cock. Her lips come to mine as her hands move against my chest. She lowers slowly, kissing her way down my body and sliding my underwear off so she can wrap her hand around my dick.

"I love every part of you." Her voice is smooth like silk. "I love how you make me feel. How you look at me. Everything with you is better."

My fingers move through her silky, chocolate strands, and tighten at her scalp. "All I want is to give you everything."

She smiles. "And I want to give to you too. Now, be quiet and don't wake Austin."

Her head lowers, eyes staying on mine as she takes me into her mouth. Her wet, hot tongue slides over me, and I have to bite back a groan. She bobs up and down, using her hand along with her mouth. Her tongue moving at the same time along the underside makes me fist the sheets. God, she feels incredible.

I need her. I need to do something before I lose my fucking mind.

I grab her hips, pulling her up toward my face and tear her panties off. She moans around my cock, sending electric pulses through my body.

To keep myself from blowing too early, I think of anything other than the incredible sensations of her mouth.

My solution is to pull her pussy near me, inhaling her musky scent and how turned on she is. "I'm going to make you come," I warn.

My tongue slides against her seam and then up to her clit. I hold her right where I want her, not allowing her to move her hips as I drive her crazy. With her mouth wrapped around my dick, she moans and sinks down even farther. I focus on her, not the intense sensations pulsing through me each time I hit the back of her throat.

It becomes a battle of who will drive the other to the brink faster, and I work hard to win.

Not that there are any losers here.

Still, I want her to come. I want to taste her as I take her over the edge.

Devney tries to move her hips away, and I hold her even tighter, flicking and sucking until she lifts her head and falls apart.

I keep at her, taking all she gives as her legs give out and she rests against my leg.

Then I flip her over, staring down into her brown, sated eyes. "We're not done."

She grins. "I'd hope not."

Her legs open, and I sink into her heat.

We stay connected, eyes, hearts, and I swear, she owns my soul. Gone is the frantic fight we just had, and I move in a steady rhythm, not wanting this connection to break. Right here, she's mine as much as I am hers. Our secrets are bared, and I want her to know I will do anything she needs.

I'll fight.

I'll surrender.

I'll do anything other than lose her.

"I can't lose you," she says as tears fill her beautiful eyes.

"You won't."

Her hand grazes the stubble on my cheek. "I love you so much, Sean."

I close my eyes and push deeper. Needing her to feel me, feel how much we are a part of each other. "You're not going to lose me." I will the words to be true.

She lifts her head, kissing me softly, and that one touch is too much. I can't hold back. All of my control is gone, and I come harder than I ever have before.

For long minutes after, we lie in a tangle, panting but holding each other close.

This is the first Christmas in ten years that I don't feel apathetic about the holiday. I spent the last two weeks getting gifts, paying my sister-in-law to wrap them, and working to make this holiday perfect for Austin and Devney.

I really hope she loves what I got them.

"Let's go make sure everything is ready," Devney says as she starts to get up.

I follow her, tossing on my shorts and grabbing her ass as she walks past me in her robe.

We get to the living room, and she gasps. "Sean, you did this?"

When she had gone to bed last night, the tree was decorated minimally from our attempts the other night, and while we had tried to make the living room look a bit more festive, there wasn't much we could do with what we had.

So, I recruited some people to pitch in.

I tuck her into my side, looking at the Winter Wonderland in front of us. "I had help."

Now, the living room is filled with decorations. Stockings are hung in front of the fireplace, there are lights around the windows, red poinsettias sit on the end tables, and the tree is now upright, thanks to Connor.

"The tree!" She gasps. "How did you . . ."

"Connor."

She smiles. "He built that?"

"Begrudgingly, but yes. He worked on it and brought it over last night. All my brothers helped get this done for you."

"You're making it incredibly hard for me."

I turn so she's in my arms and cup her cheeks. "That's the end goal. I told you that I wouldn't let you go without a fight. I told you I would make this so the only option is me."

"And what happens if I can't leave?"

I rub my thumb against her smooth skin. "Then we make a new plan, but either way, we're going to have a lot of Christmas mornings."

She lifts onto her tiptoes and our lips meet. "I knew you were trouble the first time we met."

"Well, thankfully, you ran toward the trouble."

"And look at me now."

I give her another kiss. "Caught by a man who has no intention of letting you go."

"Maybe I like being caught."

"Maybe I like catching you."

"Maybe we were meant to catch each other."

I smile down at her. "I'm glad we finally did."

"Me too."

"Merry Christmas, my love."

She rests her head on my chest. "You're the best Christmas present I've ever gotten."

thirty-four

"Here, open this one!" I say to Austin as he smiles without sadness for the first time.

He grabs the present and tears it open. "Wow!" The joy in his voice makes me feel hopeful for a better road ahead of us. "You got me a new glove."

I eye Sean with a smirk. "Not just any glove. We had this one made for you."

"You did?"

Sean nods and then takes it to show him. "See here, this is an extra padding that will help you recover the ball from the glove faster. And this . . ." He points to some other area. "Is where you can adjust it for the next few years."

"This is so cool!"

The two of them talk a little more about the intricacies of the ridiculously expensive glove, and I lean back with my coffee. This morning has been amazing. I woke up in Sean's arms, made love to him, came out to the best surprise, and have been snuggled in the living room with the fire blazing.

Of course, I miss my brother and Hazel, but I'm trying to allow myself a little piece of happy. Austin is my son. Regardless of the fact that he's always been my nephew, I've had these moments where I think . . . maybe my mother was right.

Austin and I are having our first Christmas morning where we woke up as a family.

There's a sense of right that fills me, but there is also guilt because my brother is gone and it's why I'm experiencing this.

"Aunt Devney?"

I look up from my mug. "Yeah?"

"Are you okay?"

This kid is the sweetest thing. "I'm fine, I was just thinking of the present I got for Sean that I want to give next."

"Oh!" Austin perks up.

I get up and go to the window, making sure the present has arrived. Jasper had been working on it for the last few weeks, and thankfully, a few of his friends stepped in once we lost him. I had forgotten about it until they called two nights ago to say it was done. Last night, his brothers had offered to make sure it made it here without Sean knowing.

I dip under the tree, careful not to touch it too much in case the homemade stand doesn't hold up. I grab the small package and nerves hit me. Getting him gifts has always been so easy, but I agonized over what to get him this time. Searching for hours to see if there was something that would say all the things I want to say.

I love you.

You mean the world to me.

I don't know what I'll do when you leave.

Of course, nothing seemed adequate, so I went with something that I thought might heal something else.

"What is this?" Sean asks.

"Open it."

He pulls the wrapping off and looks at it. "A key?"

God, I hope this doesn't backfire.

"Yes, and please know that if you hate this, I won't be up-set. I just . . . well, I thought that maybe you'd want something that . . . well, like I said, if you don't like it, that is *totally* fine." I'm rambling, but I don't care. I want him to know I really won't be offended.

"Okay . . ." He draws out the word.

I take his hand and lead him toward the window. There sits a black 1973 Chevy Camaro. "It's not the same. I didn't want to fix what you had because . . . I didn't think you'd want that. But this one"—I look out at it—"was in great shape when we found it. An old man a few hours away had it in his garage, and well, you were cheated out of yours. Jasper almost wept when we went to get it. The guy we bought it from just wanted someone to love it like he did. We did a few mechanical things to it because it wasn't driven much. No project or laptop be-cause . . . well . . . you know." I try to joke at the end as my body tingles in anticipation at his reaction.

He stares at it, not speaking or blinking or moving, and I gnaw on my lower lip. I have no idea if he's happy or wants to throw something. I look to Austin, who is just as nervous as I am, only he has no idea why.

"I wanted you to have something that was taken from you," I explain, hoping he isn't upset. After another minute of silence, I start to break. "Sean? I'm sorry. I shouldn't have . . . I just . . ."

"Stop." His voice is soft but stern.

My heart races, and I fight back the urge to cry. I was stu-pid. I should've known better, but when I talked to Connor, Jacob, and Declan, they all thought it was really great. It wasn't the car, it was new. It was taking a horrible thing and giving him back the past that was stolen because of their abusive father.

I don't know why I didn't just get the stupid baseball card that would've been zero risk.

Nothing in our relationship has ever been played safely, and I wanted our first, and possibly only, Christmas to be special.

The air releases from my chest, and I take a step back. Sean's hand darts out and grips mine, weaving our fingers together.

"I'm not upset," he says, still staring at the car. "I'm . . . stunned. No one else would understand what this means, but you do."

My eyes meet his, the green irises are brimming with unshed tears. "This was supposed to make you smile."

His head shakes slowly, and he turns to face me completely. "I am smiling under all the layers of what you see . . . I just can't because I don't know how else to control myself."

"You're happy?"

Sean pulls me tight, squeezing and then kissing the top of my head. "You have no idea."

"Can we give her our present now?" Austin yells.

He releases me but leans down and gives me a sweet kiss before saying, "Thank you, Devney. Just . . . thank you."

Relief that I didn't totally screw up floods my veins, and I grin.

"Now," Sean's voice shifts back to the lightheartedness I'm used to, "this is a big present. So, you need to sit."

"Really? I have to sit?"

They both nod. "We wouldn't want you to fall over," Austin explains.

"How thoughtful."

Austin continues on like I didn't speak. "We talked a lot about it. Sean wanted to get you something else, but I really felt this was the best present."

Sean takes over the conversation. "You're not all that easy to buy for, sweetheart. There were a lot of clues you were tossing out."

I laugh once and grab my coffee. "Really? I think the list I gave was pretty easy."

They look at each other and grin. "Who needs to go off a list?"

Oh dear God. This is going to be a shitshow. "Yes, who shops from a list when trying to get the other person what they want? Oh, I know, Santa?" I take a sip of the caffeine goodness.

Austin rolls his eyes. "Really, Aunt Devney, I'm not six. I know that Santa isn't real."

I choke on my coffee. "Sorry. I didn't know . . ."

Sean laughs before bringing us back on topic. "Anyway, we agonized over what to get, but we ultimately decided we had to go big or just forego Christmas altogether."

"Well, now I'm intrigued." I sit up a bit and put the mug down. "What is it? A plane? A boat? Oh, maybe it's the new video game I wanted."

Austin rolls his eyes. "A plane?"

"Well, a girl can dream."

They chuckle. "Well, a plane is involved."

I look to both of them. "What did you both do?"

Sean scoops Austin up and carries him over to me. "Give it to her, little man."

Austin extends an envelope. "Here."

My heart beats a little harder as I take it from him. I have no idea what this could be, but they both seem extremely excited.

I lift the sealed lip, moving slowly and drawing out their obvious anticipation. "I wonder what it is."

Austin sighs. "Rip it open!"

I laugh and do as he says. There is a card with Mickey on the front.

When I open it, it has three park passes to Disney inside.

"We're going to Florida!" Austin yells and grips my hands. "We're going to Disney and then to Universal and then we're going to see the beach!"

He looks like he could burst from his skin. "This is too much."

Sean shakes his head. "We could all use some sun. Don't you think?"

I look out at the freezing, snow-covered ground and smile. "I think so."

"Good," Sean says and then pulls me to my feet. "Get packed, we leave tonight."

"What?" I shriek. "Tonight?"

Austin laughs. "Sean and I packed our bags two days ago."

"What if I said no?"

Sean and Austin share a look. "You? Say no to the two of us? We're irresistible."

Oh, now I've heard it all. "Yeah, we'll see about that."

"Too late to argue, our flight leaves at nine tonight and we head to the airport right after we go to Connor's."

I get to my feet and give him a kiss. "Thank you."

"No need to thank me, sweetheart. There's nothing I wouldn't do to see you smile."

"It's so romantic," Syd says as she clasps her hands to her chest.

"Connor and I haven't gone anywhere. We didn't even get a honeymoon."

I look at Ellie with a brow raised. "You were pregnant."

"Doesn't mean I didn't want to be whisked away."

I laugh and pop another cookie into my mouth.

Syd shrugs. "I didn't get one either. But we got married in city hall with no one even aware of it. And, truly, I was already swollen and uncomfortable."

"Well, this isn't a honeymoon," I remind them.

It's a trip. A vacation with an ulterior motive, but . . . I'm not going to look the gift horse in the mouth.

"Could be . . ."

I glare at Syd. "It's not. It's . . ."

"It's Christmas." Ellie nudges me. "Magical things happen around this time of year. I know you're fighting it, but can you honestly say you don't want to find a way?"

Of all the people in this town, I thought she would be the one on my side. "You have a child who is about the same age as Austin. How would you handle it?"

Ellie lifts Bethanne in her arms a bit higher and pats her butt. "I would follow my heart."

Yeah, that's super easy to do.

I tell her. "My heart doesn't give Austin stability."

"He needs love too," she adds on.

"I love him."

Syd's hand rests on my arm. "No one is saying you don't. You also love Sean, and Sean loves you and Austin. There's no break in the chain. I'm not telling you to move there, I'm just telling you to think of what you stand to lose if you don't."

I lean back, grabbing another cookie and stuffing my mouth with it. All of this is so hard. I feel as though I'm sacrificing Austin's security just to be happy—again.

He may never know that I'm his birth mother, and I've accepted that, but I never want him to question my devotion to him.

Ellie clears her throat. "Anyway, let's talk about now. No need to get ahead of ourselves."

The porch door swings open. "Well, if this isn't the prettiest group of women ever assembled."

"Jacob!" Syd yells and rushes forward. "You made it! I was so worried."

"Please, you don't have to worry about me, I'm a super-hero."

I get to my feet. "Or a super idiot."

He grins. "That too." Jacob's flight was delayed, and we weren't sure that he'd make it in, but I'm so glad he did. He pulls me to his chest and squeezes. "I'm so sorry about your brother, Shrimpy. I didn't know Jasper all that well, but what I did know, I respected."

I hold him a bit tighter. "Thanks, Jacob."

"Any time."

He releases me and then pulls each of the other girls into a hug. This Christmas is now complete. All the brothers are together, and the family is under one roof. I know it isn't my family, but they've always sort of felt that way. Our lives were intertwined at a young age and since they're so close in age, it felt like a pack.

I've missed my pack.

"Now, I want to see my nieces and nephew, spoil them rotten, and make sure I'm the favorite."

And some things never change.

thirty-five

"So, you're going to be in Florida, but I still have to sleep in the fucking tiny shed in the woods?"

Declan laughs and lifts his bottle to me. "It's now a rite of passage."

"The fuck it is."

"You're supposed to be some big, strong, superhero dude. You can't handle living in a box with very little warmth?" I ask.

Jacob flips me off. "You're not going to be home!"

"That doesn't mean I want you invading my space."

He huffs and looks to Connor for help, but he just shrugs. "Seriously? Not even you'll side with me. Wait!" Jacob claps. "Connor never had to sleep in it."

"I also had to repair the main house, which was a hundred times worse than the tiny house when I first got there. So, yeah, the luxury that you assholes are enjoying is compliments of me."

Connor does have a point.

"Whatever, this is some bullshit."

"Be mad, brother, but you're not staying with Sydney and me," Dec adds just to dig the knife in a bit deeper.

"I have a newborn and a wife whose mood changes very rapidly," Connor says with a grin.

"And I just don't want you in the house." I really have no good reason other than to piss him off.

Jacob flops down onto the couch. "I hate you all."

Ellie enters the room holding Bethanne. "Are you boys going to help with dinner or just let the women around you do it all?"

"I offered to help, but Connor said you didn't need any." I speak first.

If looks could kill, my brother would have me filleted like a fish.

"Well." She glares at him. "You can finish cooking for us."

He gets up and kisses her on the cheek. "You know I would never say that."

She smiles up at him. "I do, but you're still going to help."

They share a look that makes my heart actually fucking ache. They love each other so much that nothing could ever stand between them—not distance, time, another person, or an obstacle. They love each other enough to figure things out, even when they seem insurmountable.

I feel that way.

I would battle a hundred men if that was what it took to keep Devney.

Ellie touches my arm. "What's wrong?"

"Nothing." I shake my head, trying to not think about the

possibilities of the future.

"Sean, come on, talk to me. I'm your sister."

"I've gained a few of those in the last year."

She laughs. "Yes, you definitely have. I'd like to think you're excited about it."

"Definitely."

I love them both. Ellie is the perfect complement to Connor and Syd has always been Declan's counterbalance.

"Then talk to me," she encourages.

"Yes, tell us all your feelings so we can fix them," Jacob chimes in.

"You watch it." She points at him. "I have to talk to you about something too."

"Oh, please, talk to Jacob," I insist.

She smiles at me and then turns to him. I really do like my new sister-in-law. "There's a new kid at the school who is having a rough time. His dad was a SEAL who was killed in combat."

Jacob glances to me. He doesn't have to say it, I know what he's thinking . . . it's what we feared would happen to Connor. Each time the phone rang while he was deployed, a part of me wanted to puke. The three of us hated the fear.

"I'm sorry to hear that."

Ellie reaches for his hand. "I know you're very good to your fans, and it turns out that he's your biggest one. His mother took the new guidance counselor position at the school, and when she found out I was an Arrowood, she asked if maybe you'd just come meet Sebastian. I didn't promise anything."

Jacob lifts his other hand. "Say no more. Whatever you want me to do, I'll do it. I'd be happy to help a kid whose dad is a hero."

She lifts up and kisses his cheek. "You are a good man,

Jacob Arrowood."

He pulls her in for a hug. "Better than these fools combined."

"Yeah right," Devney says as she walks into the room. "You are a charmer with a silver-tongue, but you're not fooling anyone."

I throw my arm over her shoulders, bringing her close to me. Right where I want her. "God, I love you."

She beams back at me. "I love you too."

"And . . . I'm going to vomit." Jacob makes a gagging noise.

"You wait, Jacob. One day, you'll meet a girl who will knock you on your ass, and I can't wait to see it," Ellie says before nodding at Devney.

"And when it does happen," I say, not taking my gaze away from Devney, "I hope you're half as lucky as I was."

She rests her head on my shoulder, and I pray I can hold her close enough to keep her.

"This is the best day after Christmas ever!" Austin says, and I wish I could see the park through his eyes.

As a kid, there were no family vacations or even the mere idea of coming to Disney. Our trips were out to the pasture to camp, which was fine for us, but when I got out of Sugarloaf, I wanted to do it all.

The day after I moved to Florida, I came to Disney for the first time.

"I'm glad you're excited," I say as I touch the top of his head.

"You're the best, Sean."

"I sure do try."

He grins. "Can I go over to the store?"

Devney nods. "Just don't go too far, okay?"

Austin, who has become a pro in his wheelchair that I rented for the trip, wheels off to check it out without even a reply. Since we got here, he's been the buoyant kid I met a few months ago. He's smiling, talking nonstop, and there's a sense of excitement that has been missing.

"Thank you," Devney says as she watches him.

"For?"

"All of this."

Her smile is worth every penny spent. "You don't have to thank me."

"I think I do. Even if this is all . . . extravagant." Devney's voice is soft as she looks around.

"No, this is Christmas. I wanted us to have whatever we wanted."

She moves toward me. "All I wanted was us."

"You have that."

I can see the hesitation in her eyes. "What about his leg? I mean, it's going to suck."

"Everything is fine, sweetheart. I talked to his physical therapy team, and he knows his limits. We got the wheelchair and this way we get onto the rides without having to wait!"

I called the doctors before booking this to make sure he could do some of this and it wasn't like dangling candy in front of a diabetic. He said that as long as Austin wore his brace, used crutches or a wheelchair, he would be okay.

Roller coasters are a no-go, but anything else should be fine. Luckily, the kid doesn't even like roller coasters, so there's nothing he's missing out on.

Plus, Austin knows the easier he is on healing his body, the faster he'll be back on the field. For a kid who just wants to play ball, telling him to take it easy will go one of two ways. They either go too fast or they baby it. Austin seems to be on the latter, which is a good thing. You can push someone to start doing more, but trying to scale them back is often a challenge.

"I know, and he's great, but . . . I don't know. We would've been fine with a regular flight or a normal room, and we didn't need all these . . . perks."

I shrug as I pull her hips to mine. "I'd rather spoil the shit out of you."

"I know what you're doing."

"And what is that?"

She lifts one brow. "You're trying to get me to love Florida as much as I love you so I'll agree to move."

She would be correct. "Is it working?"

"I've been here for fewer than twenty-four hours."

"But hasn't that time been spectacular?"

Devney plays with the string on my hoodie. "You're spectacular."

"This we knew."

Her laugh is effortless. "You're a mess."

"Yeah, well . . . it's what keeps things interesting."

Austin makes his way back over just as they start to open the gates. Devney moves to push his chair for him so he can put all his focus on looking around. Neither one of us misses the way his eyes light up, and it's that expression that makes all of this worth it.

We aren't stressed about anything and can just enjoy our time.

When we get back, the issues will still be there, and we'll still have to handle them, but for now, none of that matters.

"This is so cool! Mom would love to go on . . ." Austin trails off, the excitement in his voice fading.

Devney places her hands on his shoulders, and I move so we're eye level. I remember that feeling. When you wanted to have your mother there, but she was gone. I would have that pause so many times that I would want to scream, cry, or punch someone. She should've been there when I got an A on a test. I wanted her smile when I hit a homerun. It was gone, though, and there was no getting it back.

"Your mom would love to go on what?"

"It doesn't matter."

I wait until Austin looks up at me. "It does. It always matters, and you can't let her memory go. What's going to get you through this is remembering her and what she said and what she did. It's hard, and there will be days when remembering hurts so much you will just want to forget, but she loved you and would want you to think about her."

Devney comes around and kisses the top of Austin's head. "Don't ever forget them, Austin. I won't. Jasper would've loved to see all of this. He loved cars, building things, and his family. Imagine all the things he would say if he could see that castle."

Austin's eyes lift to it. "He would wonder if they used the right nails."

We both laugh, and Devney takes his hand. "Yeah, and he would ask if they prebuilt any of it."

"He was weird," Austin says with his thoughts a million miles away.

"He was, but I loved him very much."

Austin looks back at her. "Me too. I miss them, Aunt Devney."

"I miss them too."

He throws his arms around her and she presses a kiss to

each of his cheeks.

"I love you with my whole heart," she tells him.

"I love you too." He looks up at me. "I love you too, Sean."

My throat feels tight as emotion starts to choke me. He's part of her. He's her child, and to love her means to love him. I don't know when it happened, but there's not a doubt in my mind about how I feel about Austin. I want to be there and a part of not only her life but also his. There will be sacrifices, but I'll make each one if it means I can be there.

I pull him in for a hug, wishing I could say everything that's in my heart. Instead, I say the one thing that means everything to me. "I've got you, Austin."

"What does that mean?"

I hear Devney hiccup and see the tears falling down her cheeks as she explains. "It means that no matter when, no matter what, he'll always be here."

"So, it's like saying I love you?"

She nods and then palms my cheek. "It is."

I take her hand in mine and then Austin's in the other. "When we were kids, it wasn't cool to say I love you to a girl, so I told her that I had her. I'd always have her. I'd make sure she was safe, and if she needed me, I would be there. It means I love you and you don't have to worry."

Austin smiles. "I've got you too then."

"Yeah, kid, you sure do."

thirty-six

Who knew that vacations were so damn exhausting? I sure didn't.

Orlando was a ton of fun, and we were able to get all the parks in as well as shopping. Now, we're in Tampa.

Not just anywhere in Tampa.

We are at the ballfield. I'm pretty sure Austin is about to shit himself, but he's trying to stay cool. "So, is anyone here?" he asks as Sean helps him into his chair.

"Not sure."

He knows.

He asked a bunch of his friends to meet us here, and Austin is going to lose it. I am both excited and nervous. I haven't met any of his friends other than Tyler Shaw. He was one of those unforgettable players. Sean admired him, and they were on an all-star team together. Apparently, Tyler was some hot-shit pitcher, and Sean was happy to be behind the plate instead of in front of it, trying to hit off the guy. I couldn't keep my eyes off him, which completely irritated Sean, but that was a perk at the time.

"Well, either way, I don't care. I'm going to step onto a real major league field!"

The first thing that comes to my mind is that I wish his father could see this.

Jasper dreamed of this moment. He worked his ass off to give Austin everything he could ever need. Baseball wasn't just about Austin. It was what bonded the two of them. When it was clear that Austin fell hard for the game, Jasper spent months learning about it. They watched games, talked about statistics, and had a plan to visit every field in the States. That will never happen for them.

Instead, Austin will do this without him.

Sean takes my hand. "You okay?"

I shove down my sadness and do what I can to focus on the joy that is coming from my . . . son.

"I am."

"He's going to freak."

"He is."

We are grinning as we follow Austin through the main gate.

Sean explains everything as we go through the halls. Since it's the off-season, the place is quiet, but there's a heaviness around us. Like, peoples' hopes and dreams live here and are just waiting to be discovered.

"Whoa!" Austin says as Sean stops the wheelchair in front of a door. "Is this your locker room?"

"Sure is."

"Can we go in?"

He laughs. "Of course."

Inside is about what I would expect it to look like, only the lockers that line the walls are all pretty much empty. He stops in front of the third on the left. "This is mine. Usually, we have uniforms gear in here, and it's . . . smelly."

Austin chuckles. "But it's the coolest place."

"I remember the first time I walked in here. I felt just like you do right now." The two of them share a brief moment, and then Sean points. "Through there is the field. You ready to go out?"

"I was born ready."

I swear that boys are all the same. "Well, let's go then."

The excitement is almost too much as we enter the tunnel that will drop us right onto the field. When we emerge, it's like the light is shining down upon us from the heavens. No wonder little boys dream of this. It's like the movies . . . only real.

Two guys come running toward us, and I hear the hitch in Austin's breathing.

"Oh my God. It's Jack Carter and Knox Gentry!" Austin's voice cracks on the last name.

Sean grins. "These are my buddies, and they wanted to come meet you."

Tears fill Austin's eyes, but he doesn't let them drop as Sean makes introductions and we move farther onto the field.

"Oh, wow!" Austin's voice goes higher. "You're friends with Easton Wylder?"

"Yeah, he and I have trained together. He thinks he's better than I am, but you know . . ." Sean winks, and Austin goes back to staring at the field.

"Is that Chase Stern?"

"It sure is."

"He's the best shortstop in the whole league!"

"Don't let Knox hear that . . ."

Austin covers his mouth and then looks around. "This is

the best day of my life."

In the wake of the most horrific tragedy, Sean was able to give him a miracle. Instead of Austin being closed off, stuck inside, and remembering all he lost, he was given a gift. A moment where all the world could be okay again.

Sean lifts him into his arms. "I'm glad, buddy. I really am. Now, let's go give these guys a run for their money."

He takes off, running toward the base, and the tears that didn't fall from Austin's eyes drip down my cheeks. In that moment, I know that my heart will never be the same again.

"You ready to see where I live?" Sean asks as he pulls the car into the underground garage.

"We are!" Austin answers. "This is so cool. I'm getting to go to Sean Arrowood's house and see where he lives and sleeps and dreams of baseball."

And Sean's back to being a hero and baseball god, not that he ever really lost that status. Hell, if anything, he's probably reached walk-on-water status. Austin and Sean are two peas in a pod. They speak the same language, and it's incredibly endearing to watch.

"None of that crap, we're friends," Sean tells him and then parks. "Also, no snapping or gramming or whatever it is you kids do. This is a social-media-free zone."

"He doesn't have social media," I say and then turn to him, suddenly not so confident. "Do you?"

He laughs. "Dad said I wasn't allowed until I was forty."

"Good plan," Sean agrees.

The three of us head into the elevator, and he punches in a

code. "If you want to go in or out of the apartment, you need the code, okay?"

"My birthday?" I ask him.

He doesn't look the least bit embarrassed. "It's a date I never forget."

"Because you stole my last cupcake?"

Sean smiles and then gives me a brief kiss. "I'll steal a lot more than that."

He's already stolen it, but I don't tell him.

We ride up to the top floor, and when the doors slide open, we walk out and right into his apartment.

Wow.

I try to take it all in. This place is magnificent. The floors are white marble with plush rugs in areas to define the spaces. There is a huge television on the wall with a sectional that looks as if it were made for the place.

Sean walks deeper into the apartment, and I follow. The kitchen is one hundred percent him with the dark gray cabinets and white countertops that make it masculine and soft at the same time.

"Want anything to eat?" He opens the cabinet and grabs a bag of chips, holding it up.

"I do!" Austin yells.

He hands it to him and then points to the living room area. "There are three gaming systems in there, you go play, I'm going to show Devney around."

"Do you have the new baseball game?"

Sean smirks. "The one that hasn't released yet?"

Austin nods.

"It's in the PlayStation."

Austin is off, wheeling himself over with a smile on his

face.

"This place is incredible."

He shrugs. "I had a designer who lives in the building do it. You know my version would've been a card table and a recliner."

"Well, she did amazing."

Sean looks around and shrugs. "Nicole is great. She understood me and didn't ask many questions, she just sort of did it."

"Nicole?" I ask with a bit of jealousy.

"Her name is Nicole Dupree who is my very married, very motherly designer." He pulls me to him and wraps his arms around my waist. "You're the only woman for me."

"You say that, but . . ."

"But nothing. I mean it."

God, all of this . . . it is too much. This week, I've had the best time. We've laughed and have spent so much quality time together. Sean and Austin hung out, and I could see the bond forming between them. I have just one more week before I owe him my answer, and I don't know what to do.

I want to say I'll just pack up and go, but the main thing holding me back is that I don't think that Austin could endure moving here. Not when the season is going to start soon and he'll be gone. We'll be here, in this town—with no one.

I'm not sure that Austin could adjust. I feel like such a fool. I should've protected him. A mother would've known to do that, which just further shows how shitty of one I am.

Sean takes my hand. "Come on, let me show you the rest of the apartment."

Apartment my ass. We walk around, and it becomes clear that this is a house on a top floor. It's huge. There are four bedrooms, four bathrooms, and we're standing at the entrance to his room.

Dear God. It's bigger than the living and dining room combo.

"Uhh, this is . . ."

"It's pretty awesome, but it's nothing compared to the view." He walks over to the windows and hits a button. The shades rise, and my legs move of their own accord so I can get a better look. "It's . . ."

"Beautiful."

I turn to look at him, but he isn't staring out the window. His eyes are trained on me. I feel the heat flood my cheeks and turn away.

I've known him my whole life, and I didn't think he'd ever look at me this way. A wave of sadness hits me because it isn't fair. I love him. He loves me. We could be so happy. We have every foundation for a good relationship and he's perfect for me. I can see the life we'd share. The way we would be a family because Austin loves Sean, and Sean adores him. We could be more, but how?

We move here only to have Sean start baseball season. It's all too much. "Why couldn't this have been another time?"

"What do you mean?" he asks as he lifts his hand to brush the hair off my face.

"When there were no complications. Nothing that was muddying things and fighting to keep us apart. If the accident . . ."

"Didn't happen, then you wouldn't have Austin."

"I want to have you both."

My chest aches because I already know that my heart may want Sean, but my head will always choose Austin. I can't move down here as some girlfriend who is going to mooch off him. There has to be stability financially for me, and that isn't here, even with the assurances that he could help me find a job.

Not to mention, all of Austin's family is in Sugarloaf. Hazel was an only child who lost both her parents to cancer, so all he has left is my parents and me.

"Dev, why is this one or the other?"

"Because I don't know how to have both."

"I still have a few days to show you how you can, please don't choose yet."

I lean my head against his chest, listening to his heartbeat. "I hope you come up with a solution that works."

His hand rubs against my back. "So do I."

thirty-seven

Tonight is our last night in Tampa. My absolute last opportunity to make her see what life could be like here. I've tried to think of everything that it would take, and I really have nothing else, nothing but my heart and the truth.

We are finishing a movie and then heading to Riverwalk.

The mood feels strained today. It's as though we know that, tomorrow, reality returns. Austin will start back at school, Devney will go back to work, and I'll be planning to head back here.

Time that I thought would drag on for eternity has passed in the blink of an eye.

Six months can't be all I get.

It just can't.

The movie ends and Devney shifts. "Did you still want to go out?"

I look to Austin. "What do you think?"

"I want to stay here."

At this point, I'm fine either way. "Okay. We can stay in. Our flight isn't until midafternoon, but maybe we need to rest a bit."

He shakes his head. "No, I mean here. I want to stay in Florida."

I keep my gratefulness at a five because I know Devney well enough to understand that this won't help my case. However, I'm not going to dissuade him either. If he wants to move here, and I want them to move here, then she's the only one holding us back.

Devney looks to me, but I just raise my brow. Not a chance. "Austin, we've had a great time here, but our home is in Sugarloaf."

"No, my home *was* in Sugarloaf. Right now, I don't have a home."

"That's not true. We have the house you grew up in or we could go stay with Grandma and Grandpa once Sean leaves. Or I could get a new place for us. It's hard and things are . . . difficult, but you have a home . . . with me."

Austin crosses his arms over his chest and looks away. "I want to stay here. I like it here."

I can practically feel the despair coming from her. She's trying so hard to do the right thing, and no matter how much I want to win this one and have her move to Florida, I will never be the bad guy in her story. She needs a partner. Someone who will have her back, and that will always be me.

"I know you want to stay here, and I love having you, but we don't have to make this choice now. Either way, we'd have to go back to Sugarloaf tomorrow."

His lip trembles, and he scoots toward his wheelchair. "I wish I never had to go back to that stupid town."

"Austin . . ."

He glares at Devney, but all I see is a reflection of the scared kid I used to be. "No! I hate it. I hate that I can't go home. I can't play baseball. I can't do *anything*! I don't want to go back to school and tell everyone how my dad and mom were killed. I don't want to talk about the accident. No one here knows. I'm happy here, and I don't cry."

"Right now, you have limits," I say gently. "Whenever we get hurt, we have to heal. You've been doing great, and next week, you go to crutches. After that, you'll walk again. After that, you'll run. It's about taking steps, and the same goes for when you deal with grief."

A tear falls down his face as he gets himself into his chair. "I just want to go to bed."

Devney releases a heavy sigh. "I'm sorry you're hurting, buddy. There's nothing I wouldn't give to be able to take your pain away."

He looks over at her as he pushes himself away. "You could let us stay here, but you won't."

She goes to get up, but I grab her hand.

"Let him go."

"He's so angry. I've never seen him like that."

I wrap my arms around her and pull her close. "He's going to be angry. He has every right to be angry."

Her head rests on my shoulder. "I wanted to say yes. I wanted to tell him we would stay here forever and make it work."

My muscles tense because I know there's a but coming. "And?"

"I can't."

"Can't or won't?"

She sits up and moves back a little, but she doesn't retreat too far before she's twisting her fingers through mine. "Can't. God, I want to. If it were just me, I'd pay someone to pack my shit and mail it to me, but it's not just me. Austin might be angry, but think back, Sean. What would you have done if your father had packed you boys and made you leave?"

"Was he coming with?"

She shakes her head. "My point is that you needed me. Declan needed Sydney. Connor needed you and Jacob. Jacob needed to be in Sugarloaf. It was the only place he felt like he had your mother. That farm was your savior as much as it was your hell."

My hell had nothing to do with the farm and everything to do with the devil who was left to raise me.

"The fuck it was. I hated that town. If I had the chance to take you with me, I would've gone anywhere to escape. You're not protecting him by forcing him to stay there to be closer to Jasper and Hazel."

Her breath comes out in a huff as she gets to her feet. "You think I want this? That I want to let go of the man I love more than anything? None of this was supposed to happen. I was finally getting my chance at love. We were . . . God, I was going with you. A month ago, it wasn't a question that I was going to be sitting next to you on the flight here. I would've figured everything out, but it's all changed now! I have Austin to think about."

"And what about what he wants?"

"He's ten! Of course he wants to be with you! Who wouldn't? You're amazing, funny, sweet, fantastic in every damn way, and you play baseball. You're the dream, Sean. You are what women pray for."

"Yet, you're ready to wake up? You don't have to have me as a dream, Devney. I'm the reality, and I'm willing to give you everything."

Her head falls back as she looks to the ceiling. "I can't do this."

Then she stands and walks away, going back into the bedroom. I didn't want to fight, but I can't let this drop. We have to have this out. All of it needs to be on the table so we can work through it. Giving up now seems so stupid.

I follow her, closing the door behind me. "We need to finish this talk. You can't just walk away like that."

"Nothing is going to change, Sean! I'm still going back to Sugarloaf. I'm not coming here. I can't do it!"

"Why?"

"Because!"

I step closer. "Why, Devney? What are you so afraid of?"

"*You!*" she yells and throws her hands up. "I'm terrified of coming here and what happens next."

"We'll figure it out!"

Her head falls back, and she groans. "It's just so easy for you, isn't it? What about me, Sean? What do I do?"

None of her questions make sense. "What does that even mean?"

"It means I move here, take Austin away from the only family he's ever known, and what? How do we adjust to everything? I can't handle all of this change in one freaking month. You're asking me to come here and flip our lives upside down."

This is such bullshit. "Your life is already upside down! I'm here, willing to help you find a new center. I'm asking you to move in with me and *marry* me! I want it all, Devney, and I want it with you. I'm not trying to make it harder! I'm trying to make it easier. I can give you everything you want, but you won't fucking take it."

She jerks back as though she's been struck. "What did you say?"

"I want it all. I want you, and I want Austin. I love that kid. I would never do anything to hurt him."

"Before that."

"What?"

Her breathing is rapid as she moves toward me. "You said you want me to move in with you and . . ."

I don't hesitate. "Marry me."

"You have to be joking, right? You didn't just fight propose to me. That is not . . . you're angry or scared."

It came out, and I wasn't thinking, but it's the truth. I want her to be my wife. I want us to build a life and a family together. It just wasn't how I meant to say it. Still, I won't lie. I can't hold back, not if she's determined to walk away from us. "No, I'm both of those things, but this wasn't just something that magically came to me. I want to marry you. I think I've known it my whole life, but I refused to even consider it. This wasn't just a six-month thing for either of us, this was forever. You don't walk away from the person you're meant to spend your life with. I want to marry you, and I'll get down on my knee right now if that's what it takes."

She steps back, but I move with her, not allowing distance. "I don't want you to marry me because you're afraid of losing me."

"If you think that's why, you haven't been paying attention." I head toward her, eyes locked on her as they ask a million questions. "I want to marry you because I love you more than any man has ever loved another woman. I want to marry you because I want to wake up each day with you beside me. I would make you happy, give you the world. I'll stand by your side when you falter and when you win. There won't be a day that you're alone because I will always be here."

"You say that, but your job takes you away more than three-quarters of the year. I'll be down here alone with Austin while you're flying all over the country playing baseball. Don't you get it? I need help and my family more than ever. My parents, Syd, Ellie, your brothers are all there, but you won't be. You're asking me to give up everything for you, and what do you lose? Nothing."

Deep down, in the depth of my soul, I know she's right. I am asking her to come here, and then, the season will start. I'll train for ten hours a day, then preseason starts. When it's the actual season . . . I'm gone all the time. Life won't be easy with me, I know this, but she is only seeing what she will be giving up and is blind to everything she'll be gaining.

Many major league guys have families. They make it work, just like we can.

"There is sacrifice in every relationship, Dev. We all have to adjust, but I'm not asking you to give up a damn thing," I say through gritted teeth. "I want to give to you."

Devney huffs and steps back. This time, I let her. "You think that, and it just shows how you're not seeing this picture the way that I am."

"Yes, I'm delusional because I love you and Austin."

"No, I love Austin. I have loved that baby since the minute he was born. I loved him so much that I gave him up. I gave him a home with parents who could do better than I ever could." Tears fall down her cheeks, and a sob wretches from her throat. "I had to give him up when he was an infant, and I don't have to now. I'm not going to make a choice that will only hurt him."

"And how is lying to him the best option?"

I know I'm hitting low, but if this is my last chance to say it all, then I'm going to swing for the fences and pray I make it over.

"What did you just say?"

"You're lying to him. He is your *son*, Devney."

"I'm well aware of what he is to me."

"Well, then why aren't you taking his wants into consideration. He doesn't know the full story, and he's lost because he thinks he lost his mother when he hasn't."

"He has lost his mother." Her voice is low and full of rage. "He lost the only mother he's ever known. I might have given birth to him, but I've always known my place in his life. Don't you dare try to use that against me."

She's right. I'm being a complete ass. "I'm sorry." I move to her, wanting to take it all back. "I'm just . . . I can't lose you, but it feels like you've already given up, that you aren't even willing to try. How can you not be falling apart at the idea of us ending? How is this so fucking easy for you?"

Her gaze falls to the floor, and she shakes her head. "None of this is easy, but I'm trying to do the right thing."

"And I'm just trying to show you that you don't have to choose between Austin and me."

She looks up, eyes filled with sadness and regret. "We both know that's not true."

"So, that's it?"

"I don't want it to be."

"Well, you're clearly not changing your mind, so now what?" I ask, knowing that there is no more time for us. She's resolved to staying in Sugarloaf, which is the end of all we have.

"Now, we go home tomorrow, and I move out." Tears graze the skin of her cheeks in a steady stream as she walks to the door. "I need to check on him, and . . ."

"Don't do this."

"I don't have a choice."

I step forward and place my hand on the door so she can't open it. "There's always a choice. Whether we like it or not, we have options. I love you. I love you, and I will do whatever it takes to make you happy here, but you have to be willing to take a chance."

Devney's hand moves to my chest. "I've made my choice,

now you have to accept it."

With that, my palm falls from the door, and she opens it. I feel her loss even though I don't watch her go.

Minutes pass, and I feel empty, knowing that what we've had we won't ever find again. The laughter, friendship, and connection that I've only hoped could exist for me is gone. I stand, unmoving and trying to come up with any other options.

I don't know how to let her go.

I don't know how to give up.

I can't move until I have a solution, and there has to be one.

"Sean! *Sean!*" Dev yells with so much fear in her voice that my heart accelerates, and I run.

thirty-eight

"What's wrong?" Sean bursts through the door, and my breathing is so labored I can barely speak.

"He . . . he . . . he's not here!" I finally get the words out as panic grips me.

I thought I knew fear when he was born, and the accident taught me that was a lie. This has shown me that I had never really known what fear was before this moment.

"What do you mean he's not here?" Sean looks around. "Austin?" he calls out, but there's no reply. "Austin!"

We both dart out of the room, but I've already searched the living room, kitchen, and bathroom and there wasn't any sign of him or his crutches.

"Austin!" I scream as my hands shake and I try to move his suitcase and blankets, hoping he's just . . . hiding. But deep inside, something tells me he isn't.

He was angry when he went to bed, and I just pray to God he didn't hear us fighting.

Sean's voice continues through the apartment as we both search. I rush toward the kitchen where he's standing.

"Anything?"

I shake my head. "Where could he have gone?"

"I don't know. Maybe he just went downstairs. He couldn't have gotten far on crutches."

"We don't even know when he left! God! He could be lost!" My heart pounds, and the terror builds higher. This was such a mistake. I never should've let Austin go to the room without talking to him. He's in pain, and I let him down.

"We'll find him."

I'm glad he's so sure. I look over, grab my cell phone, and dial Austin's number, only to hear the ringtone blaring from the couch.

Of course, he didn't take his phone. If he had, I could at least have tracked it or done something.

"Sean . . ." I don't know what I'm asking for, but I'm so afraid, and he's the only person who might make this better.

He moves to me, hands on my shoulders. "Okay, think about this, we've been in Tampa a few days. There were two places he loved, the baseball field and the beach. I say we check the field first."

I look out the living room window where the ballfield is visible.

It makes the most sense, and if he's on foot, it's the best option.

"Let's go," I say and start to head to the elevator.

"One of us should stay here in case he comes back."

I can't do that. "There's no way that I can sit here and wait. I can't!"

He takes my face in his hands, holding us so we're eye to eye. "I'll find him. If he comes back, call me. I swear to you, Devney. If he's out there, I will bring him back."

My throat goes tight as the fear gets stronger. "He's just a little boy . . ."

"I know, I'll bring him back. Stay here and call me if anything happens, okay?"

I nod. Sean brings his lips to mine. "I love you."

That is something that will never change, no matter what choices I have to make. "I love you."

He grabs his keys, phone, and wallet and then heads out the door. I make my way to the couch and sink down, gripping the blanket and crying harder than I ever have before.

Twenty minutes later, my phone rings. I sit up, head pounding as I wipe the tears from my face. "Hello?"

"He's not here. I'm going to the beach now," Sean says quickly and slightly out of breath. "I let the staff that's here know to look out for him, and if they see him, they'll call one of us. I think you need to call the police."

My hope dissipates like early morning fog as I stare out the window. He's lost. He's alone and probably scared without any idea of where to go. I don't even know the address to this place, so I doubt Austin does.

God, please protect my baby.

"Please find him," I beg.

"I'm trying. I'll check the beach and keep looking. I'm on foot because I don't know how else he would've traveled. I'll call you soon. Call the police, we need all the help we can get looking."

I hang up with him and immediately dial the police department, and they explain that they're going to send a car over.

My body trembles, and I start to pace. I have no idea what to do or think. Everything feels so helpless. I debate calling my mother but decide against it. I don't want to worry her or give her anything else to hate me for or, heaven forbid, give her a reason to try to take Austin away from me. Until I know something, I'm going to avoid that.

Instead, I call the voice of reason.

"Devney?" Syd's voice sounds like I woke her.

"Syd . . ."

"Is everything okay?"

"I'm sorry if I woke you."

"No, please, it's fine. I must've fallen asleep after I fed Deacon."

"I lost him," I say as I start to cry.

"Lost who? Sean?"

"Yes, but that's not what I mean."

She clears her throat. "I don't know what you're saying. Who did you lose if we're not talking about Sean?"

I drop my head down, feeling so much shame and sadness. "Austin. He ran away or wandered off. I don't know."

"Oh, God. When did he take off?"

I fill her in on the events of the night and things leading up to my calling her. I tell her everything. I confess that Austin is really my son, that I've been lying to everyone, and how absolutely terrified I am that he found out about it because he overheard Sean and I fighting.

"I'm so sorry I didn't tell you," I say between sobs.

"You have nothing to be sorry for, Devney. What you did .

. . well, I can't imagine, but it is nothing that you owe anyone an explanation for. That boy is incredibly lucky to have you and Hazel as mothers."

I laugh once. "Please. Hazel never lost him."

"You didn't lose him, honey. He was angry and took off. You have no idea if he knows the truth about you being his mom or he was pissed because he wants to stay in Tampa. I know you're struggling, and if I were there, I'd come hug you and do whatever I could."

I know she would. Sydney has been one of the best friends anyone could ask for. She gives her time and counsel no matter what, and she always give it with kindness.

"We have to find him, Syd. I don't know what I would do if something happened to him too."

"Sean won't quit. He loves that boy just as much as you do."

"I fought with him," I confess. "I told him I couldn't move here and that I couldn't take Austin away from his home, and then he said he wanted to marry me."

I shake my head and feel as if everything is caving in and ready to suffocate me. We had the best vacation, and it ended in the most epic failure.

"You'll both get over it and get your heads on straight. Emotions are high and deadlines are never a good thing—unless it's work. When Austin comes back, just hold each other. The three of you are more of a unit than you think. Lean on each other."

There's a buzz down at the door. "I have to go."

"Love you, Dev."

"Love you too."

I hang up and touch the button I think is the intercom. "Hello? This is Officer Covey with the Tampa Police Department. We got a call about a missing child."

"Yes, I'm Devney Maxwell. I'll buzz you in." At least I'll try to.

After a few attempts, I get the code in, and two police officers enter. One must be Officer Covey, since she's the only female. She's shorter than I am, blonde, and very pretty. The man with her is huge.

"Hi, Devney, I'm Heather, and this is my partner, Brody. Can you tell us about what happened?"

I lead them into the kitchen and we sit at the table as I go over everything. She takes notes while her partner calls over the radio some descriptions of Austin. I do my best to keep it together, but each minute that passes feels like a lifetime. I'm terrified something happened to him or that we'll never find him.

She puts her notebook down and gives me a soft smile. "I can imagine that you're going crazy, but we have the entire department on the lookout."

I nod, fighting back tears. "I should've . . . I don't know."

"It's easy to play that game, but we'll do everything we can to find him. I don't have kids, but I'm an aunt, and I know how I would feel if it were one of them."

My eyes meet hers and the tears spill over. "He's my nephew, well, he is and he's also my son. I'm not making sense, and it's complicated, but that boy is my entire world. I need him back."

"Do you have anyone who can wait with you?"

The only person I want is Sean, but he's out there now. "No, my boyfriend is out searching for him too. I'm here in case he comes back."

"Is there anywhere that you think he would be?"

"Sean went to the ballfield, but he called and said Austin wasn't there. He's headed to the beach now. We've only been in Tampa a few days and we didn't really go many places. I just . . . he never should've left! He knows better! He's a smart kid, and this is not like him."

Heather takes my hand in hers. "How about this . . . I'll stay here with you, we'll talk, think things out, and Brody will go walk around the area?"

She has no idea how much that means to me. Sitting here, worried and unable to go anywhere to look for him, has been so hard. I just want answers. I want to do something, help in some way, and I can't.

All that I can do is think of all the worst-case scenarios, and each one leaves me sick to my stomach.

"Thank you."

She squeezes gently. "We'll do everything in our power."

She doesn't make promises she can't keep, and I hear the underlying concern in her voice.

There's a chance they won't find him.

There's a chance he's gone.

And that's what has me terrified.

thirty-nine

Fuck.

Fuck, I have to find him. I run up and down the beach again, hoping to spot him, but nothing. There's a pit in my stomach that grows deeper each second. I've called all the guys that came to the field yesterday and they're out looking too.

Someone has to have seen him and called the police. I think about going on my social media and making a plea for help, but that would make it worse. God only knows the responses and judgement that would come. If I thought it might help and people would truly behave right, I would, but then I know Devney would be upset.

So, I just stick to the plan and think.

No one has called to say they've seen him at the ballfield, but that's where my gut says he is.

It's where I would go when shit would get bad.

And if he heard anything, he'd feel lost and know that's where you're found.

I release a deep breath and start to make my way back there, not going on anything but a hunch.

The field is huge and there are many places he could hide. I need to keep moving and look.

As I'm jogging there, my phone rings. I swipe without even looking at the number.

"Hello?" I stop running, working hard to regulate my breathing.

"Hey, it's Zach. I was just calling to see how it's going with the horse."

"I can't talk now, we're in the middle of a crisis and . . ."

"Oh, what's going on? Is everything okay?"

I rub my hand over my face and keep walking. No, nothing is okay. Everything is falling apart, and I'm the one to blame.

I give him the brief version of all the shit that's changed since he was out here. No fluff, just details. "So, I'm dating a single mother."

"I relate. It's hard coming into that."

"That's not the crisis though. Austin ran off. We were at my place and Devney and I got in a fight . . . he wants to stay here, and she isn't on board. I don't know . . . it's all so fucked up. I said stupid shit, and we're not sure if he heard . . ."

"I've been there. Literally. Exactly where you are. Just take a deep breath."

I do as he says and then look around. "I don't know what the fuck to do. I love this kid, and I love his mother, and now he's out here because he's upset."

"I get it. When Presley returned a few months ago, one of the boys wandered off. It was fucking hell. We were in the woods, searching for him for hours. Then, a few months later,

Logan overheard something he shouldn't have. It was difficult, but be honest and talk it out. Kids are resilient, I promise. Look, my best guess is he went somewhere to feel close to himself . . ."

Zach and I speak baseball, as does Austin. "He's got to be at a field somewhere."

"Try the ones he knows and then look for a local park or a game going on. I don't know, it's just what I would do if I were him."

"Same. Thanks, Zach."

"Call me and let me know when you find him."

I agree and then hang up, making my run back to the field.

When I get there, I ask again if anyone has seen him. I don't get the response I was hoping for, but I go in anyway.

I rush through the same way I took when I brought them here the other day and emerge by the dugout. I scour the field and don't see him.

"Austin, where the hell are you?"

I turn around to head back out, and that's when I see something that shouldn't be there. Over at the very end of the dugout is a silhouette.

My heart begins to pound, and I run over and find him just sitting there, arms wrapped tight around his stomach, head down.

A part of me wants to yell out, but I don't. I've been him before—broken, sad, lonely, and unsure of what to do. Back then, there was a little girl who would just come sit beside me. She didn't say anything, she just let me know she was there, and it was enough to let me know I would be okay.

So, I'll follow her example.

I send a quick text to Devney before I make my way closer.

Me: I found him. He's okay. I'll bring him home soon.

Two seconds later a response comes.

Devney: Thank God. Hurry please. I'll let the police know.

I slip my phone back in my pocket and take a seat next to Austin. He looks up at me, eyes puffy from tears, and then he puts his head back down. I lean back, crossing my legs in front of me, and just let him come around.

After a few minutes and a lot of looking over at me, he speaks.

"You're upset."

"I'm not upset. I was terrified that something happened to you."

He wipes his face. "Is Aunt Devney mad?"

"No, she's not mad. She's relieved you're okay and probably upset, but I don't think she's mad."

Austin sighs and then adjusts his leg.

"Where are your crutches?" I ask.

"I left them outside the park. I couldn't get in with them."

I tell myself not to get angry at that. "Are you hurt?"

He shakes his head.

Well, at least there's that. Still, I need to get to the bottom of it and then get him home. "Why did you run off?"

His gaze goes to home plate and then back to me. "I don't want to go back to Sugarloaf."

"Why?"

"Because everything there is sad."

I remember feeling the same way. Bad things happened there. People died there. Fathers became abusive assholes and ruined the lives of kids. It was the place where dreams were crushed, and mothers were lost.

Telling Austin how wrong he is or that it will be better won't change the fact that, to him, it's the reality of his life.

"Aunt Devney and I aren't sad."

He looks over. "I heard the truth."

The dread in my stomach tightens, and I do everything to make him say it. If he heard the truth about him not moving here, then I'm not going to be the one to tell him that Devney is really his mother.

"What's that?"

"That Aunt Devney isn't my aunt."

I was afraid of that. Still, I won't lie to him, but this isn't my conversation to have. So, I'll tell him how I feel about the whole thing and maybe he'll be able to understand.

"Life is hard. When you're a grown-up, you have to decide what's right and wrong at that moment. As a kid, you just feel and do something, not knowing the consequences."

"Like running away?"

"Yeah. And even when you grow up, you still make bad decisions and sometimes, when you run away from your problems, you never really get to stop. It happened to me, when I was in college, something happened, and instead of doing what I should've, I made a different choice and ran. It's taken me a really long time to finally be able to stop."

"Was I what you were running from? Are you my father?" he asks.

"No, I wish I was, though."

"You do?"

I nod. "You're a great kid, and I love Devney very much.

However, if you were my son, we would've made a different choice. You might have never had your mom and dad in your life the way you did. I think you should talk to your aunt. Let her explain, and maybe you can both find a way to understand, but running away is never the right answer."

"I'm sorry." His lip quivers, and my heart breaks a bit.

"I know you are, buddy. How about we go back and let Devney fuss over you?"

"She's going to be so upset."

"She probably will be, but if she didn't love you so much, she wouldn't have known you were gone or be as worried as she is."

I scoop him up and carry him to where he left his crutches. I don't know how he got all the way over here without them, and right now, I don't want to know. He's safe, and I didn't have to break my promise to Devney.

The rest, we can figure out.

When the apartment door opens, Devney practically lunges at him, pulling him into her arms. Tears fall between the two of them, and she just keeps touching his face.

"You're okay? Nothing is hurt?"

"I'm okay."

"You're sure? Did you check him over?" she asks me.

"I did. He was fine. He's upset, but he'll be okay."

The police officer walks toward us. "I'm glad you are safe, little man. I have to get back out there."

Devney looks up at her and smiles softly. "Thank you for

everything. Thank you guys for not giving up and for staying here with me."

"Not a problem." She looks back at Austin. "You don't run off again, okay?"

"I promise I won't."

"Good. You've got a lot of people who love you."

"Yes, ma'am."

She nods at me and then heads out, which leaves the three of us alone with the elephant in the room.

Devney wipes her face with both hands and lets out a deep sigh. "I don't know what to do with this, Austin. I'm not sure if I should yell at you, cry, ground you, beg you to never do this to me again, or . . . I don't know."

He looks up at her, shame filling the brown eyes that mirror hers. "I just didn't want to leave."

"That's no excuse to run away."

"I know that, but then I heard you . . . I was just going to ask you guys a question and . . . I . . ."

She looks up at me, and I nod, letting her know it's what she feared. "You heard I was really your biological mother."

Austin sniffles as she cups his cheek. "How could you lie to me all this time?"

"I'll go in the other room so you two can talk," I offer, but she grabs my hand.

"No. Stay. Please."

"If that's what you want." I sit at the table, unsure of how this will go. When I was his age, I was a tornado, and no one knew which way the path would go.

She takes a seat, moving it so we're both in front of her. "I never wanted you to find out like this, Austin. Never. It was honestly something I never thought you'd need to know, but things changed for all of us after the accident."

"You promised me that you'd never lie. You swore that I could always count on you!"

"And I didn't lie. I told you I loved you. I told you I'd always be there for you and that, no matter what, you were the most precious boy in my life. I kept that promise, Austin. At least I've always tried to." She tries to take his hand, but he doesn't let her.

"If you loved me, you would've kept me! You never would've let me go to live with anyone else."

I sit here, hating the hurt in Devney's eyes and knowing how hard this must be for her. The shame and sadness she's felt over her decision can't be easy.

"No, I love you so much that I gave you to my brother and sister-in-law, the two people who I knew would love you every bit as much as I would but would be able to give you all the things I couldn't. I was young and stupid and beyond sad. Your biological father and I haven't spoken since the day I told him I was pregnant. I did the most impossible and incredibly difficult thing in the world when I handed you over. I cried, but I knew, deep down in my soul that it was the right thing. If I kept you, it would've been because I wasn't strong enough or didn't love you enough to do what was right for you."

He slams his hand on the table and tears fall. "Stop saying that!"

He reminds me so much of myself when I was young that it's hard to watch. The anger at life not going my way was sometimes too much to take. Right now, he has an outlet, and it's Devney.

She tucks her brown hair behind her ear and releases a deep sigh. "I know you're angry, and you have every right to be. But I also want you to know that I stayed in Sugarloaf because I needed to be close to you. I was so lucky to get to be a part of your life, go to your games, hug you, teach you to ride a horse, and all the other things we shared. You have been my world from the minute I knew I was pregnant, but part of doing the right thing for the person you love the most is letting them go where it's best for them."

Her words hit me in the chest like a boulder. This is what she has been asking of me and I've been unable to do it. She can't move here because of him, and I can't ask her to because I love her more than anything.

She has to put him first, just as I have to do that for her.

I look to her, tears falling freely down her cheeks. "Love is a sacrifice that we make at the expense of our own wants. We think of the other person's needs before our own and act knowing that, even if it hurts us, it's what we need to do." Devney's lip trembles, and I focus back on Austin. "If she didn't love you the way she did, she would've made different choices that maybe would have meant you never played baseball. Maybe you would've stayed in Colorado, and who knows where you would all be. I know you're in pain, but you have the most amazing gift of all. You had two parents who loved you as though you were theirs, and you have your mother here, getting to love you with her whole heart."

"It was all a lie. Everyone lied to me. They weren't my parents."

I lean down so we're eye to eye. "What makes a parent isn't just where you come from, Austin. I had the most amazing mother and the worst father imaginable. He was cruel and hit me and my brothers because he was so angry and hated himself. I would've given anything to have someone like Jasper as my dad."

"You wouldn't have hit me," he says as he stares at Devney.

"No, but I couldn't have given you anything close to what your parents could, and that's what they were, Austin. They were your mother and father. I know it's hard to understand, and I'm so sorry you're learning about it like this, but I know you believe that I love you and that they loved you too."

He looks down and nods. "I do."

"And in your heart, you know I will always be here for you."

He shakes his head again. "I just don't understand, and I'm . . . sad."

She puts her finger under his chin and lifts it. "And that's okay. There are still times when I don't understand stuff, and I'm a grown-up. Days that I struggled so hard when I had to drop you off at home, but then I remembered that you were in the best place. You were so loved and happy and I got to be with you anytime I wanted. Your mom and dad never told me no when it came to being with you. All the things we did, we did because the three of us loved you so much, and we always put you first. Do you know how lucky you were to have them too?"

"Would you have ever told me?"

Her shoulders slump a bit. "I don't know . . . I like to think I would have, and I thought about it. It was your seventh birthday, and you were so sick you couldn't get out of bed, do you remember?"

"Yes."

"You had to go to the hospital, and they wouldn't let anyone in other than the parents. It was the first time I hated that I couldn't tell anyone that I was also your parent, but I knew it was a selfish reaction. Your mom and I talked about telling you around a certain age, but . . . I don't know, Austin. I might have told you, but we may never have either. If your mom and dad were alive right now, we definitely wouldn't be having this conversation, but a part of me is glad you know. You are my son. You're my whole world, and there's nothing I won't give up for you."

Including me.

She's being his mother just like she's always been, choosing the welfare of her child over herself.

It's what my mother would've done.

Austin looks back to Devney and wipes his nose on his arm. "I'm sorry I ran away, Aunt Devney."

"I'm sorry I hurt your heart."

The two of them sit there, looking at the other. How I never saw their resemblance before is beyond me. They are mirror images right now. Both broken, scared, and afraid of trusting what could be.

"Austin," I say, hoping to ease the tension, "there is nothing I would've given to have someone love me like a mother would after I lost mine. You have a gift right in front of you. Someone who loves you, has been there for you, and will always be. You can be angry and hurt, but you can also know that your parents loved you so much that, if they were ever gone, they wanted you to be with Devney. You can choose to let this destroy how special your bond is or you can figure it out together."

His brown eyes look to me, and while they are heavy with sadness, there is also a spark of hope in them. He loves his aunt. He always has, and now there's a new dynamic to them, one that is more complicated than just grief. It'll take time, but they will be able to make it through it together.

He moves into her arms, and she crushes him to her chest. The two of them cry, holding on to each other. Something wet drips down my own cheek.

She looks up at me and mouths the words, *Thank you.*

It's me who should be thanking her. For giving me hope. For giving me love. And for giving me the best few months I've ever had, even though it means I won't get more.

forty

"Is he asleep?" Sean asks as I enter the bedroom.

He's sitting up, back against the headboard, reading on his phone. I try not to notice how incredibly sexy he looks, but I fail. He always looks this way. No shirt, a dusting of scruff on his face, and hair haphazardly disheveled from running his fingers through it. But it's the eyes that get me. They're green with flecks of yellow around the edges and the dark black rim that makes me feel as though I can see into his soul.

"He is."

"Good. You guys talk more?"

I nod and make my way toward the bed. I'm not sure what I'm supposed to do. Our fight earlier left things in a very strange place. I can't remember a time when I didn't know what to say to fix things between us.

Sean sighs and pats the bed. "I don't want to make tonight any harder on us."

"I don't either."

"Then just let me love you, Devney."

God, that sounds good. "I need you to hold me," I tell him.

He puts the phone on the table beside him and lifts the covers. I don't hesitate before climbing in. My body gravitates toward him like a magnet, needing the person who is my other half. I lie on his chest, listening to the sound of his heart as his hand travels up and down the length of my spine.

Words aren't needed for us to know how the other is feeling. I can taste the relief and also the sadness of all that happened and all that is yet to come.

"Sean?"

"Yes?"

I run my hand across his stomach and pull myself tighter. "Thank you for finding him and bringing him back."

"I would've searched the world if that was what it took."

There's nothing this man wouldn't do for me, and I'm a fool for even thinking of letting him go.

"Can we rehash all of this when we get back to Sugarloaf and just have tonight for us?"

Sean shifts, and I'm forced to look into his eyes. "Not another word, Dev. I've got you for tonight. Just trust me."

I trust him with my life.

His hands move to my face, cupping me as though I'm breakable. The tenderness he uses warms me to the tips of my toes. Sean would never hurt me. He'd break himself in half before ever allowing me to be the victim.

I watch the myriad of emotions dance through his eyes. Love, hope, sadness, fear, and then desire.

Oh, the desire is strongest, and he pulls me to him at the same moment I move toward him. Wanting him has never been an issue.

It's keeping him.

I won't allow my thoughts to wander there because he's mine right now, and I'll always be his.

Sean's lips move to mine in the sweetest kiss. There's heartbreak and longing mixed with love, and I cling to the last. Tonight, I will love him like there is no tomorrow. As though our days like this are everlasting and we don't ever have to say goodbye.

We kiss slowly, letting our tongues glide together as one kiss turns into another. His hand moves into my hair, tilting my head so he can get a better angle. Kissing him is like that first breath of air in the morning. It's filled with hope that the day can be great and ushers in the feeling of peace that washes over you. I want to kiss him forever, allow myself the serenity that comes from being in his arms.

"I love you," he whispers against my cheek. "I love you, and I am going to make love to you tonight."

I lean my head back and let out a soft groan when his lips move to my neck.

"You're so beautiful. I could do nothing but look at you all day and find something new that I find perfect."

"I'm not perfect."

"You are for me."

His mouth covers mine, stopping the words that were going to escape my lips. He's the one who's perfect.

I wasn't lying when I said he was the dream, because he is.

He shifts, his weight braced above me, and he lifts my shirt over my head before he removes my bra. When Sean looks at me, his eyes are a liquid fire that threatens to melt me. "Perfect." His voice is husky before he moves his head to lick my nipple.

My fingers thrust into his hair, holding him there as he takes it into his mouth. He sucks, licks, and flicks it before moving to the other side.

"Sean." I moan his name when he does it again.

"Tell me what you want, Devney."

"You."

He chuckles. "Good thing, sweetheart, because you're going to have me. Do you want me to make you come?"

Is that really a question?

Sean doesn't give me a moment to respond before he moves his mouth back to my breast.

"Do you?" he asks again before going to the other side. He moves one hand down to my pants and slips inside. "Are you wet for me? Do you want me to touch you here, sweetheart?"

"Yes."

I want it all. I am so overwhelmed and in need that it's too much. Thinking is beyond me when his finger moves to my clit.

"Does that feel good?"

My hips move, and I nod. "God, yes."

He drives me higher, moving faster in a steadier circular motion. I feel the peak coming quickly, and I want to run to it, fly off the edge, and free fall, but right when I'm cresting the top, he stops moving.

The free fall back to the bottom is so fast that my eyes fly open and I struggle for breath. "Sean?"

"Yes, sweetheart?"

"Why did you stop?" I look around to see if there's a reason like my nine-year-old son in the room or something.

His nose runs along the column of my throat. "Because I'm going to draw this out for as long as I can."

"Please, baby," I whine, needing him to touch me again.

He pulls my shorts off and kisses his way down. "Sit up,"

he orders. "Lean on your elbows and watch me."

I do as he says, pushing myself up as he lifts my knees.

"Don't take your eyes off me or I'll stop. Understand?"

I nod.

Sean takes the awkward and shyness away from me. I don't feel self-conscious when we're together. I feel empowered and beautiful . . . as if I'm the only woman in the world he wants.

His strong hands move my knees apart, and I watch as his tongue licks at my clit. I want to close my eyes, not because it's not incredibly arousing to watch but because I am overcome with pleasure.

The need for him to keep going keeps me from doing it.

He watches me watch him, and it's so hot that I could catch the house on fire.

My teeth bite into my lower lip as he brings me back up the mountain. He pushes me higher than before, moving the peak farther away than it was before. Each swipe of his tongue thrusts me up. God, I can see it.

I moan, keeping my eyes on him, watching him love me with his mouth. And then it's too much, and I can't hold back anymore. Each glorious second feels like heaven, and I never want to come down.

Head on the pillow, I pant as I feel him enter me in one thrust.

My eyes open, wanting to memorize every second. "I love you," I tell him.

"Say it again."

"I love you."

He pushes deeper.

"More," Sean demands.

"I love you. I love you. I need you. I'm yours!" I say the words with every ounce of my emotion. It's all true. I love him more than anything. I need him so much, I'm afraid of losing him. I'm his, and I always will be. No matter what happens, that will never change.

His hands frame my face, and his green eyes are pleading. "Stay with me."

Confliction tears through me so hard that it hurts. My head is at war with my heart. I want to stay. I want him forever. Our life could be so beautiful, but the fear screams at me, telling me not to speak.

I fight for the words . . . the ones that my soul is desperate for me to say. To tell him I'll stay by his side and we'll work it out.

He pushes harder, deeper, as though he knows he has to pull it from me. It is the most connected to another person I've ever been. It's like our bodies are talking while our mouths can't.

Sean entwines our fingers and then stretches so my hand is pinned to the pillow above my head. We're touching from the tips of our fingers to the edge of our toes. Not a part of me isn't his right now.

He thrusts again, and I feel him begging for me to give him the answer. He's fighting for me. For the life we want.

I open my mouth to say it, but nothing comes, and then I feel him fall apart. He yells as he comes, and then I feel him leave me.

forty-one

"Well, this is the last of it," Devney says as she holds the box in her arms. Austin is in the car, buckled up and ready to return to his house.

"It seems like it."

She kicks the dirt and releases a heavy sigh. "Will you come by at all?"

I would move the world if I thought it would change things, but it won't. It is selfish of me to ask her to move to Florida, and I won't do it. We could try to do it long distance, but we know it won't work. It'll be hard enough on her trying to get Austin settled here. I can't ask her to travel at all, and my schedule is unyielding.

"I'd like to, but I don't know . . ."

"If we should?"

The break in her voice tears at my soul. "I don't mean it like that. I just don't want to make this harder on you."

"I don't think that's possible. This is absolute torture right now."

"It's not easy for me either."

She looks to the car and back to me. "You're my best friend, Sean. Please tell me that we didn't destroy twenty years of history in a few months. I can't . . . I can't lose you, and you promised I wouldn't."

I step toward her, and my hand moves to her cheek so I can caress the soft skin with my thumb. "You will never lose me, but I am going to have to figure out how to stop loving you like this."

"I don't know that I ever will," she admits.

"I might not either."

A tear trails down her face, and I wipe it away. "Don't cry, sweetheart. This is the right thing, no matter how much it hurts. You have to think of Austin, and I will always do what is best for you."

Her beautiful eyes shut, sending another stream down her face. "All I want is to drop this box and fuse myself to you. I want to beg you to stay even though I know you can't."

I shift, letting my hand drop as my heart pounds relentlessly. "I can stop playing."

"No." She shakes her head. "Absolutely not, Sean Arrowood. Baseball is your child. I wouldn't ask you to stop playing for the same reasons you wouldn't ask me to leave Austin behind."

"Baseball isn't everything."

"No, but you're not ready to give it up."

"I would for you."

"I won't let you."

And that's where my final Hail Mary begins and ends. Not to mention, if I broke my contract, it would cost me millions of dollars in penalties. All of this is so fucked.

My brother makes his way over and takes the box from her hands. "I'll go talk to Austin while you two say goodbye." She looks up at him with so much pain that Jacob winces before dropping a kiss to her temple. "Take your time."

There is no time. That's the fucking problem. I have a few weeks left here before my time is up and so is everything that matters in my life. I will have to walk away, and I feel as though my heart is tearing from my chest.

I love her. She's everything good in my world, and she's leaving. My world will never be the same again.

"I don't know how to say goodbye to you."

There is no barrier between us, and I step closer, pulling her to my chest. I hold her tightly, breathing in the soft scent of her shampoo. "We never say goodbye."

Her fingers tighten as she clings to me. "Thank you."

"For what?"

Slowly, her gaze lifts to mine. "For loving me."

"I'll love you forever."

"And I'll always have you."

I nod and release my hold. I have to be the one to do what's right. One of us has to be strong even though I hate that it has to be me. "You should go. God only knows what Jacob is teaching Austin."

Her smile looks pained, but she nods. Her lips part as though there's something she wants to say, but I take a step back.

There's nothing to make this easier and nothing we haven't already said.

We love each other, want each other, need each other, and yet, we can't have each other.

When we landed yesterday, we knew this was the end of

the road, and now, I have to watch her make the turn.

Devney gets to the door, opens it, and looks back at me one more time. She lifts her hand to wave, covers her mouth, and disappears.

I don't hear or notice my brother make his way to me. I just stand here, watching her taillights fade down the drive.

His hand rests on my shoulder. "I'm sorry, Sean."

"It was never going to work."

"Don't say that."

"It's why I never fought for it before. It's why I fucking lied and refused to let my feelings become more than friendship. Fuck! I knew this was a bad idea." I shove his hand off me and go out to the porch. I sit there, hoping the car will reappear.

He sits beside me in the rocking chair, quiet and so damn loud at the same time. Each time he looks at me, I can feel his disappointment.

"What?" I snap after I catch him looking at me again.

"You're sure it's over? There's no way you can work this out?"

"Yup. It's over."

"I don't get it."

I release a heavy breath through my nose and stare out at the dirt that is trying to settle back down. "Me either."

In fact, I don't get anything in life. My mother's death was horrible. Then there was our shitty ass father who beat us, killed two people, and almost destroyed all our lives. I mean, why the hell not lose the girl I love? What's one more thing at this point?

"She left because Austin is her son? I don't get it."

"It's complicated."

Jacob and I have always been close. I've told him everything, and he's been an open book to me. I don't know if it's because Declan always seemed so much older, so when I was with him, I tried to be cooler and more mature. When I was with Jacob, I was me. I could be calm, funny, and just laugh at life. Connor was the youngest, and he looked up to us, so we bossed him around.

And even though he's the one I'm closest to, I don't want to tell him anything. I want to scream, throw things, and leave this shithole of a town.

"Then uncomplicate it."

"Well, why didn't I think of that?" I ask sarcastically. "I mean . . . that's just fucking brilliant. I should go and make things easier for Dev and me because you mention it. Now, how to take the situation and make it better . . . any ideas, genius?"

"For one, you could stop being a dick and grow up."

I ignore him and lean back in the rocker, moving to the beat of my broken heart. Pain is my constant friend. It reminds me that it was real and I'm living through it.

After a few minutes of silence, Jacob speaks again. "Austin was upset."

"So am I."

"When we were sitting in the car, he just kept asking why you couldn't be his dad."

I blow out a deep breath. "Because I don't deserve the kid."

"You don't deserve Devney either right now. In fact, the only thing you should get is punched in the face."

"Try me," I taunt him.

He laughs with a shake of his head. "Yeah right, pretty boy. We all know you're not a fighter. Back to the issue of why you are a fucking idiot." I groan, wishing I had Declan's temper or Connor's right hook. "Want to explain why you let her go?" Jacob asks with a bit of annoyance in his tone.

"I didn't *let* her do anything. I tried to salvage it, but she was intent on going."

"Right." He nods. "I see. Makes total sense. When she was standing there crying it seemed like she was really excited about it. I hope my exit from this town is the same."

He doesn't see anything, and I might kill him. "At least now when you move back in a few weeks, you can stay in the house. Hell, go get your shit now because I can't stay here."

It's too much of Devney, and I've had enough heartbreak. She is everywhere in this house. The scent of her shampoo lingers in the shower, her laugh echoes in the kitchen, and her warmth is all over the bedroom. Only it's just my imagination because, not even twenty-four hours after we returned from Tampa, she left.

It's as though everything we shared disappeared with the dust from her tires.

"You're not a quitter, Sean. All the things that have come your way, you've found a way through."

"I can't make her love me."

He shrugs. "I don't think that's her problem."

I lean back in the rocking chair, not giving a shit that it's fucking freezing outside, I feel nothing. The numbness is welcome.

"She left, and that was her choice." She asked me to accept her decision, and that's what I'm doing.

"It's not as if you don't know where she's going."

"So what? You want me to show up there and beg her. I have some fucking pride." Something comes flying at my head, but I'm quick enough to bat it down. "What the fuck?"

"You need something to hit you upside the head, you fucking dumb shit."

"This isn't my fault."

"Maybe not," Jacob agrees. "I still think you're both idiots. You love her. She loves you. She's got a kid who loves you, and I'm pretty sure you love that kid. So, what's the damn problem? Marry the girl."

Oh, the kicker in that statement. "I told her I wanted to! She left anyway! You just watched her go. Do you not think I'm dying inside? I love her more than anything, and she left."

"You told her you wanted to marry her?"

I glare at my shit-for-brains brother. "You were supposed to be the smart one."

"Okay, asshole, let me rephrase that. Did you ask her to marry you or just let her in on the fact that it's something you wanted to have happen?"

"I told her."

"Not the same. I thought you were supposed to be the sweet brother with all the moves? Turns out, I got that trait."

I roll my eyes and huff. "Jacob, I'm usually able to handle this, but today . . . I'm done."

"Listen, I'm not trying to give you shit, I'm saying that it's a very different thing to tell a girl you want to marry her and asking her to marry you."

I don't know how he thinks I would ask her that when it was clear what her answer would be.

"That would make me an idiot if I asked."

"What the hell does that even mean? You're an idiot now!"

"She didn't want to marry me. Devney made up her mind once she got custody of Austin. We both knew how this was going to end. Sure, I wanted to think there was a chance I could sway her, but there wasn't. I was a fool to think I should ask it of her, and I have no right to push her."

In some ways, I don't blame her. She's in new territory and needs the support. I would be gone a lot, but I would've done what I could.

"You know? I think she's right," I tell Jacob with the defeat in my voice.

"What?"

"She was smart to walk away. All I can give her is a beautiful home without me in it. I'd be gone all the time, and she'd be in Tampa, raising Austin alone. It was never going to work. No matter how much we both wish it would've, we were starting at a disadvantage."

Jacob is quiet for a minute, assessing me. "Something tells me that not even you believe that line of bullshit."

"Spring training starts soon, and I have to start preparation for it. We'd have a few months, if that, before I was gone all the time. It's better this way."

"Yeah, totally better," Jacob agrees. "I mean, why the hell would you want to take her down there? I see what you mean about breaking up now being better. It's smart, man. Let her go. You know, I'll be here for the next six months, I'll take care of her."

I shift, ready to pounce, but the asshole is grinning. "Fuck you."

"Yeah, well, wake up, Sean. You're a fool if you think this is the right move. I've always been on your side. You are who helped me through all the crap after the accident, and I owe you, so here's me paying it back. Go get her. Marry her. Sit on her front step until she lets you in. Camp there if that's what it takes. If you love her, figure it the fuck out. No one in this world knows you like Devney Maxwell, and she's the one for you."

"I know that."

In every fiber of my being, I know she's the only girl I'll ever love. It doesn't matter who I might meet down the line, they'll pale in comparison. It would be cruel of me to even try, so I'll stay the way I've always been. No other woman will ever touch my heart, they can't anyway because she took it with her.

"Then stop this shit."

I blow out a heavy breath, the fog filling the air around me. "And how do I fix the issue?"

"Which one?"

"That she won't go to Florida, and I can't stay here. I'm in the middle of my contract and I can't get out. So, please, tell me how do I fucking fix this, Jacob? Because, right now, I don't see it. If you can figure it out, I'll be all for it because I don't know how to live like this. She's my fucking world."

He shrugs while leaning back with a cocky grin. "Finally, you ask the important question. You know, it's too bad you don't have an agent to help trade you somewhere like Philly or New York, huh?"

forty-two

"He leaves in a few days," Ellie reminds me as if I wasn't already incredibly aware of it.

I didn't want to come to this playdate. I knew that it was going to be an ambush the second she had Hadley call and ask me to come hang out with her. I can't say no to the girl, and Ellie knows it.

"By the way, having your daughter set this up was well played."

Ellie doesn't bother to look the slightest bit apologetic. "We do what we must. Back to the point I was making . . . Sean leaves soon."

"Yes, I know."

"And you're letting him go?"

I'm not *letting* anything happen, I'm . . . barely existing. I'm lost, drifting, and I miss him so much. I don't know how to live like this, and maybe I'm making a huge mistake. Ellie must understand to some extent.

"Can I ask you something?"

She smiles softly. "Would I have gone if it was Connor?"

I nod.

"I want to lie and tell you no," Ellie confesses. "I can't do it, though. I have the power of hindsight and know that life without Connor isn't the life I want. I have a family and love that I thought was for non-broken girls because of him. So, if you asked me now with two kids and a house, the answer is yes. But if you had asked me when I was living with an abusive man who made me think I wasn't worthy of love, then it probably would've been no."

Her honesty stuns me. I believed the answer I was going to get was all bubbly and without pause, but she gave me two answers from warring standpoints.

It's been two weeks without Sean, and I am hollow.

My heart aches for him. I roll over at night, tears on my pillow, reaching for arms that aren't there to hold me.

And I'm living in my brother's house, which is harder than I ever imagined. He's everywhere I look, and I can see the hurt and longing in Austin's eyes. All of this sucks, and we miss Sean.

"I don't know how to fix it, Ells. I really don't. Austin needs the stability that Sugarloaf can give him. To move him would be a huge mistake. Sure, he thinks he wants to be with Sean, we both do, but Sean isn't just some normal guy with a normal life."

"No, he isn't."

"And that means that even if we go there, we'll be just as away from him as we would be if we stayed here."

She looks into the living room where the kids are playing and then to me. "That's fair, and you don't want to try long distance?"

"Would you?"

Ellie shakes her head softly. "No, I wouldn't. If I couldn't have all of Connor . . ."

"It would be better to learn to live without him," I finish the sentiment.

"I guess."

I release a deep breath through my nose and turn away. I don't want to start crying again. It hurts too much. The idea of no Sean in my life is like cutting off an arm. He's been my constant, and everything I feared about falling in love with him is coming true.

Gone is the easy friendship that has been my companion through the dark times. He took the light when he stole my heart, and nothing will be the same anymore.

I miss my best friend.

I miss the man who knew my thoughts just by the look on my face.

I feel like I'm falling without a net, and it's scary.

"The worst part is that Sean was my person. He was the other half that made me feel secure," I say without looking at her. "I was afraid of losing that, but I took that chance anyway, and look where I am now."

Ellie gets up and comes around the table, her hand covers mine. "You're not alone. I know that we're not the same as Sean, but we are here for you, Devney."

"I know, I do, but Sean became so much more."

"He became the other half of you," she says, understanding layered in each word.

"Yes."

"Then, as someone who has screwed up more times than she can count, I can tell you that you shouldn't lose that. The road ahead is hard, but if you both want this, you can find a way to make it work. Connor and I didn't have it easy. God knows Declan and Sydney didn't. You and Sean are different, though. There's nothing standing in your way but yourselves."

I look at the little boy in the other room, arms crossed over his chest as Hadley tries to give him one of her toys—forcefully. He's the reason I can't go, and I'm okay with that. Austin is my son, and there's nothing I won't do to protect him from further pain.

"Maybe you see it that way, but that kid has been through a lot in the last few months. He's lost both parents, had surgery, and found out his aunt is really his mother. I won't add more on top of that."

She nods. "I remember being the same way. I thought that Hadley couldn't handle more change. She had watched her mother . . . well, go through hell, for sure. I convinced myself that, for her, I had to push back against a relationship with Connor."

"We're not the same," I tell her.

"I know. I just want you to know that, whatever you decide, Connor and I are here for you. You're not alone, and if there's anything you need, don't hesitate to ask."

"Thank you, Ellie."

"Don't mention it."

We sit and talk a bit more. She explains some of the school things for Austin that I was struggling with. We've been trying to get into a routine, but it's hard. He's angry and doesn't want to do his homework. Not to mention, he can't play baseball, and he's upset he wasn't there when his team won their last tournament.

It's been difficult, and I want to make it better, but I don't know how.

"Sean!" I hear joy in Austin's voice for the first time in a few days.

"Hey, little man!" There's a squeezing noise, and I look over to see Austin wrapped around his neck.

I quickly avert my eyes. Here I was, wishing I could see him and thinking about how much I miss him, but now that he's here, I'm not ready.

I haven't seen or heard his voice since I left. Neither of us has reached out, and I can't blame him.

Just the sound of his voice makes me ache.

Ellie looks to me and then gets to her feet, her head nodding as she goes to the doorway. "Hey, Sean."

"Ells." He kisses her cheek. "Sorry to barge in . . ."

"You're not. I just thought you'd be coming by later, that's all."

Then he turns to me, and I rise. The pull to him is too great. Our eyes meet, and two weeks' worth of pain, longing, and sadness washes over me in seconds.

He gives me a crooked smile and makes his way to me. "Dev, it's good to see you."

The knot in my chest gets tighter, and I fight back tears. I won't cry, not when I'm the one who left. "Good to see you too."

He stops just close enough for me to catch a trace of his musky cologne. "You guys doing okay?"

"Yeah, we . . . we just stopped over so Hadley and Austin could hang out."

"I see that."

"Are you having a good visit?"

I wish I were visiting you. I long for you every night. Please, find a way for us to work because I'm dead inside without you.

"Yes, it's been good to see friends," I say and hope he hears the slight dig.

He's my friend, and I haven't seen him. Two weeks of

looking over my shoulder, wondering if the ding on my phone would finally be him, and wondering if I'd see him anywhere in town.

A part of me was convinced he disappeared without saying goodbye. It might have been easier if he had.

"I'm sure it is." There's a wash of guilt that crosses his face. He knows I meant him.

Good.

"I've been in meetings."

Ellie's eyes jump between us as we volley the conversation. "Did your meetings go as you hoped?" she asks.

The look that passes between them leaves me curious. "They were productive."

Ellie clears her throat. "I'm going to take the kids out to the barn. Give you guys a chance to get this awkward conversation out without the walls having ears."

"Thanks, Ells."

She pats his arm and winks at me. "Anything for you two."

Once we're alone, I feel dizzy and have to fight the urge to throw myself into his arms and refuse to let him go.

Instead, I stand statue still and stare at the man I love.

Time has done nothing to diminish how much I want him. I don't know that a million years could lessen the feelings I have.

No, what we share is something that will never change.

I know. Right here, right now, that I can't watch him walk away again. Somehow, I have to have him. I love him enough to have him in whatever way possible.

"How are you?" I finally ask.

Sean takes a step closer. "I'm miserable. Lonely. And I miss the only person who matters in my life. How about you?"

My head jerks back, not expecting him to be honest. "Sean
. . ."

"No. I'm not going to lie to you. I'm miserable. I miss you,
and I love you. If that makes me an asshole, then that's what
I am. I knew you were here, so I came. Want to know why?"

I look up at him, the walls feeling as if they're closing in.
"I can guess."

"Can you?"

I nod. If he feels even half as bad as I do, I know why he
came. He couldn't stop himself. "I hate this. Now what?" I
ask, feeling nervous.

"Now, we talk."

I want to fall to the floor and weep. "Talking changes nothing, Sean. We've talked, and we're back here each time."

"Then you listen, and I'll talk."

He pushes the stray hair from my face, and I resist the urge
to rest my fingers on his strong chest. I long to feel the muscles
beneath that shirt, the strength in his arms, and the shield he
provides around me.

There is nothing about him I don't want and need, I just
hate that he lives there while I'm stuck here.

"Does this not hurt you?" I ask. "There has to be a way to
make it stop, right?"

"You have no idea how much pain I'm in without you,
Devney. You can't fucking fathom how much I miss you, but
we're going to talk. I'm not rehashing anything we haven't
already said."

Hope blooms in my chest, but it fizzles when I remember
there isn't anything we haven't already talked about. The situation is the same as it was two weeks ago, only now, having to
stand here and look at him sends new cuts through my tattered
heart.

Still, I'm unable to push him away. I will take the scars

because he's worth the pain.

He extends his hand to the table, and I sit. There's no way I could outrun him if I tried, and I'm not going to squander the chance to stare at him.

His thick, dark brown hair is in disarray, and his green eyes look tired, but there's a mix of hope in there. The scruff on his face is a little longer, but no less sexy. Sean is even more gorgeous . . . because he's here.

"Okay, I'll listen."

He sits beside me and takes my hand in his. The feel of his skin against mine is a balm that heals a damaged part of me. It's sad that this simple gesture can both break and mend me. I'm a fucking mess.

"For a long time, I've loved you. Loved you more than I loved the girl who bought me a bat and made mud pies. Maybe it was because you did that. Still, I fought it. I found excuse after excuse to resist the feelings I had for you. I dated girls who looked like you, told myself it was just a coincidence, and put you in a box in my heart. I couldn't open it, I couldn't even think about touching it because I knew, once I did, that would be it." His thumb brushes against the top of my hand, and I fight back the tears once more. "You didn't just open it, Devney, you tore it apart, threw it out, and took up residence in my whole fucking life. There is not a part of me that doesn't belong to you. So, I can't do this without you. I can't go back to the way it was because that life doesn't exist anymore." There's no fighting them anymore. The tears fall, and he pulls me into his arms. "Don't cry, sweetheart."

"Don't make me love you any more than I do because I can't. My heart can't love you more. It can't contain it, and you're killing me. I'll find a way to do long distance or something, but I need you."

He takes my face in his hands and stares at me. Those green eyes penetrate my soul, and then my hands are mirroring his. I hold him, needing to see him, really see him again.

Page 365, the one for me.

I have never thought love like this was possible for me, and now I'm here.

"I understand what you need. I know why you can't come to Florida, and honestly, I'd be the worst asshole imaginable if I asked it of you."

"But . . ."

"You have to do what's best for Austin."

He told me he wasn't going to rehash old points, and now, we're sitting in Ellie's kitchen, and I'm sitting on his lap crying.

My hands drop. "Again, Sean. Again we're back here."

"We're not. Listen to me, we're not." He leans in, kisses my tears, and then my lips. "I love you, Devney Maxwell. I love you more than you will ever know, and that's why I'm no longer playing for Tampa."

I gasp, my stomach drops, and I want to throw up. He didn't. Please tell me he didn't quit or do something stupid. Not for me. Not when this has been his dream since he was Austin's age. I've been on the receiving end of living the life you never wanted. I can't watch him do that.

"Sean, you can't!"

"I can, and I did."

Sean smiles at me, but all I can feel is the regret that surges through my body. He has no idea what he's done. How much he'll regret it. "I don't want to be the reason you give up your dream."

"You're the one who said I have to choose one or the other, Devney, and I choose you. Each time. Every day and twice on Sundays."

"I won't let you do this!"

He just smiles wider and leans forward to rest his forehead to mine. "It's already done."

I close my eyes, breathing in deep as I brush my nose against his. "Why? Why would you?"

"Because you're the one for me, Devney Maxwell, and I won't live without you."

"You're going to hate me. Maybe not today or tomorrow, but one day, you'll see me as the girl who stole your dreams instead of your heart."

"Never, sweetheart. Not possible. Besides, you didn't ask the right question."

I pull back, not sure what the hell he means. "What question?"

"How did I do it?"

My eyes narrow slightly as confusion fills me. "Do what?"

"Get to keep you, not move you and Austin to Florida, and still have baseball."

Air fills my lungs as I feel like I can breathe for the first time. "How?"

"I requested a trade to Philadelphia."

forty-three

I wait for her to say something, but she just looks at me, head tilting side to side.

"You're coming back . . . to Pennsylvania?"

I shrug as though it's no big deal because, the truth is, it isn't. It wasn't even a question. As soon as Jacob said it, it became the only option.

Move here.

Be with her.

Be happy.

Who cares that this town makes my skin crawl and memories of my father are everywhere? I need her.

Devney is what matters, and so long as I have her, I can live here . . . where she is.

It may have cost me a lot of stress and arguments with my agent, but we got it done. I'll take a lot less money, but none of it matters as long as this is a solution to the problem we had.

"I am. I have to pack my shit in Tampa, sell my condo, and then . . . I don't know . . . I'll need a place to live. Any ideas?"

Her smile lights up the room. "You're going to move here?"

"That's the plan."

"For how long?"

"Forever."

She launches herself into my arms, which knocks us both back to the ground. Her lips are on mine a second later, and I crush her to my chest.

"You're serious?" she asks between kisses.

"Completely." I roll us so I'm on top and look down at her. "There's nothing that I wouldn't do for you, Dev. When I said I had you, I didn't mean as long as it was convenient."

She touches my cheek with a grin. "I was trying to talk myself into going with you. Somehow, some way, I knew I had to be with you. It just . . . it seemed so impossible."

"It still won't be easy. I'll have to travel, but when I'm home, I'll be right here."

"I can deal with difficult. I just can't deal with not having you at all."

I bring my lips to hers again, needing to kiss her. For two weeks, I went without her, and now that I'm here, it's like opening my eyes for the first time. The light is bright and pure, and there's a sense of hope in the air.

"Well, thank God you're not my wife," Connor's voice comes from the door.

I look over. "Do you mind?"

"Considering you're in my house, on my floor? Yeah, I kinda do mind."

Devney's cheeks redden, and she pushes me off her and then I help her to her feet. "Sorry, Duckie."

He rolls his eyes. "It's fine, Shrimpy."

And then she does the same. "I hate that name."

"Yeah, I'm not too fond of mine either," he quips.

"I love mine."

They both turn to me, faces showing their displeasure as if I were the one who handed out the nicknames instead of Declan. I'm the only one my asshole brother spared. I don't know why, and I've never been stupid enough to ask.

"Which is why no one uses it," Connor says with his arms over his chest.

"Say it."

"No."

I smirk at my brother. "Come on, you know you want to."

He flips me off.

"Dev?"

"Not a chance."

I sigh dramatically. "It's fine. I'll say it myself . . . Stud. I'm the stud. I'm studly, manly, and the guy that all girls just can't help falling for."

"Oh for fuck's sake. He meant it like you're a block of wood in the wall."

I shrug. "If it makes you feel better to think that . . ."

"Either way, you want to make out with Devney, do it somewhere my kids won't walk in and see it."

I pull her to my side and kiss her temple. "Fine by me."

Her head shakes before she lays it on my shoulder. "He's stupid."

"Yeah, like wood."

"Do you think you could watch Austin for me?" Devney asks Connor. "Just a few hours."

"Sure . . . is everything okay?"

She looks up at me, a mischievous smile on her lips. "Yeah, I just have some wood I need to tend to."

And this is why I love her. Well, this and many other reasons.

"So you're moving in here? Where the fuck am I going to stay? Back in that damn shack?" Jacob asks as he rubs his hands together over the bonfire.

All four of us are together again. We are all living in the same town, at the same time, after we swore it would never happen.

"Devney sold Jasper and Hazel's place, and we took a vote for whether we could stay in the house until we decide if we want to build on the land."

"I didn't fucking vote."

Connor laughs. "That's because you don't count."

Declan nods. "You were in Hollywood, it was done in person."

Jacob groans and flops into his chair. "I hate you assholes."

"Feeling is mutual."

Within just a week, she was able to list and sell the property to a new family that was staying in a temporary home while they looked for a place. The father, Luke Allen, was killed overseas on what should have been a routine mission, and his wife, Brenna, moved here so the kids could be near their family.

Luke was a good guy, and I played ball with him on our high school team. When we heard about what happened, we made it a point to try to help them out. Connor helped get

Jasper's place updated a bit while I worked on getting all the animals rehomed, Jacob was able to get the kids some signed stuff that no one asked for, and Declan pulled some strings to get Brenna the house without paying extra fees or whatever.

All I know is that Devney took the money, and now Austin has a college fund set aside.

"Well, if I have to stay on Arrowood land, then I'm staying at Declan's house."

"The hell you are."

"You have four bedrooms!"

He shrugs. "I don't have enough space for your ego."

"Oh, please."

"I have to agree with him," I tack on. "It's only gotten more inflated since you signed that movie deal."

"Listen, the kid who thinks you're amazing is Brenna Allen's son," Connor explains while grabbing a drink.

Jacob rubs his hands in front of the fire. "The kid Ellie told me about? That's Luke's son?"

"One in the same," Dec affirms.

Apparently, Brenna's youngest son, Sebastian, is a huge fan of Jacob's. His one wish was to meet him and we've all been helping to make sure that happens, only Jacob has a big heart and wants to do more.

"Wow. I didn't realize. Connor, did you serve with him?"

Connor shakes his head. "I didn't know he was in the navy. Apparently, he was a fighter pilot and his plane went down during a training mission."

"Crazy," I say, feeling the mood dip a bit.

"Yeah, I feel for the kid. I'm hoping to spend some time with him and make this a little easier for him."

"Nothing like having a fake superhero as your new best friend," Declan says and raises his glass.

"Instead of an old fart with a hero complex?" Jacob counters.

This is going to get ugly—fast.

But I'm really not one to get in the middle of things, so I lean back, letting the fire warm me as the two of them trade jabs.

Tonight was supposed to be a night where we drank beer, made jokes about the women in our lives, poked fun at Jacob for being the last single brother standing, and generally spent some time bonding. Know whose idea it was? The women in our lives.

They're under some misguided notion that we need to spend more time as a family unit since the last nine years was a shitshow with varying degrees of a mess.

"How long before Declan punches him?" Connor asks, leaning in.

"Maybe another five insults."

"Twenty bucks says he makes it ten."

I grin at my brother. "You're on."

"So, when are you going to pop the question to Devney?"

My head jerks because I haven't told anyone about the ring I bought this morning. "How did you know?"

He smirks with a shrug. "I guessed. But do yourself a favor and don't wait. Soak up every possible moment you can with her. I think about Dad a lot lately with that. I think he squandered his time, thinking she'd always be around, and that was why he snapped."

I don't give a shit why he snapped, but the one thing we've never been able to say about the bastard was that he didn't love our mother. When she died, he was gone too. I think about how I would feel if it were Devney and for the first time in my adult life, I can empathize with that loss.

I would be broken.

Declan gets to his feet and puffs out his chest.

Connor leans in, and I do the same. "I'm going to win," I mutter.

He scoffs. "Just one more, Dec . . ."

Come on, Jacob, go for the jugular.

"You're just jealous that Mom loved me more, I'm better-looking, and I didn't spend eight years pining after a girl who I was too big of a pussy to go back to!" Jacob yells while pointing his finger in Declan's chest.

And then . . . Declan snaps, and I put my hand out for my twenty bucks.

Nothing like Arrowood bonding time.

forty-four

"Where are you taking me now?" I ask Sean as I sit in his car with a blindfold on.

"You'll see when we get there. No peeking!"

Tomorrow would've been the day that Sean went back to Florida. I can't help thinking about it or wondering how I would feel had he actually gone. I'm grateful he didn't.

"I just want a hint."

He takes my hand in his and chuckles. "We'll be gone for eleven days."

"Eleven days?" I yell, tossing my blindfold off.

"Devney!"

"What? You didn't say anything about *days*! You made it seem as if we were going on a date!"

He groans under his breath. "So much for a surprise."

"What about Austin?"

"Austin? What? He can't just feed himself?"

I glare at him, but he ignores me. "I'm serious."

"Trust me, woman. I dropped him off at your parents' house, who know exactly where we are going. Austin is also well aware, so calm yourself."

I lean back in my seat, indignant that I really don't have anything to be upset about. He thought of everything—as usual.

"I'm calm."

"And you've ruined the surprise."

"Were you driving to where we're going for eleven days?"

He huffs. "No."

"Then I didn't really ruin anything since, even with the blindfold on, I knew I was in a car."

Sean keeps riding down the highway without replying. We pull into the small airport, and excitement hits me. Wherever we are going, it involves another trip on a private plane. I am really going to have a hard time ever flying commercial again if he keeps this up.

I rack my brain, trying to figure out if I've ever mentioned somewhere I'd like to go, but there have been so many dreams shared between us. Like, I know that one of his bucket list places is to go to Ireland to see where his grandmother was born. And the Maldives, which is pretty much on everyone's bucket list. I know we won't do either of those because of the flight time, so it has to be somewhere reasonable.

After popping the trunk, he makes his way to my side of the car, opens my door, and extends a hand. "My love."

I smile and place my palm in his. "Kind sir."

When I get upright, he gives me a sweet kiss. "You can call me sir later."

"If you deserve it."

"Oh, I think I'm going to more than earn it."

"Yeah?" I taunt.

"Oh, yes."

I tap his nose and wink. "We shall see."

We board the plane and get up in the air without my finding out where we're off to. There's a part of me that doesn't care because we're going on a trip—alone. I wouldn't give a shit if we just circled in the sky. Sean pulls me to the couch so that my back is to his chest and his arms are holding me close. He's quiet, seeming to be lost in whatever is on his mind.

Neither of us speak much, just enjoying the silence. It's one of the things I love most about us. There isn't a need to fill the void because we're just comfortable together.

One of the pilots exits the cockpit and heads our way, and I smile when I recognize him from the last time I was on this plane. "We'll be making our descent in about thirty minutes."

"Great, Sam, thank you."

"It's my pleasure."

"Sam?" I call out.

"Yes, Ms. Maxwell?"

"Where exactly are we arriving at?"

He smiles, looks over at Sean, and then shrugs. "I'm not sure, ma'am, I'm only the second in command."

"Traitor."

Sean laughs. "Sweetheart, I knew you'd try to ask the flight crew, so I tipped them to ensure you were kept in the dark."

I grumble under my breath and hate that it's nighttime and I can't look out the window and try to guess where we are.

Another few minutes, and I'll figure it out.

We land, and when we deplane, the warm air hitting me

has a smile tugging at my lips. "It's hot here."

He nods. "It is."

"And I smell the ocean."

"Nothing gets by you."

I slap his chest. "Jerk."

Sean's laugh is low as he takes my hand. "Come on."

We start to walk to where there's a limo waiting. I can hear the swaying of the palm trees in the warm wind. It's paradise, and I start to realize where he brought me.

My hand clings to Sean's bicep, and I fight back the urge to squee. I can't believe he whisked me away to an island without me knowing. "You know, this is a pretty extravagant pre-Valentine's Day present."

He chuckles. "This isn't a present."

"No? What would you call it?"

Sean's lips press to the top of my head. "I'd call it the beginning."

I have no idea what exactly it's the beginning of, but it's definitely off to a good start. If all beginnings are this way, count me in.

But then I think about how our entire relationship has gone, and I realize it's always been this way. When we were little, we were instant best friends. It didn't matter that I was a dumb girl or that he was a stupid boy, we were just Sean and Devney. As we grew up, we didn't let other people interfere with our relationship, he was my number one and I was his. If he was dating someone I hated, he dumped her. I never really got to date because of his overprotective ass, but I know, in my heart, I would've done the same.

Sean and I have never really struggled. We're both adventurous, like to laugh, and lack reservations when in regards to the other. It's probably why I fought against loving him as more than a friend.

I knew that this would be us. We'd fall so hard, so fast, so deeply in love that there would be no going back.

And now, here we are . . . on an island—together.

We approach a driver, who opens the door for us.

"Mr. Arrowood, my name is Dennis, and I will be your driver to the resort."

"Thank you, Dennis. This is Ms. Maxwell."

He kisses the top of my hand. "Ms. Maxwell, allow me to be the first to welcome you to St. Lucia."

My heart pounds faster. "St. Lucia?"

The world seems to fade around me as I stare at him, waiting to see if this is a joke. Sean gives me a sweet smile that says it isn't a joke and, in fact, it was very purposeful. "Twelve years ago, my best friend wrote me a letter about her dreams, do you remember?"

I nod with tears in my eyes. "I do."

"Do you remember what you wrote?"

"That I wanted to have a destination wedding."

"Where?"

"Here," I whisper, hoping the wind will carry it into the universe to make it true. He remembered. He brought me to the place I wanted to stand in the sand to say the words that would bind me to the one I was meant to stand beside all my days.

He lifts his hand, brushing back my hair. "Yes, here."

"Sean, we don't . . ."

"No, we don't, but I sure hope you will."

My heart pounds against my chest as he reaches in his pocket. "I hadn't planned to do this here." He looks around the airport. "I had a whole plan, but I also shouldn't be surprised because we both suck at planning."

I laugh because it's true.

When his hand emerges, there is a huge ring between his thumb and pointer finger. "Devney Maxwell, you are the only woman I would ever give a ring to. You're the beginning, middle, and I hope you'll be there until the very end. I want to love you, raise kids with you, and spend every day making you happy. Will you do me the incredible honor and let me be your husband?"

A tear slides down my cheek as I take in the moment. I want to remember it always because it's when my world made perfect sense. "Yes. Yes! I will marry you! Here! Today?"

Sean hoists me into his arms, pushes me back against the car, and fuses his lips to mine. After what could be minutes or even hours, he stops and looks at me. "Not today, sweetheart, but in five days, our families will arrive, and then, yes, you will be my wife."

I take his face in my hands and kiss him again. "I love you."

"I love you. Now, get in the car so I can get you to the room."

I smirk and tap his nose. "Yes, *sir*."

epilogue

"You're getting married. Jesus, you're all fools," Jacob says as he fixes my bow tie.

"You say we're fools, but I say you're the fool."

"Maybe so, but . . . I don't know, man."

There is no doubt in my mind that this is the right thing. She's the right one. The only one. I have never been this happy or as sure of anything in my life. Well, other than baseball. My brothers, their families, Devney's parents, and Austin arrived last night. We had a very loud, very boisterous dinner together and prepared for today.

It's going to be a small wedding, but everyone who matters is here.

Ellie and Sydney are with Devney and the boys and I are all here, waiting for the wedding planner to let us know it's time.

Sydney is standing up for her, and Jacob is my best man. Picking between my brothers wasn't easy, but Jacob just felt right. Plus, it might be the closest that man gets to an altar.

"You won't question it if she's the right girl, you know?" I ask.

"Maybe. I just haven't found her yet."

"No, but you might."

He laughs. "I'm busy as hell. I live a pretty odd life. What woman wants to have her day invaded by cameras when she goes to the grocery store? It just is not what I would ever sign up for."

"You did sign up for it."

"Yeah, yeah. But I'm not a woman. They're odd creatures who want weird things."

Sometimes, I think he just wants to be alone. "Like love, security, and family?"

Jacob shrugs. "Exactly, all shit that I can't provide."

He's wrong, but telling him that isn't worth it. "Did you get the tiny house set up?" I ask him.

"I did, such a bunch of bullshit. I don't know why I can't just stay in your place."

"Well, first off, I'm about to be a newlywed and don't need my pain-in-the-ass brother in my house. Second, because we all had to do it, and third, I just don't like you enough to care if you're miserable."

"Whatever."

He's a freaking baby. "What are you planning to do in Sugarloaf while you're there?"

"I don't know. I met Brenna Allen two days ago."

I have no idea where he's going with this.

"Luke's wife?"

He nods. "She came by the farm the other day, looking for Ellie, not realizing who lived on what part of the land and where their house was. Anyway, she's real nice and was mentioning something about her son and a play."

I raise an eyebrow. "And that made her nice?"

Jacob flops down in the chair. "No, she was nice to look at."

"Jacob," I warn.

He puts his hands up. "I know. I wasn't going there. I'm just making a statement. It's been a long time since I've seen a girl who literally took my breath away. Anyway, she's excited about the plans I have for Sebastian."

Jacob doesn't just make statements. "I don't want to see you get hurt."

"Me?"

I nod. "Yeah, you. The last time you fell in love, it ended with my having to fly out there because you wouldn't get out of bed."

He and another actress were pretty serious. Of course, he didn't tell anyone other than me since Declan and Connor would never have understood. With me, it was different, I get him. When we lost our mother, Jacob handled it horribly. On the outside, he was a tough kid, good-looking, popular, and took everything in stride. The truth was a very different story. He was a mess. He didn't want to eat and sought ways to piss my father off to take the beatings he felt he deserved. It got better as we got older, but his pain was always there.

When the accident happened, Jacob regressed.

It wasn't until he met the actress that he started to turn his life around. She was beautiful, funny, and gave him the illusion of love that he needed. When she left him for the director, he broke.

"That was a long time ago."

"Not that long, Jacob."

He sighs. "I'm not in love with this girl. I don't know her and have had one conversation about her kids. All I said was she was gorgeous, and she is. She has this fiery red hair and dark blue eyes. I'm just saying that she's naturally pretty. But I'm not in love with her. She's a widow and dealing with her kids."

"Okay, if you say so."

It's been years since he mentioned a woman at all, and him doing so tells me it isn't as innocent as he says.

"I do, now, let's talk about how my brother is getting married to the woman of his dreams. In six months, you got the girl not to only fall in love with you but also to marry you. I think you definitely have the most game out of any of us."

I laugh. "It wasn't a game."

He slaps me on the shoulder. "I know. I'm happy for you."

There's a knock on the door, and no one waits to enter, they just do. In comes the rest of my brothers and Austin. He's in a tux with his pants fitted around his brace.

"You look good, buddy."

He extends his fist, and I bump it. "You do too."

"You ready to be my other best man?"

He nods. "I'll do a good job, I promise."

"You'll be much better than that dope." I turn to see Jacob glaring and then shrug as though he knows it's true too. "Are you sure you're okay with me marrying your . . ."

"My mom?"

I nod, unsure of whether he is really okay with thinking of her that way. It's been a rough few weeks, but they are doing their best. She told him he didn't have to call her that, but he said it was the truth and that he loves her. So, sometimes, he calls her Mom, but other days, it's Aunt Devney. No matter what, we're all trying.

"I'm happy about it. She really loves you."

"I really love her. I love you too, Austin. I am going to be whatever you want me to be. Your friend, your coach, and maybe someday, you'll see me like a dad too. I won't ever try to take your dad's place, but I will always be here like that for you."

Austin's arms wrap around my waist, and I hold him to me. This kid has been through hell, but he won't have to worry with Devney and I by his side. We'll do right for him, and we'll give him the love that he had with his parents and a secure home. Something I never had.

"Thank you, Sean."

"You don't have to thank me for being so easy to love."

He laughs. "Does this mean I have to be nice to Hadley?"

Connor and I burst out laughing. "I'll tell you a story about a girl and a boy who were very much like you and Hadley . . ." I squat so I'm on his eye level and hold his shoulders as I tell him about how I met his mother and why having a girl best friend is the best thing in the world.

Declan comes over, clearing his throat. "It's time."

Each one of my brothers gives me a hug and then leaves. It's surreal to think that, in just a few minutes, Devney will be my wife and Austin will be a son to me.

"Ready?" I ask him.

"I'm ready."

I give him a wink, and we head to the beach. Once we get to the sand, I lean down and scoop him up. We get to the end of the aisle, and Devney's mother is there.

"Can your soon-to-be son-in-law and grandson escort you to your seat?"

Her lip quivers as she wipes at her eyes. "That sand just

keeps getting in my eyes."

"I understand. I'm sure I'll get a bit in mine too."

She takes my elbow and we bring her to her seat. When I draw to a stop, she doesn't release her hold. "You are the exact person I hoped would marry my daughter."

"I don't know that there was ever a chance of it going another way."

Her hand taps my arm. "Chance is a funny thing, which is why it's better never to leave it to that. We have to cherish each moment because time is fleeting. Promise me that you'll always remember that."

"I will."

She leans in and kisses my cheek. "Make each other happy."

I head over to my spot and wait. Austin and Jacob stand behind me, Jacob holding him so he doesn't have to try to balance on crutches.

"Big moment," Jacob says.

"It is."

Then I see her. She's wearing a long pink dress that Ellie and Sydney found in her size. This was the big question mark I had, but Devney has never been the traditional girl. When she wrote about that wedding, she said she wanted to be on the beach in St. Lucia, wearing a long dress that blew in the wind. She wanted just her family and close friends there and a chocolate cake.

So, that's what she got.

I was very specific on what the dress needed to have, and they delivered.

As she walks toward me, the skirt blows, acting as a sail guiding her right where she belongs—next to me.

There are tears flowing down her perfect face, but her

smile tells me she's happy. I watch her, coming with grace and love shining in those brown eyes.

Her father stops her, kisses her cheeks, and then places her hand in mine.

"Hi."

She smiles. "Hi."

"You look beautiful."

"You have made me so happy."

"This is just the beginning, Devney Maxwell."

Her head tilts to the side, lips tilting into a coy smile. "I much prefer Devney Arrowood. Marry me so I can be who I was always meant to be."

I don't care about tradition, rules, or anything else. I pull her into my arms and plant my lips to hers. There are hoots and laughter around us as I kiss my bride, ready to do it for the rest of my life.

acknowledgments

To my husband and children. You sacrifice so much for me to continue to live out my dream. Days and nights of me being absent even when I'm here. I'm working on it. I promise. I love you more than my own life.

My readers. There's no way I can thank you enough. It still blows me away that you read my words. You guys have become a part of my heart and soul.

Bloggers: I don't think you guys understand what you do for the book world. It's not a job you get paid for. It's something you love and you do because of that. Thank you from the bottom of my heart.

My beta reader Melissa Saneholtz: Dear God, I don't know how you still talk to me after all the hell I put you through. Your input and ability to understand my mind when even I don't blows me away. If it weren't for our phone calls, I can't imagine where this book would've been. Thank you for helping me untangle the web of my brain.

My assistant, Christy Peckham: How many times can one person be fired and keep coming back? I think we're running out of times. No, but for real, I couldn't imagine my life without you. You're a pain in my ass but it's because of you that I haven't fallen apart.

Sommer Stein for once again making these covers perfect and still loving me after we fight because I change my mind a bajillion times.

Michele Ficht and Julia Griffis for always finding all the typos and crazy mistakes.

Melanie Harlow, thank you for being the Glinda to my Elphaba or Ethel to my Lucy. Your friendship means the world to me and I love writing with you. I feel so blessed to have you in my life.

Bait, Stabby, and Corinne Michaels Books—I love you more than you'll ever know.

My agent, Kimberly Brower, I am so happy to have you on my team. Thank you for your guidance and support.

Melissa Erickson, you're amazing. I love your face. Thank you for always talking me off the ledge that is mighty high.

To my narrators, Andi Arndt and Joe Arden, you are the best and I am so honored to work with you. You bring my story to life and always manage to make the most magical audiobooks. Andi, your friendship over these last few years has only grown and I love your heart so much. Thank you for always having my back. To many more concerts and snowed in sleepovers.

Vi, Claire, Mandi, Amy, Kristy, Penelope, Kyla, Rachel, Tijan, Alessandra, Meghan, Laurelin, Kristen, Devney, Jessica, Carrie Ann, Kennedy, Lauren, Susan, Sarina, Beth, Julia, and Natasha—Thank you for keeping me striving to be better and loving me unconditionally. There are no better sister authors than you all.

about the author

Corinne Michaels is a *New York Times, USA Today, and Wall Street Journal* bestselling author of romance novels. Her stories are chock full of emotion, humor, and unrelenting love, and she enjoys putting her characters through intense heartbreak before finding a way to heal them through their struggles.

Corinne is a former Navy wife and happily married to the man of her dreams. She began her writing career after spending months away from her husband while he was deployed—reading and writing were her escape from the loneliness. Corinne now lives in Virginia with her husband and is the emotional, witty, sarcastic, and fun-loving mom of two beautiful children.

books by corinne

CPSIA information can be obtained
at www.ICGtesting.com
Printed in the USA
LVHW080357030920
664964LV00018B/1546